# Addicted in Blood

## OF BLOOD AND DREAMS - BOOK 3

### KIM ALLRED

STORM COAST PUBLISHING, LLC

ADDICTED IN BLOOD
Of Blood and Dreams, Book 3
KIM ALLRED

Published by Storm Coast Publishing, LLC




Print edition May 2023
ISBN 978-1-953832-20-7

*Faithless is he that says farewell when the road darkens.*

J.R.R. Tolkien

*Prologue*

THE BEAST LUMBERS through the dark, deserted streets. He stops and lifts his nose. His blood stirs at the scent. He doesn't run, but his pace quickens as he moves toward his prey.

They're close.

More than one, and his hunger calls to him. Ravenous. Burning. Unquenchable. And the beast rages from within, demanding to be fully released to hunt and eat.

He turns down an alley. His prey stands in the shadows. Two of them. They carry long sticks, but he is not afraid.

He slows, slipping through the darkness like his prey, his movements silent. Yet, they turn toward him. Somehow, they know where he is.

He stops, sniffing one last time. The scent is sweet. The meal worthy.

He springs, and as if perfectly choreographed, a blinding white light fills the sky. The shadows are gone, and so is his prey. He falls back and snarls, raising an arm across his face, shielding his sensitive eyes from the light as fierce as the noonday sun.

Someone calls a name. A distant memory flickers. The voice—at first familiar and then not.

He backs up and then runs. The voices trail behind—urgent and incessant.

The corner. He must get to the corner. Safety. Without warning, a net falls from the sky. It barely misses him, the edge brushing against his back.

He runs and runs until his legs are leaden and the streets are far behind him. There is nothing but forest and the cool ocean air. When he reaches the familiar den in the base of a large cedar tree, he crawls in and pulls his knees to his chest. He chafes against the pain that permeates his joints.

The beast howls with hunger.

I ZIPPED up my duffel bag then dropped my overnight bag on top of it. Devon didn't mention how long we'd be in New Orleans, but knowing him, if I didn't pack the right clothes, he'd simply buy me new ones. It was annoying but saved on shopping and worrying about what to bring.

Last night, after my introduction to Lyra, Devon's sister, who'd been living in secret on the third floor like a bad family secret, Devon and I had discussed our next plans. Number one on his list was finding the person who could explain my dreams. My mother had given him a name and a city, now we just had to find them.

He'd wanted to get an early start, so I was surprised when I woke to find the sun already up. He must have decided to let me sleep in, and while I didn't want to look a gift horse in the mouth, I could have slept on the plane.

I moved the two bags to outside my bedroom door, knowing Sergi or Lucas would have them put in the car. There wasn't anyone in the dining room, so I backtracked to Devon's office. The door was closed, but I knocked and waited a full minute, surprised when he didn't respond.

I knocked again, then turned the handle and peered in. If he was in a conference with his personal guards, I wanted to give him enough time to shout an order to close the door. When that didn't happen, but a cacophony of voices immediately ceased, I threw the door wide.

His entire cadre of personal guards—Simone, Sergi, Lucas, and Bella—stood around Devon's desk. Jacques, who always seemed to tag along with Bella, his usual partner, was also present.

Devon's chair was empty.

"Where's Devon?" A pit opened in my stomach when they all stared at me, leaving me shaky with a rapidly growing anxiety. They didn't have to say it. They were hoping I knew.

"That answers that question." Sergi rifled through a folder on Devon's desk.

"Come in, Cressa." Simone's face revealed nothing.

I walked in and leaned against the sofa that faced the cold fireplace, telling myself it was to keep distance between me and the vamps and nothing to do with my unsteady legs.

"He was supposed to have someone wake me for an early flight." The words trickled out of my mouth as if his cadre didn't know his schedule to the minute. Based on him not being here, I guessed not every minute.

"Someone must have seen him leave." Simone sat in his chair and rummaged through his top drawer. "He usually keeps his calendar in here."

"He left my room about twenty minutes after he introduced me to Lyra." I inched along the sofa, worry overtaking any concern that I was alone with five well-trained, highly dangerous, agitated vamps.

Everyone but Sergi turned to me.

"Let's save that for another time." Sergi turned back to other files on the desk.

"Where's his tablet?" I had to ask, though they probably covered that before I arrived.

"We haven't located his phone or tablet." Lucas seemed more troubled than the others. "Taking his phone makes sense, but he doesn't always take his tablet." He jumped up and moved to the espresso machine. Though no one had asked, he started making drinks. "It was my turn to watch Ginger, and I left before six."

Simone continued her search in a drawer to her left. "I was at Oasis until Sergi called this morning. The last time I spoke to Devon was a couple of days ago."

Eyes turned to Bella and Jacques, and though I expected Bella to respond it was Jacques who spoke up. "We had the day off and had gone down to the city." Which meant San Francisco, a couple hours' drive south of Santiga Bay. "We got back around two a.m. Instead of staying at the mansion, we continued on to the safe house."

"The sedan was pulling out of the driveway when we drove past," Bella finished the story. "We both thought it was Sergi."

Lucas dropped cups of espresso in front of Simone and Sergi, then picked up the phone. He whispered something into it, waited a moment, and hung up before moving back to the coffee bar. "The sedan is still gone. According to Mateo, Devon didn't say anything about where he was going or how long he'd be gone. He was polite, but there was an edge to his tone." He shrugged. "That could be Devon on any given day."

"What about GPS tracking?" I asked.

Sergi shook his head. "All GPS tracking is removed from cars, phones, and tablets."

Of course. I'd been told that before. "I assume everyone checked their messages?" My question sounded lame. Of course they would do that, but sometimes in the heat of the moment, the simplest of things were overlooked. I reached for my back pocket, a reflexive habit, then remembered I'd stuffed my phone in my overnight bag after checking for messages. There hadn't been any.

No one seemed to think the question was stupid because they all nodded.

"Ah, here it is." Simone closed the drawer to the right. "That's unusual." Her blank expression didn't falter. She never let her emotions show when she was working, but I caught the glance she gave Sergi, and the pit in my gut turned into a hole the size of a meteor. A massive meteor. Like apartment sized. I could only assume by her earlier statement that Devon never left his calendar in that drawer. Was that a message in itself or just a sign of being distracted?

She flipped through the pages until settling on one that would either reflect yesterday or the entire week. I couldn't see the pages, so it might have been a monthly calendar. I found it odd that he would use a paper calendar rather than his tablet. Perhaps he kept two calendars for some reason, then I remembered him writing letters with a fountain pen and linen paper. A man caught between two worlds—the old and the new.

"He doesn't have any meetings listed for last night or this morning." Sergi stood behind her, reading over her shoulder. He pointed to something. "What's that mark?"

Simone frowned. "He left a message. This is strange. He hasn't used symbols for some time."

"Symbols." Sergi moved back to his tablet. "I'm not sure I still have the legend to decipher it."

Bella moved to lean over the desk. "Don't bother. I recognize it."

Sergi's brows rose. "You weren't even around when we used symbols as messages." He didn't appear to think she was lying, he was just curious. A ding from his tablet distracted him.

"Devon asked Jacques and I to use the old system when we started trailing Venizi. He didn't want anything traceable." She jutted her chin toward the calendar. "That symbol means he's taking a secret meeting with someone who isn't a friendly."

"Is there a message drop to know who he was meeting with?"

"Sometimes. But usually not until we knew the information was good."

"I don't think we have to guess anymore." When Sergi looked up, his face was one I never hoped to see again. It was a strange combination of fear, anger, and disbelief. "Council member Boretsky was found dead this morning, his throat ripped out. Devon's sedan is in the parking lot."

He stared at Simone. "They found a vial of Magic Poppy in the front console."

# Chapter Two

"NOT POSSIBLE." Simone's tone left no confusion of her certainty.

"Dammit. This was exactly what I was afraid of." Sergi dropped into one of the chairs in front of the desk.

"Explain." Simone stern response confirmed she was playing full-on House leader, and Sergi wasn't questioning it. No one was. I wasn't surprised. She was, after all, the one being groomed for her own House.

Sergi leaned back, his tablet laid forgotten in his lap. If any vamp could look like a whipped pup, he would have been last on my list. He appeared to have the weight of the world, or at least his House, on his shoulders.

He spoke to the room at large, his gaze unfocused. "Devon and I have been following the deaths of rogue shifters in the Los Angeles area with a tip that Magic Poppy might be showing up. One of Decker's fighters had been dosed without his knowledge."

Bella paced, and Jacques seemed to curl in on himself. I wasn't sure what Magic Poppy was, but it obviously wasn't good. Yet, something nagged at me. I'd heard the term before but couldn't remember where, maybe from one of the dreams.

Simone's fangs dropped. "Why didn't I know about this?"

If her growing anger worried Sergi, he didn't show it, but I found a seat closer to the fireplace and out of everyone's direct line of sight. If I had any sense, I'd sneak out before the discussion heated up, but I didn't for two reasons. The first was that it was like coming upon a traffic accident. Some need to quench a morbid curiosity. The other should have been a concern about my future in a world without Devon, and perhaps part of it was. But the more honest truth was that he'd become a fixture in my life. One who I was becoming to know and understand. Someone who would be missed. I blinked. How could this have happened?

Sergi released a long sigh and gripped his tablet. It appeared even the cadre kept secrets from each other. "Decker told us about his fighter the night we tracked Underwood while you and Cressa were in Los Angeles. We met with Elijah, the alpha of the Humboldt pack, who was acting as The Wolf's representative. He was the one who'd heard of the drug cropping up in SoCal. But it was different this time.

"No one had purchased it. From all accounts, each vampire had been secretly dosed. Some, like Decker's cage fighter, just once. Others more often. We don't know why or who was doing it."

"Do they think the shifter killings were related to the Magic Poppy?" Lucas edged up in his seat. If the cadre had been anxious about Devon's disappearance, this new mystery, and whatever implications it held, refocused the group. This appeared to be something they could work with—or distract them from the more critical issue of Devon being at the scene of a gruesome murder.

"We believe so, but the initial blood samples from the scene were inconclusive as to whether it was shifter-on-shifter attack since the dead shifters were rogues, or whether vampires were involved." He ran a hand over his head then sat up and straightened his collar, as if suddenly remembering he was Devon's head of security. "Devon was concerned about two things. The scene at the shifters' house mirrored the shared dream of the shifter massacre he'd had with Cressa. It just wasn't the northern pack." His gaze locked on each vamp in turn. "He worried about his own past with the Poppy and wanted more information before bringing it to the rest of the cadre."

I watched the group, not understanding Devon's history with this Magic Poppy. Then I couldn't keep my mouth shut. "Does this have anything to do with the Blood Poppy?"

All heads turned to me, and I reconsidered a swift exit from the room when a couple of them seemed to have forgotten I was there.

"Most vampires believe the Magic Poppy is created from the Blood Poppy, though no one has been able to determine how." Simone gazed at me with one of her looks that said she was trying to figure out what to do with me. Or more accurately, how I could be used in this current dilemma. "What you need to know I'll keep brief. Some time ago, Devon was addicted to the drug, and it took him many decades to get clean. The House was almost lost during that time. Once on the highly addictive drug, it brings out our beast to a point where it can't be controlled. Devon will be very dangerous. I can't emphasize that enough."

My initial concerns just torpedoed to nuclear proportions. "So, someone dosed Devon." My analytical mind took over, considering the situation as if I was planning a job and searching for the best way in. My worry for Devon temporarily pushed aside, giving me something I could work with rather than fall apart. I could freak out later with a bottle of tequila at Ginger's condo. For some reason, I still couldn't think of it as part mine. "The obvious person would be someone who knew he'd been addicted before, which is why they left the vial in the sedan. The question is why would they do that?"

"To get him out of the way," Bella quickly responded as she continued to wear a path in the carpet. "Who's the dead Council member? Did he side with Devon or Venizi?"

"We're getting ahead of ourselves, though I think you're on the right track." Simone stood and turned to stare out the window, the blinds barely open to the morning light.

"We need to consider all possibilities." Sergi seemed to have regained his composure now that the initial shock was wearing off. "We know what Devon is capable of. We also know his restraint, which is why we know this wasn't him, but we aren't the ones that have to be convinced."

As if in answer to his statement, the desk phone rang, and Simone turned to pick it up. "House Trelane." She listened for a few seconds and responded with, "I understand," then hung up.

The excitement at having a lead to work with had been sucked out of the air. I didn't understand why.

"That was a summons." Her tone was even, almost robotic. "The Council has scheduled a meeting to determine the fate of the House Trelane. A representative has been ordered to Council chambers this afternoon."

Everyone began talking at once, something I'd never seen them do. My earlier anxiety returned as if turbocharged.

"Enough." Simone stood with fists planted on her hips like some comic book hero.

"This is too soon." Sergi was angry.

"Well, it tells us one thing." Lucas remained levelheaded, suggesting what everyone else had to be thinking. "Venizi isn't losing any time. The question is whether this was simply good timing on his part or he's behind the murder. What better opportunity to seize control of the Council and destroy the Trelane name in its entirety."

"When a House leader goes missing, the Council has waited months before making such a decision." Bella's pacing had increased until Jacques put out an arm that didn't stop her but slowed her down.

"It's been some time since a member of the Council has been implicated in the killing of another." Sergi was back on his tablet. "I'll send you the background. That event was witnessed by several others, and even then, it was months before the Council made a decision on the House."

"I'm not sure I'm familiar with that incident. What was the final decision?" Simone pulled out her own tablet and appeared to be taking notes at the speed of light.

"It was a hundred years ago. The House was a smaller one but had deep roots going back centuries. The House survived under the leadership of a distant cousin."

Their legal precedents wouldn't matter. I wasn't sure why I believed that, but the infighting between the Houses had grown deep. Maybe the Council didn't see it—or didn't want to see it.

"Didn't you say there was an outbreak of this Magic Poppy?" Although I'd asked the question, I'd expected to be ignored.

"Your point, Cressa?" Simone's steely gaze caught mine, but underneath it was a flash of hope. Unfortunately, I was going to disappoint.

"If a vial of it was found in Devon's car, and the Council gets wind of this Poppy outbreak, will someone connect the dots and assume Devon is creating the drug?"

I'd expected denials or anger, but the room turned deathly silent.

"I believe the outbreak to be small enough to miss the Council's attention, but I wouldn't be surprised if Venizi is aware of it." Sergi's earlier emotions were neatly tucked away as if he'd never had a momentary lapse. This was his area of specialty, and his focus had returned. "Devon had a theory that all the various issues we've been working—Venizi's increasing control of the Council, removing Devon's censure as a Council member, the Poppy breakout, this illusive book, the *De første dage*, written centuries ago— were all somehow related. He couldn't explain why. It was instinctual." He turned his gaze to me. "Even the myth of dreamwalkers, which apparently isn't a myth at all."

"Then the path ahead is clear." Simone returned to the desk chair and reviewed a sheet of paper she'd pulled from Devon's spiral-bound calendar. "Devon had listed assignments before his meeting with the Council member." She lifted her hand when the others began grumbling. "We'll assume for the moment that he chose to attend this meeting, regardless of who requested it. Sergi will attempt to determine that answer. We need to see if there's a traceable link that can confirm Devon's suspicions. I'll work with the Council and buy as much time as possible to find answers."

"We need to determine which side the Council members are on." Sergi's expression was blank as he added something I hadn't considered. "And which of our allies are still with us after this morning's discovery."

"Agreed." Simone leaned back and tapped the arm of the chair. I couldn't read what she was thinking, but it wasn't difficult to pick up on the anger mixed with agitation. She didn't like chaos. "For this afternoon, I'll need Lucas, Bella, and Jacques to go with me."

"I should go as well. You'll need a show of force." Sergi couldn't be more surprised than I was on Simone's decision to go without her head of security.

She shook her head. "We don't know the motive for killing a Council member. This could be subterfuge for something else. Someone believes they have weakened us, leaving us open for an attack. But we are not weak. I need you to lead should something unforeseen occur at Council. If we return, then we continue with Devon's plans."

"And if something unforeseen occurs?" I had to ask. Whether I was part of the family or not, this catastrophe impacted me and Ginger.

"Then, in all likelihood, we'll be dead, and the House will be dismantled. Which reminds me. Sergi, we need to know where the police are with the Underwood investigation. Specifically, how much trouble is Cressa in?"

*Chapter Three*

I PACED my room as wired as the day Devon had given me blood after performing a pirouette through a second-story window. Someone had framed him. The truth sang through my blood, though it was most likely the several cups of espresso Cook had sent up to my room. Devon's mission hadn't been moving at record pace, but we'd been uncovering new leads and making progress, as slow as it seemed.

We'd discovered a book that might hold the origins of vampires, and we hadn't been the only ones searching for it. Then out of the blue this Magic Poppy showed up. The timing was just too perfect. With everything moving forward, why would Devon toss it all away by dabbling with the Poppy, especially after introducing me to Lyra?

Devon loved his sister and worried for her. It was evident with how gentle he'd been with her. Somehow my dreams were a connection, which was why Devon had dug into my past. He'd only hinted at it, but it felt right. Our planned trip to New Orleans to search for my father and Colantha Dupré, a name my mother had given Devon, might have provided more answers.

I picked up a crystal statue and threw it against the far wall. It gouged the drywall before thudding to the carpet. Of course, I would pick up something that was more useful as a paperweight than something that would shatter into a million pieces as my emotions were currently doing.

After wearing a trail through the plush pile, I stared out my window and down at the grave markers. Lyra had been the one visiting them that first night at the manor. And it made me wonder all over again who'd been buried there. I turned away from that mystery and fell across my bed.

Simone had shooed me out of the office a couple hours earlier, claiming it was cadre business to determine how to deal with the Council. I didn't argue. Lucas would eventually tell Ginger, but the waiting game was going to drive me loony.

Before leaving the office, I managed to learn one thing. Decker was out looking for Devon. I'd only met the shifter once. He owned a shifter fight club called The Den. I didn't know his history with Devon, other than Decker had once saved his life. If someone could find him, it would be a shifter. Lucas had once mentioned they had excellent noses, but so did vamps. One more thing I couldn't help with.

I stared at the ceiling for another five minutes before Simone's comment about Christopher floated back. Was I a suspect in his murder? More importantly, and something I should have thought of immediately, how was my mother taking the news? From what Devon had said, she knew about Christopher's infidelity. She must have known something about his shady business dealings if she'd been saving for a way out. I'd never given her enough credit.

The police had to have notified her by now. When would the questioning start? Sergi thought they'd wait a couple of days, but I wasn't so sure. Christopher was well-known in the community, and I had no doubt his murder would be a priority for the mayor, who would put pressure on the chief of police. Would they care if they found the real murderer or be satisfied with someone close enough? A chill ran down my spine. With everything going on with Devon, I wasn't sure the cadre would take my plight as seri-ously as they would if Devon was here. I considered the cadre my friends, but when it came down to it, I wasn't sure the feeling was reciprocated.

I scrambled off the bed, grabbed my cell, and then sat by the window, this time staring at the ocean and a lone sailboat heading north. This call would be easier if I were closer to my mother. Rather than let any further procrastination set in, I dialed April's number. She hadn't returned any of my calls before the murder, what were the odds she'd take my call now?

I counted the rings. After the fourth one, I waited for voice mail to pick up and was surprised when I heard April's sniffles.

"Hello."

"Hi, April. It's me." When she didn't hang up or respond, I continued, "I wanted to tell you how sorry I am."

Her ragged breathing mixed with background conversations. They weren't loud enough for me to pick up specifics.

"How dare you!"

"April..." My hand trembled.

"Don't say a word. You have no right to call here. Not after what you've done." Her voice was shrill with a touch of hysteria.

"It wasn't me."

"You've always had it out for him. Now the police know it, too. How could you? I trusted you. This is all your fault." The last part was the most hurtful. Probably because she screamed it at me —all her anger and loss fresh and in my face.

I listened to dial tone for several seconds before dropping the phone on the cushion. But it was nothing more than a smoke-screen hiding April's words. "And the police know, too."

What had she told them? Somehow, Christopher had turned her against me. Whatever he'd told her, it must have been major for her not to confront me. This was worse than I'd thought, and with Devon gone, it was highly questionable whether the cadre would cover me.

I hugged my knees to my chest, my forehead resting on them as I sucked in air. I was in trouble and more scared than I'd ever been.

The chirp from my phone made me jump. It took a second to pull out of my self-pity before I searched for my cell. I stared at the number—April. She must be calling to apologize. Of course, I couldn't have killed Christopher. Certainly not the way he'd been found.

"April?" I answered.

A pause. "No, Cressa. It's me."

Mom.

And suddenly I was crying. "I'm sorry, Mom. So sorry. But you have to know it wasn't me. I swear it wasn't me."

"I know."

I wiped my nose. "You do?"

"Of course, I do. But April is very angry. She saw you with the necklace."

I didn't remember showing it to her.

"The police showed us a picture of the sketch that had been in the limo with Christopher. She said you showed it off the day of your graduation."

"But I didn't." I would always remember that day. "I put it in my picture box right after you gave it to me. It was packed in my duffel." I spit out a dry laugh. "She must have snooped."

"Following in her big sister's footsteps?" Mother quipped. She seemed rather cheery a day after her husband had been brutally murdered. "I suppose that was inappropriate."

"For being honest about my thieving ways or because you don't sound like a grieving widow." I could have bitten my tongue for the rash comment, but her short laugh surprised me again.

"Did your friend tell you about our meeting?"

She was talking about Devon. "Yes."

"And that I was aware of Christopher's infidelities?"

"Yes."

"You must have been aware of the dangerous men he'd been

associated with. You've always mistrusted him. And for good reason. Over the last week he'd become frantic over finding the necklace, but he wouldn't tell me why. I told the police Christopher was scared of someone who was searching for it. They know I gave you the necklace and that it belonged to you ever since your father gave it to me." She sighed, the catch in her throat loud enough for me to hear. Maybe I was naive, but I didn't think it had anything to do with Christopher. "It was the best I could do to make amends."

I considered everything she said. "It's enough."

Her chuckle was self-deprecating. "Hardly. But it's a start." She whispered something I didn't understand, then I realized she'd been talking to someone else, probably with a hand over the phone's speaker. "I'm sorry, Cressa. There are people here. I don't know what April might do, but you should destroy your phone."

"It's not traceable, but I'll see about getting a different one."

"I don't know if the police know about your friend. Either way, it's only a matter of time. Find yourself a good lawyer. The mayor is in a hurry to have this closed."

"Thank you, Mom."

"I couldn't let you think the world was against you." A long pause that I didn't know how to fill. "I love you."

And for the second time in less than an hour, I was listening to a dial tone. A long breath rushed out of me and the tears fell. She still loved me.

I replayed the conversation over and over. There wasn't anyone who could tie me to Devon. But I was still in big trouble, and Mom was right—it wouldn't take the police long to track me down.

Letty, who worked with Cook in the kitchen, brought me a tray with coffee and blueberry scones. It was a thoughtful gesture from Cook, and I placed the tray in front of the hearth. A comforter and my sweats weren't able to stop the chills, so I started a fire and curled up on the sofa.

I sipped coffee and nibbled at a scone while I considered my options. Sergi was adamant about obeying Devon's orders for me to go to New Orleans. Simone seemed to agree. If the police did find where I lived, they might think I ran. Even if this had been a planned trip, I'd been at the murder scene. The cops had seen me there with Devon and Sergi. There was one detective that knew Sergi. Would they keep their mouth shut? If they knew Sergi was a vamp, there was no doubt they would. No one wanted to end up like Sorrento.

On one hand, I didn't want to leave town. Not with Devon out there somewhere. Was he scared, or was he already the mindless beast searching for blood? There had to be more to the Poppy addiction, and I needed someone to explain it. On the other hand, if Devon was as dangerous as they all claimed, it would be safer to let Decker and Simone handle it.

My indecision was interrupted when my phone chirped again. I didn't think I had any more tears left until I heard Ginger's voice.

"Oh my god, Cressa. Lucas just told me about Devon. Are you okay?"

I wasn't sure why I had to think about it. "No."

After five minutes of crying and Ginger's encouraging words, we hung up, and I stared at the dying embers for another five. Then I stood and shook it all off before changing into slacks and a light sweater. I was Devon's Blood Ward and thief. I didn't wallow —I reacted.

In my haste to be proactive, I screeched to a halt when I reached the first floor to consider the best place to start. I detoured to the kitchen where Cook was playing with dough, and Letty was in the corner washing dishes.

"I wanted to thank you for the scones and coffee."

Cook gave me a sympathetic nod. "Comfort food keeps the brain functioning in harrowing situations." He gave me a long look. "These are dark times indeed, but our Father is strong. He will be found, healed, and brought home to us. It has happened before; it will happen again."

His words pulled me farther into the kitchen. I helped myself to another cup of joe from the urn that never went dry before dropping onto a stool across from him.

"Can you tell me more about those earlier days?"

He considered my question as he folded the dough, broke it into pieces, and continued to knead a section. "I wasn't here during that time and only know what I've heard from others. I'm not one for telling tales."

When I just nodded, obviously disappointed, he leaned toward me and lowered his voice. "But considering the current situation, it's probably best you know what little of the facts I know."

I nodded and glanced toward the door to ensure no one was eavesdropping. "I'm not interested in rumors. Before this morning, I'd been aware of Devon's addiction to Magic Poppy. What I can't remember is where I'd learned of it—one of the cadre or one of my dreams."

"Well, no matter." He continued to work the dough as he spoke, his furry brows drawn down. "Devon's parents were killed in a freak accident about, oh my, it must be a hundred years ago now. It was a terrible tragedy that rocked the foundations of this great House. Devon had been away for several years, building relationships with other Houses as he began filling the role as the successor. But that is another story.

"The word at the time was that he wasn't prepared for taking control of the family business and the stress wore him down. In truth, there were many stories on why Devon took his first dose of the Poppy, but that's all it takes. It's quite addictive and weakens the mind, giving the beast more control. After a time, the beast takes over completely, leaving little of the man behind.

"It required sheer mental willpower to come back from that. Decker helped, though I don't know the specifics. He gave Devon a place to live and a job. Eventually, Devon returned home and filled the House seat on the Council."

He placed the dough in a bowl and covered it with a towel. "If he did it once, this cadre will see him through it again. You must trust in them—and in Devon."

I laid a hand on his arm. "Thank you. Before I came here, I lived close to the Hollows. I've seen firsthand what addictions can do to a person. This time, the Poppy wasn't his decision. I'm convinced of that. He's strong. We just need to find him and bring him home."

He patted my hand. "And perhaps that is all it will take."

"Maybe so." I picked up my mug and was almost to the door when I turned back to him. He was already cleaning off the counter and pulling over a basket of apples. "Thank you again for the scones and the information."

"Devon has one more thing he didn't have that first time."

"What's that?"

"He has you."

# Chapter Four

I STROLLED out of the kitchen, sipping coffee and thinking about what Cook had told me. Devon's parents had been killed while he'd been building House relationships in preparation for becoming the successor. I wasn't sure what that all entailed, but Anna could fill me in on the succession process. It hadn't been part of the course material up to now.

Losing parents was a horrible tragedy and could lead one to finding comfort in drugs or alcohol. I'd seen it happen before, but somehow I didn't see it with Devon. I snorted before taking another sip of coffee. It wasn't easy to wrap my head around it, but the tragedy happened a hundred years ago. That was a lot of years for a person to change. But I was thinking like a human. Was it the same for vamps? That seemed like a question for Lucas.

I must have been meandering without any thought to a destination because I ended up in the solarium. No one had lowered the shades, and the sun filled the space, the ocean sparkling in the distance. The warmth of the room drove away any remaining chills, and I credited the strong coffee for removing the fuzz from my brain.

I'd stopped by the kitchen to get directions to Sergi's office then forgot after Cook agreed to tell me about Devon's earlier addiction. I stared out the window, my mind whirling with ideas as I considered how I could help with the current situation, until a sound spun me around. There was no one there.

Whether from the quick spinning motion or a stab of sunshine, a headache slammed into me so hard I dropped to one knee. Somehow, I didn't spill a drop of coffee. For a split second, an image of a forest came to me, and just as quick, it was gone. Before I could question what happened, a scraping sound came from the far side of the room.

I followed the noise to an open door across the hall. Curiosity overrode any thoughts about the headache that was already gone. When I peaked in, expecting to see Greta or Letty, I found Sergi searching through boxes.

"I was on my way to find you but realized I didn't know where your office was." I inched my way into the narrow closet that held rows of shelves that filled the walls. Sergi pulled down a box from a back shelf before turning around.

"It's across the hall from the security room. Something tells me you know where that is." He never looked my way as he set the box on the floor and dug through it.

I smiled. I'd searched the entire first floor for the security room the first day I came to the mansion. Sergi knew his way around security systems, which had been confirmed by the top-of-the-line system most financial institutions and museums would wet their pants over. I vaguely remembered a closed door across from the room, but the mansion had dozens of doors, and I'd only peeked through a handful.

"I do know where that is, but I've only been down there once."

He closed the box and put it back before pulling down another. "Was there something specific you needed? I haven't heard from Simone and don't expect to for another few hours."

His gruff response didn't bother me, even if it was harsher than normal. I watched him flip through files, and as much as I was dying to ask what he was looking for, I knew better. He was frustrated about Devon. Maybe even afraid, which didn't make me feel any better. It made me feel worse.

"I need to go to New Orleans."

He stopped and peered up at me. "Why?"

"It's what Devon wanted, wasn't it?"

He closed the box and pushed it under the bottom shelf before standing. I glanced at the other boxes that were all labeled with dates. Most of them stretched back decades. He wiped his hands on a rag, not wanting to get any dust on his black dress pants and blue tailored shirt. Not that I could see a speck of dirt on anything. Greta found time to keep the closets spotless. That was just nuts.

"With Devon in trouble, you find this the best time to flee?"

That pissed me off. "You know that's not it. It was Devon's wish for me to learn everything I could about dreamwalkers and the necklace. Even Simone said we should stick to Devon's original orders."

He shook his head and tossed the rag onto a shelf. "I don't need to be reminded of Devon's or Simone's orders. I want to know why you want to go. What does Cressa Langtry hope to discover in New Orleans?"

I hadn't expected the question. I'd assumed they'd balk if I dragged my feet about going. Now I was getting the third degree because I said yes too easily. But when I studied Sergi's face, I didn't see the mocking expression typically reserved for our training sessions. He wanted to know if I had skin in the game, or if I found it easier to run and avoid the difficulties the House was facing, or the police investigating Christopher's untimely murder.

I sucked in a breath and gave him what he wanted, though I avoided his gaze. "At first, I didn't know I was the one creating the dreams. They were intimate. Too intimate to discuss with anyone, even Devon." When I gave him a quick glance, I caught his nod, which encouraged me to continue.

"The necklace obviously impacts the dreams, though I have no control when I wear it. And the dreams, prescient or not, are getting darker." I closed the door and leaned against it. "Did Devon tell you I'd been in his head when he killed Sorrento?"

When his eyes narrowed, I held up my hands. "I wasn't controlling him. Nothing like that. It was more—" I considered my words, "—more like hitching a ride. I was a passenger, observing what was happening, but I witnessed much of it through his eyes, as if I was him. Sometimes with my own thoughts, but then I'd feel his rage." I ran my hands through my hair. "God, I know how that sounds." I finally looked at him and held his gaze. "I need to know how to interpret these dreams, maybe block them if necessary. It might help Devon if I understood them more."

He considered me. Seconds turning into a minute, then another. "Now is not the time to share a dream with Devon. I don't know how this dreamwalking works, either, but the last thing you want is to meet the beast, especially in your dreams."

"But that's just it. Right now, I can't prevent what I dream. I have no control over what scene I drop into, and I don't know how to wake myself up. What happens if I meet the beast and can't stop the dream? If I can learn to control it, I can break the connection if I need to. And when you find Devon and bring him home, we'll be further along with his plans."

Muscles worked along his jaw, his expression a blank slate. "Be prepared. We leave as soon as Simone returns."

He turned back to the shelves, picking up the rag and running it over the top of the box before opening it.

"Can you tell me about Devon's previous experience with Magic Poppy?"

I didn't think he'd answer as he picked through the contents.

"It's not my story to tell, and I don't see how it will help anything you might learn in New Orleans."

That was fair. I didn't think I'd get anything out of him on the first round. But we'd be alone together for a few days, and I had other ideas how to get him to crack. Besides, giving in quickly might loosen him up for the next question.

"I get it. It's just that I'm worried about him." The anguish that leaked out should be more than convincing. To be honest, I was more than worried. I was terrified, and I needed this trip, or I'd go crazy sitting around while the cadre shut me out.

He nodded. "Get some rest if you can. I'll let you know the minute Simone returns."

I was part way out the door when I turned back. "Can I have the necklace for the trip? It won't do any good leaving it behind if I need to learn how to use it."

His lips twitched, and I could have slapped myself. Could I be any more transparent with him?

"I already have it packed. It will be available when you need it."

"You're insufferable." I didn't care that my irritation seeped out.

"I know." He turned his back on me, returning to his search as if I weren't there.

I'd bet ten bucks he was laughing at me.

Asshole.

*Chapter Five*

AFTER I LEFT Sergi in the closet, digging for who knew what, I spent an hour in the gym until my arms and legs felt like tall grass beaten down by summer hailstorms. I dragged my feet up the stairs and fell into a tub of Epsom salts, continually draining and refilling the tub to keep the water hot. When my skin was pink, I added cold water and soaked until my pruned body shivered from the chill.

Once I dried myself off, I rolled into bed and slept, thankful no dreams came. Not that I'd slept long enough for dreams. I'd been down for maybe fifteen minutes when Ginger slipped into my room. She was uncommonly reserved, and I only knew it was her from the scent of her floral perfume. She slid into bed and grasped my hand.

I squeezed back. She was worried for Lucas. I understood, and we laid quietly for some time before a knock sounded on the door.

I sprang up. Simone must be back. Ginger popped up beside me, and I blew out a disappointed breath when Anna poked her head in.

"Did I wake you?" She pushed the door open, seemingly not caring whether she had or not. I considered forgiving her since she was holding a large tray with domed lids and a bottle of wine with three glasses. She kicked the door closed with her foot then placed the tray on the dresser. "Sorry for the intrusion, but Sergi said you needed to eat, and with all the tension in the manor, I thought this might be a good time for a chat."

She shook out a small tablecloth and spread it on the floor before placing the tray in the middle of it. The wineglasses were arranged in strategic locations followed by napkins, plates, and utensils in what I recognized as one of the casual social settings I'd learned during the first week in Devon's employ.

Ginger hit the floor before me. I rose slowly, testing my spent muscles and relieved to find the bath did the trick. I wasn't ready to run a marathon, but I'd be able to walk down the stairs without falling like a limp doll.

I sat cross-legged and watched as Anna laid out warm roast beef sandwiches, homemade potato salad, and a desert of fresh fruit tossed with one of Cook's signature light sauces. Anna opened the wine with the expertise of a sommelier and poured a small amount in each glass before sliding in a stopper.

"Wow. I've never had a picnic in a bedroom before. This is perfect." Ginger gobbled the potato salad.

She was a stress eater. I was more of a stress drinker, so I started with wine while nibbling at the sandwich.

"This is certainly my first indoor picnic." Anna tittered as she moved her utensils around. "But it seemed more exciting than leaving a tray at the door. I know Cressa well enough that if she doesn't want to come down to eat it's almost impossible to find the proper lure."

Ginger laughed. "Yeah, manipulation is the only way."

When I gave her a sour look, it only made her giggle more.

"And you needed to stick around to report to Sergi how much I ate." I took another bite of sandwich, knowing I sounded like a harpy.

If Anna was hurt by my comment, she didn't show it. "That's

easy enough to see by the leftovers. Though he is worried about you." She shrugged, scooping up a fork of fruit salad. "We're all overwrought by the situation. Worry for Devon, his House, and family."

"I know that." Although I questioned whether Sergi was truly concerned or had been given orders to keep an eye on me. "I get a bit snippy when my world's been turned upside down."

"And let me tell you, I usually grab my headsets and run for my room until she drinks her way out of it." Ginger stuffed her mouth with a huge bite and still managed to give me a devilish smile.

"I'm aware." Anna nodded and pointed her fork at Ginger. "I admit, it took me awhile to figure her out. At first, her taunts bothered me until I noticed she was like that with everyone. If she can do that with Sergi and Simone and get away with it, I figured she doesn't really mean anything by it."

"Hey, guys. I'm right here. No reason to talk about me like I'm invisible."

The two of them winked at each other like co-conspirators, and I shook my head. Once most of the food was gone, and Anna poured more wine, we leaned back, rubbing our bellies like satisfied elves after Christmas dinner. I might not have been hungry, but it was impossible to pass up Cook's food.

I turned to Anna. "I apologize if you covered this in one of our lessons, but I don't remember talking about succession within a House."

She tilted her head as she considered our recent sessions. "No, we really haven't. I might have mentioned succession but not how it works. You're wondering about the rules if the leader of the House leaves no heir."

"In part. But I understand after Devon's parents were killed in the accident, he had an issue with Magic Poppy. Would there have been a question of succession then?"

Anna's face paled, but she shook her head. "Devon was the first born. The House would immediately be his. It doesn't matter what mental condition a leader is in. It's only if he or his family can't keep the House running that the Council would step in to seize and dismantle it. So his incident with the Poppy, while frowned upon by the Council, had no impact to the House, but it did lead in part to his censure, as it would any of the members."

I considered what she said. "So why is it different now?"

"If it were only the Poppy, it would make removing his censure twice as hard—almost impossible—but not eliminate his leadership." She ran her hands over her slacks before playing with an errant string from a seam. "In this case, a Council member was killed. Murder of another House leader calls for execution."

I couldn't breathe. I was thinking vamp prison, not death. I swallowed the rest of the wine and poured myself more. "Doesn't it have to be proved?" It was a reasonable question, though we all knew it didn't look good for Devon.

She nodded. "It has to be proven without any doubt, otherwise the leader will be imprisoned until a final determination can be made."

"And the House?"

"Would stay intact until that time, assuming the House was structured to support its continuance. Some Houses don't plan for these things. It's shortsighted, but since vampires live a long time, many don't worry about it."

"But Devon would have a succession plan."

"Oh, yes. That's why Simone immediately stepped in. But it's also why it will be difficult to keep the House. Many on the Council don't believe a woman should lead."

"But there are women who lead Houses, though I was told not many. Aren't there any women on the Council?"

"There are several Houses led by women, and there are three women on the Council. One is quite powerful. Her vote sways many."

"Does she like Devon?" Ginger asked.

Anna smiled. "I would say she's his only hope, but she also

follows the rule of law. It's difficult to say which way she'd lean, and Lorenzo has been gaining his own followers."

We all growled at that.

Then a thought occurred.

"How did those women become leaders if it's unusual to have a House with a woman master."

"Through succession if there are no male heirs."

A hysterical laugh burped out. It couldn't be that easy. Surely, Simone or Sergi would have considered it. "What about Lyra?"

Chapter Six

IF SOMEONE THOUGHT vampires could move quickly, they would have been impressed by Anna, a mere human, and her march to Devon's office. She was known to practically fly through the manor, even when weighed down by heavy tomes, and this time was no exception. Ginger and I huffed and puffed to keep up. For my part, it might have been the wine.

The mention of Lyra as a possible successor had lit a fire under Anna. She'd stared at me for several seconds with her head tilted and eyes unfocused. It was a bit unsettling. Then she'd sprinted from the room. When we reached Devon's office, she stopped long enough to knock. Not in her normal timid manner, but a robust knock that made me jump.

I was surprised to find not only Sergi but the rest of Devon's cadre already there. I hadn't known they'd returned, and I gave Anna a withering glare. She'd been sent up to babysit. My glower went unnoticed because she never dropped her gaze from Simone.

"Ladies." Simone leaned back from the laptop she'd been staring at. Sergi, Lucas, Bella, and Jacques were seated in a semi-circle around Devon's desk. "I'd wanted another hour before calling for you." This was Simone, the business manager for Oasis and Devon's pick for successor, and she left no doubt who was in charge. I attempted a step back, but Ginger blocked my exit.

Anna bowed her head in deference. "I'm sorry to interrupt, but something came up that I'm sure you're aware of..." She glanced at the other vampires then cleared her throat before continuing. "But Cressa asked about succession within a House." She hesitated, then straightened her posture, her chin raised. "I explained my knowledge of the protocols, but I'd been thinking about it from the position of you being the most logical member of the cadre to step in."

"We're already aware of Devon's succession plans." Simone's tone was even, though she looked past Anna to me, and her expression was clear that she wouldn't put up with any of my shenanigans.

Not one of the cadre glanced our way. Whatever happened at the Council meeting hadn't gone well. The situation was serious, the tension brittle enough to snap the most resilient in two. Somebody cue the dirge.

"The Council didn't it see it the same way," Simone continued. She sighed and waved her hand for the three of us to draw closer, and the vamps shifted their chairs to include us in their discussion. Their expressions were so grim, I had to look away.

The three of us remained standing. Anna, stiff as a board, took a spot to the left of Bella and Jacques. Ginger followed me to the bar where I leaned a hip, ready to run if needed. A room of high-strung vamps wasn't the best place for humans.

"Lorenzo came prepared, which I don't think anyone in this room finds surprising." Simone steepled her fingers, her gaze split between Anna and me. "His recommendation was simple. He wants the House Trelane sanctioned."

When Anna sucked in a breath, I didn't have to be told what that meant—we were hosed.

Simone's expression was somewhere between angry enough to kill and tired beyond comprehension. "The sanction is being held in abeyance until Devon's capture and conviction. We provided the Council a copy of Devon's succession plan since he has no direct heirs. The Council was split, and the deciding vote came from Council member Isabella Stanton, breaking the tie in our favor. Until Devon is convicted, I will remain the leader of the House, which remains intact with all of its privileges. We have two weeks to bring Devon in. If that doesn't happen, the sanction goes into effect."

"What does that mean?" I asked.

Simone's gaze didn't falter, but I could see the pain behind her stern expression. "The papers accusing a House leader of a High Crime will be filed and Eliminators will be given an arrest order for Devon. Sentinels will be sent to ensure all House activities and finances are frozen pending dissolution of the House, including the manor, all property and assets, even the family itself. Each of the family members will be given a choice of going rogue or being assigned to another House, which is typically not one of their choosing unless they've aligned with a House willing to absorb them."

A chill ran over me. This was worse than I'd imagined. Two weeks to find Devon and discover who killed the Council member. Was Oasis safe from the Council and the Sentinels, and if so, how long could an entire family of vampires be hidden?

"It's as dire as I'd assumed." Anna had gone pale, and her shoulders slumped.

I'd never asked if the human staff were considered part of the family. I decided to keep the question to myself, knowing quite well what many vamps thought of humans. Ginger, who was tearing up, had turned toward the cold hearth. It seemed selfish to be thinking of our own plight, but unless the ownership of the condo was well hidden, it was back to the apartment for us.

"If I might." Anna took a step closer to Simone. "I don't think we've considered all the options."

Simone lifted a brow then glanced at me. "Go on."

"I'm surprised I hadn't considered it myself. It wasn't until I was explaining the succession protocols that Cressa mentioned it."

It was nice of her to give me the credit, but this wasn't the time to seek accolades. It wasn't always easy to read a room full of vamps.

"Yes, yes, what's your point?" Simone must have dozens of things to worry about with finding Devon and preparing for a sanction.

"The House Trelane has two heirs—not one."

~

THE ROOM WENT DEATHLY QUIET, and all heads turned to Anna.

"Well, Lyra of course. She is Devon's full sister."

The room erupted. For the first time since I'd woken to this nightmare, hope flickered.

Simone remained silent and dropped her gaze to the computer. She was as motionless as the bronze sculpture behind her. I'd seen this before. She was deep in thought, and if she heard any of the conversation around her, she gave no indication. It was best not to intervene during her musings. I instinctively rubbed my shoulder, remembering the lesson well.

While the vamps were engaged, each talking over the other, I moved Ginger to a sofa. It was best to keep her out of immediate reach of a vamp in case they momentarily lost control. My nurturing instinct, which was nothing more than a dim flame at the best of times, took over, and I stepped up to the espresso machine. A full minute ticked by before the sound of the machine interrupted their conversations. Simone's head lifted, her gaze pinned to mine, her eyes glowing a bright yellow before they darkened to their tawny amber. The tip of her fangs extended with her smile.

"Explain." Her single word, spoken with unquestionable

authority, brought focus back to the meeting. "And continue with the espressos, Cressa. I think we could all use one."

I turned back to the machine and smiled as I whipped up cup after cup while Anna demonstrated her knowledge of vampire law.

"The succession protocols are quite clear on the matter. If anything should happen to a House leader, whether by death, killed by an enemy, or convicted of a crime, the heir of the leader is next in line. However, if the House leader has no heir, their oldest sibling gains control of the House."

"If an enemy kills Devon, such as Venizi, the House becomes his." Sergi seemed quite positive about the fact, and an arctic blast of air shot through me.

Anna shook her head. "In order for the leader of a House to take over another, there would have to have been an official declaration of war between the Houses. While the Trelane and Venizi Houses have been at odds for centuries, no documented proclamation of war exists."

"But Lyra isn't mentally sound." Lucas was the vamp expert on the law, but it was hard to beat Anna's dedication to the ancient texts. "At least not sound enough to run a House."

"It doesn't matter." Anna relaxed, falling quite comfortably into her instructor role about a topic in which she was well-versed. "As long as she's not implicated in the Council member's death, she is the legitimate heir. With a strong cadre, led by Simone, the Council won't be able to question the health of the House."

"Has something like this been done before, not just in the text, but in practice?" Simone tapped her fingers on the desk.

Anna grinned. "There have been multiple case laws over the centuries. The Council can't ignore it."

"But Lyra's condition is part of the reason for Devon's censure." Sergi, ever the faithful bodyguard, wasn't doubting Anna's words. He was head of security, and part of that role was playing devil's advocate.

"Only a minor reason," Simone responded. "One that pertains

to his Council seat, not leadership of the House." Her attention returned to Anna. "What would this do to Devon's council seat?"

"For that, we'd have to look at two different protocols, which aren't always mutually exclusive. Since Devon isn't dead, as far as we know, and at this time only wanted, not convicted, Lyra's rise to leader would be considered temporary until Devon's final status is determined. Until then, his censure would continue. If he's convicted, the House would lose the Council seat unless Lyra can show she is mentally sound."

"Why didn't the Council mention this during the hearing?" Lucas asked.

"That's an easy one." Bella had been pacing, her hands wrapped around her cup of espresso. "We spent hours waiting for the Council members to arrive. Then Lorenzo immediately raised his motion for the House to be dissolved. No one took the time to discuss protocols."

"It did seem rather hurried," Sergi agreed. "Their focus was on the dead Council member, as it should be. And while Devon's guilt seems apparent with the current evidence, there was no call for the Sentinels to investigate."

"I found that interesting as well." Simone closed the laptop. The tips of her fangs still showed, though she no longer smiled. "This has given us an opening we hadn't considered. I'll call the Council for an immediate hearing. In addition, I'll request an investigation into the Council member's death."

A new energy infused the room, and Simone took the time to look at each of us. If I could only garner a tenth of her regal stature and commanding presence. "We have many things to consider. Find seats for our three guests. We need to make new plans. Then we'll ask our new leader to come down and meet with us."

*Chapter Seven*

AFTER THE TEAM had settled down, Simone listed out the issues facing the House. The first step was gathering the precedents for a new House leader and preparing for sanction should the eventuality occur. The second was locating Devon and initiating their own investigation into the Council member's death. One thing hadn't changed—Devon's last order for me to go to New Orleans.

Sergi made excellent arguments why the trip should be set aside, but Simone disagreed. She had every expectation the Council would be forced to concede to protocols. Even if they wanted to ignore it, based on Anna's continued expertise in the area, they would have to call for a change in the ancient texts. The Council would not be able to do that alone. It would require input from other House leaders. A change of such magnitude could result in a civil war, and no one would want that.

Sergi then argued he was the best person to lead the investigation. Fortunately, he'd found Devon's phone and tablet in his bedroom and a burner was missing. I'd forgotten about them. If they'd been taken, House secrets would have been exposed. Sometimes, less technology was best.

Simone agreed with Sergi's assessment and made him the lead, giving him two hours to finalize a plan for others to act on. He could monitor the activities from his tablet regardless of where he was located. Simone would act as his second during his absence.

Ginger would remain at the manor until everything was resolved—one way or another. Lucas would be close at hand since he was given the job of preparing the House for both succession and dissolution, with Anna at his side. The cadre was well-schooled at having a plan for every contingency.

When Simone began sorting through tasks and team assignments, I grabbed Ginger and made an early exit. Ginger was still upset, and once back in her room, she cried in earnest. Cook added a sleeping aid to a glass of orange juice, which she drank without question. Then I put her to bed, promising to return soon.

I had another goal.

Since I was going to New Orleans whether I wanted to or not, I refocused my attention on learning about dreamwalkers. While I had my own experiences to draw from, there was one other who might have critical information to add.

From the first day I'd entered the manor, Devon had advised in his best don't-fuck-with-me tone that the third floor was strictly off-limits. He didn't have to state there'd be consequences. However, it hadn't been enough of a threat to stop me from sneaking up there that first week, only to be terrified when the doorknob had turned. It had seemed silly afterward, but I wasn't sure of my worth to Devon at the time, and fear of being returned to Sorrento had tempered some of my snooping.

Now that I'd met Lyra, and with Devon temporarily away, I refused to consider any other option. The same rules couldn't possibly still apply. She wasn't a hidden family secret anymore. The thought made me stop halfway up the stairs. Why was she being kept a secret? She didn't appear particularly mad or dangerous, but she was a vamp. And I had to remember that.

I straightened my spine that had begun to turn to jelly and marched up the rest of the stairs. After reaching the third floor, my pace slowed until I stood in front of the door. I didn't think I'd been breathing hard, but her voice was crystal clear behind it.

"Come in, Cressa. I've been expecting you."

That was creepy on several fronts. First, how did she know it was me? There were several humans in the house besides Anna, Ginger, and myself. Second, how did she know anyone was at the door? Humans weren't the only ones with heartbeats. I'd heard Devon's heart beat. Maybe it was my breathing, which vamps didn't do as frequently. The last possibility was one I didn't want to overthink—that she was in my head even when we weren't dreaming. It was that thought that kept me staring at the door for another solid minute before I opened it with a trembling hand. I stepped inside and closed the door. Maybe I should have left it open in case I needed a quick escape.

"Come sit over here. I do love watching the ocean, and the sun is at the perfect height to cast the warmest shade of blue."

I glanced around and realized the expansive room had been two at one time. It was decorated in both old and modern tones, with screens dividing it into smaller areas. I noted two doors that would most likely be the bedroom and maybe a closet. A large hearth held center court with several intimate seating arrangements. Signs of a kitchen could be glimpsed beyond a stained-glass screen.

Off to the side of the west-facing windows, dozens of canvases leaned against a wall. The recognizable scent of paint brushed over my nose along with something more stringent. Maybe turpentine. The mix of scents was rather pleasing. The visible canvases were a collection of landscapes, each including a man. Every painting displayed a variety of backgrounds: a simple splash of color, a boat dock, a beach cove, what looked like an arboretum, and a large tree that bared a striking resemblance to the sycamore outside the window. In every one of them, the same man had been added. Even those where his back was to the viewer, it was obvious it was him. Who was this man, and why did I feel some pull to him?

I shook it off and turned to the two sofas that faced the windows. Lyra sat in the middle of one, her back straight as a board as she stared out to sea. I circled around from the other side, so I wouldn't interrupt her view, finding a seat on the adjacent sofa.

Lyra's entire bearing had changed from the single time I'd met her, which had only been the night before. She'd been dressed in what looked like a child's nightgown and had skipped through the room before eagerly clutching Sergi's hand. Her voice had even been childlike in tone.

While I still detected the same voice, it had matured. And what she wore today wasn't anywhere near childlike. Her wide-leg pants appeared to be a soft cotton fabric that had been matched with a high-collared tunic, both a rich cobalt blue. A thickly roped necklace hung over the tunic with a medallion that didn't surprise me. It was the three-triangled symbol of the House Trelane.

Lyra didn't take her eyes from the view, and I tapped a finger against my knee. "So, you paint." I rolled my eyes. I was the worst conversationalist.

Her laugh was still the soft tinkle I'd heard before. "What gave it away?"

I grinned and released a breath I hadn't realized I'd been holding since first entering. My shoulders relaxed as I leaned back into the sofa. "I haven't seen anything like them in the house. Why aren't they hanging in every room? They look amazing from what little I can see."

"Devon thought someone might recognize them as mine and notice the time differences as the landscape around the yard changed over the years. I agreed with him."

"Does it matter if anyone recognizes them?"

She turned her gaze to me, and her eyes shimmered. "After the accident, I didn't do so well. Physically, I was all right, but I couldn't understand..." She paused and her eyes moved to some point behind me.

It killed me not to turn to see what she was looking at, but in all likelihood, she was simply staring into space.

She closed her eyes for a moment, then continued. "Sorry, I wasn't sure of the best word for my malady. Let's just say my mind was attempting to put together a puzzle from fragments of my memories, and I couldn't quite grasp what the end picture should be or why the pieces didn't seem to fit." She leaned over to the tea service I hadn't given a thought to. She poured a cup for herself and then glanced at me. "It's green tea. Organic."

I nodded, not wanting to say anything that might interrupt her story. After I took the cup, she sipped her own, running a hand over her pants leg.

"Devon says I was like that for almost ten years. No one will admit it, but having a crazy person within a House carries a stigma. Devon had already been left a great burden with running the House and holding a seat on the Council." She smiled as if it was some fond memory. "He refused to send me to a sanitarium. Did you know vampires have their own asylums? What does that say about us?" She glanced back at the ocean, and the silence extended until I thought for sure she'd forgotten I was there. "I'm sorry. I'm still not a hundred percent, though the voices don't come as often during the day."

Alrighty then. The new leader of the House Trelane is hearing voices. I shrugged it off as if it was no business of mine. Which it wasn't, but still. Voices? Of course, I was a dreamwalker, so I didn't have room to judge.

"Devon modified the house to provide your own living space while keeping you hidden from society."

She nodded. "Yes. He thought I'd recover quicker if I was around family. I don't think anyone could argue for a sanitarium over being at home, even if my activities had to be curtailed. In actuality, those first years were the quiet times. I never spoke and rarely ate. Devon made me drink blood each month to maintain my body, only allowing a reprieve if I'd eaten well since the last feeding. When I began coming out of my initial break, my actions became more volatile. Devon still refused to send me away. He searched for a healer that could treat me at home. Dozens were interviewed by Devon and Sergi before Madame Saldano came along. Not many practice the psychic arts, and those that do keep it to themselves. I think Uncle Decker found her."

I'd chosen an inappropriate time to sip tea when her last words hit me, and I almost spit the liquid across my lap. Uncle Decker? He didn't look like uncle material to me, but I'd only met him as a shifter and a friend of Devon's.

"Over the decades, the improvements were slow but steady. Most of the bad dreams went away, replaced with..." again, she struggled with the right word, "...better dreams."

I wasn't convinced she'd vocalized her preferred word, and I wondered if she'd modified it for my benefit. Either way, she had opened the door for my reason for coming here, but I decided to let her finish her story.

"I still have a few bad dreams." She set down her cup, which had begun to shake. "I think he's blocking them." The last words were whispered so low I barely heard them.

I leaned forward to ask a question when the door to her suite opened.

"Lyra? Simone would like to see you now." Sergi came from around the entryway and stopped. "What are you doing here?"

It seemed the third floor was still off-limits. And damn if that man didn't have the worst sense of timing.

"She's visiting me." Lyra stood and brushed out the soft wrinkles in her tunic. She turned to me as I stood and held out her hand, which I grasped. She pulled me close, and I could feel the strength of her grip. Not just human strong—but vampire strong. I had to remember this slight woman could mop the floor with me without breaking a sweat.

Her lips brushed my ear as she leaned in. "I know you want to talk about the dreams. But you need to visit New Orleans first.

Then we can talk." She kissed my temple then turned around, clapping her hands together. "Let's see what Simone has in store for me." She hooked her arm around Sergi's and led him toward the door.

It took me a second to remember to follow, but I didn't need to worry.

"Stop visiting the household and get your bags ready," Sergi barked over his shoulder. "We leave in fifteen minutes."

Killjoy.

*Chapter Eight*

Jacques drove us to the private airport just south of town. I swayed in time with Sergi as the sedan took the corners at breakneck speed. We were running late, and I had to make an effort not to gloat that the delay hadn't been my fault. I'd been ready, bag packed, and waiting on the front porch within the fifteen minutes Sergi had given me. I wasn't going to start the trip with him pissed at me.

First, something went wrong with the limo, so they had to bring out one of the sedans. Then Simone needed Sergi for something, and soon the fifteen minutes had grown to an hour. Sunset wasn't far away when Sergi sprang from the front door, grabbed my arm, and raced us down the steps.

I wanted to ask about the wait, but the look on his face suggested it was safer if I didn't. So, I hid my grin and watched the buildings whiz by.

"Yes. I understand." Jacques tapped the headset he always wore and glanced in the rearview mirror. "I'm sorry to bother you, but Simone called. They found Devon and have him pinned down in an alley in the Hollows. She would like us to stop by."

Sergi tugged his shirt sleeves, spending time to straighten his cuff links before he answered. "Tell her we'll stop, then call the pilot and let them know we'll be another hour."

Fear gripped me. This was good news—or I had assumed it was. But Sergi's expression was grim, and my stomach twisted at what we'd find. When I replayed Jacques's words, the only ones that kept repeating were "they have him pinned down." The sedan accelerated, which didn't seem possible with our earlier speed, and soon I recognized the streets of the Hollows.

I was expecting cop cars with flashing lights and barricades, throngs of nosy people, and a crush of media vans. Instead, the streets were quiet. Two vans were parked in an alley, and men dressed in black with matching knit caps were splitting up, some running to doorways along the street, others climbing fire escapes. They all carried rifles, and I involuntarily reached for Sergi's arm. He scooted close to look out my side window.

"What's wrong?"

"The men with rifles."

He sat back and patted my hand, which somehow made the situation worse. "They're part of Devon's assault team. The bullets are silver and only meant to slow him down, assuming they can get close enough."

"Why so few people? I was expecting...I don't know. More."

"We want this done quickly and quietly so the Eliminators aren't informed. This is Decker's doing."

That made sense. If the vamp authorities didn't know where he was, it would slow them down if the time came for them to step in. But if Devon couldn't control his bloodlust, someone could end up dead. The last thing they needed was the human cops getting involved.

Jacques parked across the street from the vans. When Sergi got out, I didn't wait and jumped out my side. And ran right into his chest. Damn, he moved fast.

"It would be better if you waited in the car." His gaze was stony. It was the death stare he gave me during workouts. It was scary. But I'd seen it dozens of times, and the effect didn't have the same bite anymore.

"I don't think so."

"Cressa—" He didn't have a chance to finish.

I stormed off toward two men in black, whom I guessed to be in charge based on their hand waving and pointing. When we got closer, I could see one of the men was Decker. Sergi grabbed my upper arm, but instead of pulling me to a stop, he pushed me forward, almost forcing me into a jog.

"We'll do this my way." Sergi's tone brooked no argument. "Stick close and don't say a word." We were ten feet away when he pulled me to a stop. His eyes appeared hollowed out in the waning light. "And prepare yourself."

My nerves flared, and I second-guessed leaving the sedan. But now that Sergi accepted my presence, he pulled me along even as I dragged my feet.

Decker turned as we approached, his face grim. "We've got two nets, but he's slipped them twice. I wanted to wait for you before firing the silver."

"Is the alley secure?" Sergi asked.

"It's a dead-end."

There were plenty of dead-end alleys in the Hollows, but that didn't mean there weren't ways to escape. Spotlights were positioned at the entrance and halfway down the narrow lane. I'd seen the glow when we first pulled up, but I'd been focused on the men with rifles. When I followed the trail of light, I gasped.

A hunched form prowled back and forth. His movements seemed labored, which made me question why it was difficult to catch him. He kept looking up, his head turning this way and that, like a dog tracking a scent.

"He's been like this for a while," Decker said. "The doors and windows have barricades, but he's been able to dodge the nets. He hasn't given up searching for an escape path, so I had the team back off."

Sergi studied the area. "How close are the men?"

"We can't get the ones on the street any closer. They're moving in from the roofs to see if they can get a clean shot."

My eyes locked on Devon. It was him, and it wasn't. I couldn't wrap my head around what I was looking at. His head seemed oddly shaped and somewhat larger. His clothes hung off of him, ripped and torn, revealing a predominant hunchback and a bulkier form. His arms hung by his sides, his fingers bent like hideous claws.

He continued his pacing, but even with the spotlights, he found the shadows, which made it difficult for me to get a better look.

I didn't remember making a sound, but Devon pivoted toward the entrance, his nostrils flaring. A low keening erupted, growing louder by the second. At the same time, a headache blasted me, and my knees buckled. Sergi grabbed an elbow and pulled me up. The pain was gone as quickly as it hit me, and I pushed Sergi out of the way so I could keep an eye on Devon.

He saw me. Our gazes locked for the briefest moment. When he took a step toward me, nets dropped from upper windows.

Devon jumped back, narrowly avoiding them. He leaned his head back and roared. Sergi pulled me back, and with one last wail, he made an incredible leap, grabbing the fire escape ladder. He swung like a trapeze artist and flew to the wall, his feet barely touching as he scrambled over it.

Gunfire opened up, and then I saw nothing as Sergi covered me with his jacket and raced us back to the car. We were blocks away before Sergi pulled the coat from me.

"I apologize, but a small crowd was forming, and I didn't want anyone to see you."

"Devon? Did they get him?" I shook like someone had pulled me out of a deep freeze, and my teeth chattered uncontrollably.

"Turn up the heat."

I assumed that was directed at Jacques. Sergi opened a

compartment and pulled out a small blanket. "Put this on until you warm up. And no. He got away."

"What was he howling about? Is that normal?" I couldn't get his image out of my head.

"No. I think he became angered because he picked up your scent."

I sat back and stared at him. "Mine? Because I'm human?" I didn't want to be scared of Devon. He couldn't know what he was doing.

"No. He thinks we're holding you against your will. His mind isn't working like normal. He's more primal now."

"I don't understand."

His expression softened, and he glanced out the front window, probably hoping to see signs of the airport. When he turned his gaze back to me, I never wanted to see the myriad of emotions that played across his features—regret, sorrow, and maybe surprise.

"Cressa. Devon was concerned for you because he sees you as his mate."

SERGI GUIDED me from the sedan to the plane. I couldn't seem to get one foot in front of the other. I barely registered the private jet, and I might have tripped going up the stairs. The chilled air of the cabin pricked my skin, increasing the shivers that never went away in the warmth of the car.

I sunk into the buttery, leather chair, somewhat embarrassed that Sergi buckled me in.

"We'll be taking off shortly, then we'll get you some food."

I nodded and grabbed the blanket he handed me. My hands shook, but my teeth weren't chattering anymore. That had to be a good thing.

Sergi sat close with his ever-trusty tablet. Was he checking on Devon?

I closed my eyes, and all I could see was Devon's beast. When vamps mentioned the beast, I'd assumed it was an internal craving for blood that drove them mad, like when you've been eating salad for weeks. Then you spot the pizza delivery guy, and you'd willingly drive over him just to get your hands on the pie he was holding. Like that, but on steroids.

It turned out going full beast was more than hunger. There was a physical change that occurred. He didn't shape-shift. It was more a bulking out. Not as much as the Incredible Hulk, and he didn't turn green, but his facial and physical form was different. More Cro-Magnon than the refined features of modern man. It must be horrifically painful. Was there a point where the physical transformation became permanent? I shook my head. Maybe he hadn't physically changed at all, and the shadows were playing tricks.

I glanced at Sergi. Part of me wanted to grill him on what I'd seen, but there was more than just the changes in his physical form that terrified me. It was that brief moment when the beast had looked at me. Had actually locked eyes with me.

The body and mind might belong to the beast, but the eyes belonged to Devon. There was only one way to interpret what I'd seen. Trapped. Fucking scared and trapped. And every time the image flashed, all I saw was Devon begging for help.

"Here, drink this." Sergi set a glass of orange juice in front of me. "We both know you're not going to eat, and you need your energy."

I glanced around. The jet wasn't climbing anymore. He tapped the table. I'd do anything if it made him go away. Without looking up, I emptied the glass, pulled my legs up, hugged the blanket around me, and dropped my forehead to my knees.

Devon's eyes were back. This time accusing. Dark clouds as wispy as shadows floated around me, gradually thickening until his gaze faded into the darkness.

"Wake up. We'll be landing soon."

A rough hand shook my shoulder. I mumbled something and turned away, but the shaking continued.

"You need coffee. Wake up."

I managed to pry one eye open as the scent of fresh brew cleared my senses. The light was too bright. My brain was fuzzy, and I was pretty sure I'd been hit by a bus. I rolled over when I heard the clatter of dishes.

The flight attendant, a young male vamp, was picking up food dishes, and from the remnants, it looked like I'd missed a succulent dinner. My stomach grumbled.

I wasn't in my seat anymore but lying on the sofa across from it. A groan slipped out as I pushed myself to an upright position while getting my bearings. The last thing I remembered—my gaze flew to the table—was drinking a glass of juice. The glass was long gone. I narrowed my eyes at Sergi, who was in the same seat as when we took off.

"You drugged me." My voice was hoarse.

He shrugged. "A light sedative. One of Cook's remedies. It was mostly you. You needed the sleep."

A glance out the window said it was still nighttime. "What time is it?"

"Almost five."

The attendant was back, placing a roast beef sandwich and fruit salad in front of me. His smile was congenial, and my return smile was most likely a sneer. It was the best I could offer before coffee, which I slurped as fast as the temperature would allow.

"I thought a sandwich would be better in case you didn't finish it. You can wrap it to go. It will be several hours before breakfast. Girard Lafitte will be entertaining us this morning."

I nursed a second cup while devouring the sandwich. I'd recognize Cook's food anywhere, and I was famished. With our destination close, it was easier to push back my concerns for Devon and focus on our mission. But whether Sergi was ready or not, we were going to have a serious sit down before we left for home.

"Lafitte, he's the leader of the New Orleans House?"

"Yes. And up until a couple of days ago, a staunch ally."

I swallowed a bite of fruit salad then took a bite of sandwich. "You think the incident, or whatever we're calling it, had a negative impact with our allies." I was licking the spicy dressing off my fingers when I noted the silence. Sergi was staring at me. "What?"

He shook his head with a small smile, but he looked at me differently. "You said 'our allies'. Not Devon's allies. Not the House Trelane's."

I replayed my words then shrugged, not wanting him to see my own confusion over my choice of words. "We're a team, right?"

He studied me for an uncomfortable minute. "Of course. It's too early to know where we stand with the House allies. Simone is determining that as we speak. Based on the fact that half the Council was still supportive of giving Devon a chance to tell his side, I'd say the jury is still out. But Lafitte will want to know why we're in his territory."

"Does he think we're here to traffic Magic Poppy?" It was said with sarcasm, but when Sergi didn't respond, I sat back, savoring the last piece of sandwich before almost choking on it. "He doesn't really think that does he?"

"He'd be wise to consider it. While the only evidence of the Poppy appears to be localized, the news that Devon is addicted again has spread like wildfire, not just in the States but across the globe. All his allies will want reassurances."

"And he's having us over for breakfast?"

"A breaking of bread if you will. Now, finish your dinner."

That was Sergi lingo for signaling the conversation was over for now, which was fine by me. After the attendant retrieved the dishes, he showed me where the seatbelt was in the sofa. Rather than close my eyes and face the horrors waiting for me, I flipped through a magazine and worked through a couple more cups of coffee.

Once we landed, and I made my way to the door, the blast of

warm, Southern humidity slammed into me. So did another blinding headache. I gripped the doorframe to keep from falling on my backside and grimaced against the intense pain. This one lasted a full minute before it receded as rapidly as it hit.

Though it was still dark, there was enough light to make out the tall trees and greenery that surrounded the airport. It wasn't until I walked down the stairs, white-knuckling the railing, and followed Sergi to a brick building that I realized this was another private airport.

Rather than going into the building, Sergi directed me to a limo parked just to the right of it. The driver and another man greeted us with a nod. Two more vamps.

Before we got in, Sergi whispered in my ear, "This is a welcoming committee from Lafitte. Don't say anything until we get to our hotel."

The limo was comparable to Devon's, and I sank into the seat, ignoring the pleasantries Sergi shared with the vamp who had climbed in with us. I watched the landscape turn from dense green foliage to an occasional house, to suburban neighborhoods, until we were driving through the empty streets of the city proper. The limo pulled into a hotel near the French Quarter. At least, that's where the vamp said we were. I'd never been to New Orleans and was sorry my first time wasn't with Devon. The sultry air seemed made for lovers.

When we walked down the hall to our rooms, which were next to each other, Sergi touched my shoulder. "These rooms were arranged by Lafitte. Until I have time to sweep them for microphones, consider your choice of words should you call anyone. Texts would be better until after our meeting with him."

I nodded, dismayed that we were being tracked so thoroughly. "Do you do this when vamps visit Santiga Bay?"

He smiled. "Get a couple hours of sleep if you can. I'll knock on your door at eight thirty." Then he disappeared into his room.

I did the quick check of the room that everyone did when first walking into a hotel room. I dropped my duffel on a luggage rack, took out my toiletry bag, and tossed it on the bathroom counter. After the majority of my clothes were hung or stuffed in a drawer, I slipped off my shoes and slid into one of the two queen-sized beds.

I tried to get comfortable, but something dug into the back of my neck regardless of how much I fluffed the pillow. Unable to sleep and somewhat obsessed with the pillow, I pulled the pillowcase off.

I jumped back.

A piece of paper fell to the floor attached to what looked like a chicken bone.

My first thought was to call Sergi. All I had to do was say his name. He'd hear me through the connecting wall. Once my heart rate slowed, I stepped closer and gingerly picked up one corner of the card.

I studied the bone first. It might have been from a chicken or any small animal. Or maybe it was human. I shivered at the thought, remembering where we were. New Orleans. Home of the Saints, beignets, Mardi Gras, and voodoo.

My hand trembled, and I dropped to my knees when I read the note.

*"Welcome home, dreamwalker."*

# Chapter Nine

THE BEAST RUNS. He'd been close. The memories from long ago returned. A time before, when the beast was free.

A safe haven.

Food. Warmth. Shelter.

Traps kept him from it. He will try a different path. But not now. There are too many eyes.

He'd scented her. His mate. They have his mate.

He roars with anger.

People run. He is so hungry, but something stops him from chasing. Instinct says run to shelter.

People are dangerous. Must stay away.

He saw her. Couldn't get to her. Save her. Not the right time. Not yet.

When he reaches his den, he slows. Another has been here. Same scent.

A dead deer lays in the soft needle bed. Same place as before. It won't satisfy, but he drags it into his den and tears into it.

It will have to do for now.

## Chapter Ten

THE NEW ORLEANS hotel was luxury at its finest. No expense spared for vamps, it seemed. Our rooms were on the executive level and the floor had a lounge with its own bar for entertaining, a buffet with made-to-order omelets for breakfast, and various appetizers provided throughout the day. Sergi sat at a table on the far side of the room near the windows that overlooked the Quarter.

He looked refreshed and polished, where I felt like crap on toast. Two hours of sleep would do that to you. I dropped into the cushioned chair across from him, and he barely batted an eye, though I caught his grimace.

He must have taken pity on me because he poured a cup of coffee from the urn that had been left on the table. I'd barely taken my first drink when a waiter set down a plate of freshly made beignets.

"Eat them while they're warm." Sergi cut into a piece, and he might have smiled when he licked the powdered sugar from his lips.

My stomach was more than ready for food, and we spared the small talk while we followed the pastry with eggs, bacon, sausage, and biscuits. I fell back, hands over my stomach as if I'd finished a

Thanksgiving feast. Our meeting with the local House leader was to be over breakfast, but if I remembered Anna's training, the meal was more symbolic than filling. When a fresh pot of coffee was delivered, I refilled our cups and waited for Sergi to start the conversation.

He tapped his ever-present tablet. "Lafitte will be expecting us in an hour."

"What's our explanation for being here?"

"To visit the Renaud Library. Lucas asked me to stop in while we're here."

"You think you might find out where Philipe Renaud is?"

He pushed the tablet aside and released a sigh as he scanned the empty tables around us. "No. But I might pick up a scent if there's concern about him. And, as you're Devon's Blood Ward, it's important for you to learn more of our culture. And what better place?"

"Even though we have a library closer to home in L.A.?"

He gave me that grin that said he knew more than me and enjoyed showing it. "There's a smaller library in San Francisco, more an annex, but it still houses many books and antiquities. It's open by invitation only. They occasionally hold a benefit there. When they built the Los Angeles museum in the 1930s that became the public museum on the West Coast, and the San Francisco library became more a warehouse. The building is too small to be much more.

"Each library holds different items. Since no one can remove the material from the library, the Family prefers to ship an item to a closer library should someone request it. That way, one doesn't have to travel as far, unless they're working on a particular project and require access to everything on the topic."

"What will you tell them you're looking for?"

"Not a thing. Lafitte needs to know why we're visiting, but not the details. Since this is your first visit to New Orleans, I will, of course, want to show you the city and all its marvels."

I nodded and sipped my coffee, glancing out the window to the few tourists already wandering through the Quarter. From what little I knew, the place wouldn't get busy until mid-afternoon. I fingered the card in my pocket. This was as good a time as any, though I'd planned a more private setting. I glanced over my shoulder; the closest people were six tables away.

I slid the note that had been left in my pillowcase across the table to him.

A brow lifted as he scanned the room. He gave me a quick glance before picking it up. His gaze shot back to me. "When did you receive this?"

"It was tucked inside my pillowcase."

He tapped his finger on the note. "Interesting."

"That's not the half of it." I slipped the bone, wrapped in a tissue, across the table.

When he opened it, he stared at the bone for a long while then turned it over, inspecting it. "This is a real bone, but not human."

I leaned over and whispered, "Is this voodoo?"

He shrugged. "Not necessarily, but I think it gives us a place to start. Although I'm not sure we'll have to do much searching."

"What do you mean?"

"They—and I don't know who they are—know you're here. My guess is that they'll seek us out when the timing and location is right."

"And how do we know when and where that is?" I wasn't a fan of just hanging out and waiting for someone to sneak up on me.

"We stick with our plan. Let them come to us. It will be faster."

"Easy for you to say," I muttered.

"Let's go. We don't want to keep Lafitte waiting."

∼

Turned out, Lafitte wasn't as interested in us as Sergi had anticipated, considering the rumors about Devon that had spread throughout the vampire community. The House leader, a long-time friend of Devon's, was approaching his limo when we arrived. After a brief introduction, the older vamp with touches of gray at his temples and a goatee kissed me on both cheeks, welcomed me to the city, and told Sergi to let him know if we ran into any problems.

Then the limo was cruising down the driveway, and we were left standing with one of his cadre.

The woman shrugged. "We've been having trouble with rogues." Her gaze locked on Sergi. "Regardless of the rumors about Devon, House Lafitte still stands with House Trelane. Enjoy our city." She gave a small bow and strode back to the house.

Once we were well down the road in a rented sedan the hotel's concierge had provided, he broke the silence. "That was unusual."

I'd been glancing at the passing houses, appreciating the ante-bellum architecture, my thoughts split between the note I'd been left and what was happening back home with Devon when Sergi's words hit. I sat up. "Unusual how?"

"Lafitte knew we had an appointment to meet with him. It's possible the issues with rogues presents a clear danger, or there was some other reason he didn't want to meet with us."

I stared out the windshield, my focus a blur as I took in what he said. "But his cadre seemed to make a point to state he stood with Devon."

"Not Devon," he corrected, "but the House Trelane."

"Meaning?"

He tapped a finger on the steering wheel. "He's putting distance between his House and Devon. He hasn't stated anything publicly and won't unless pressured to, but he's letting us know through his cadre that he's still aligned with our beliefs and has no issue with the change in succession."

"You mean with Lyra?"

He nodded.

"How would he know? Simone is meeting with the Council later today."

He smiled, which was unsettling in the fact he rarely did it. "Simone is striking first. Calling our most critical allies to advise of the situation and gain early support. Once the Council rules and the information is formally announced, Venizi will expect a moment of turmoil, assuming Simone will be playing catch-up with our allies as they storm us with questions. At most, the smaller Houses will look to the stronger Houses to get a read on the situation. With our allies in place, they'll be proactive in putting the smaller Houses at ease."

I slumped back in my seat. "I had no idea how political it got. It makes my head hurt just thinking about all the implications."

"Some have the knack to make it look easy."

"Like Devon."

He nodded. "And Simone. I think that was one of the main attributes Devon considered for a new House leader, and why she was selected as his successor." He paused for a moment, which was good, because I wasn't sure how to respond to that. If I had a question as to whether he felt slighted, he answered it. "I'm not a subtle vampire and bore easily with court intrigue. While I could step in temporarily, I'm not the best choice to build and maintain a powerful House." He chuckled, which was a surprisingly pleasant sound. "The Council would never accept me. My strength is in the role I occupy today.

"You're seeing Simone at her best, and she has so much more to learn. Even then, she's a force not many would move against. If you want to see someone with the potential to make something of themselves, keep your eye on Lucas."

I rested my head against the car seat, listening to the information on the cadre he'd never shared before, and found I wasn't shocked by his comment about Lucas. "If you'd told me that the first week I'd entered the manor, I'd be laughing right now. But these last weeks, he's really amazed me. His knowledge of your culture and history, his charm, his courage—I can see it. Was that what Devon was like when he was Lucas's age?"

He snorted. "Just the opposite. You have to remember the difference in ages. Almost four hundred years separate them. If we didn't have House Renaud to understand the importance of knowledge and keeping records of our history, Lucas, or most any vampire, would only know the stories they could beg from the elders.

"Devon was born in a time where war was common. His knowledge was steeped in battle strategies and effective combat techniques. He honed his skill at leadership during battle, using his natural ability to persuade men to follow him. When wars became less frequent, Guildford, his Father and leader of the House, became adept at the art of negotiation, and it was during those years that Devon learned the basics of political intrigue."

I wanted to broach the subject of Devon's addiction to Magic Poppy, but I had to be tactful and find the right moment. When Sergi mentioned Guildford, the only thing I knew of him was from Lyra and how he died. Devon was addicted not long after that and would be a good place to start.

"Here we are. The Renaud Library. This was the first one established in the States almost two hundred years ago."

With our arrival, I'd missed the opportunity to steer him toward Devon's addiction. I sighed and glanced out the window.

Tall brick walls surrounded the property, and similar to the one in L.A., two massive rod iron gates were open, leading to a small security booth. After Sergi flashed a card and a quick computer scan of our faces, we were allowed to proceed. The driveway curved around expansive green lawns spotted here and there with oak trees, the Spanish moss hanging from the stately branches.

The library depicted an old Southern plantation complete

with tall white columns supporting a veranda that appeared to wrap around the building.

If I'd just woken up in my room in Santiga Bay and looked out the window, I'd have no doubt I'd been transported to the South. What told me I was most likely near New Orleans were the two decorative yard posts that each sported two symbols. I recognized the style of design from the quick internet search about voodoo I'd performed after finding the bone in my pillowcase. My first hunch was that it was some type of warding or protection spell. As beautiful as the symbols were, a shiver ran through me.

Sergi slowed when we reached a split in the road. A sign for general parking showed a symbol for going left. Below that another sign showed VIP parking straight ahead where the drive appeared to take the visitor to the front entrance.

He turned left, and though there was plenty of open parking, he drove to the back of the lot where it branched off to another smaller lot. A chain had been strung across the drive, so Sergi couldn't pass, but he stopped the car and leaned toward the windshield as if trying to get a better view.

"What is it?" I leaned forward, as if I knew what we were looking for.

"The black limo on the far side."

There were five cars in the lot. Two were limos, two were sedans, all four black as midnight and polished to a sheen. The fifth car was an expensive-looking red sports car, most likely European.

"I see it."

"I think that belongs to Lafitte."

"Didn't you tell him the museum was the main reason for our coming to New Orleans?"

"Yes."

When he didn't elaborate, I kept quiet. The car wasn't moving, so he must be thinking. It was best not to interrupt. I'd learned that the hard way, which resulted in lovely bruises to my left hip and right shoulder. That didn't include the other aches that took a couple days to work out, and that was after an Epsom salt bath and time in the hot tub.

"He knows we'll be here for several days." Sergi squinted in thought. It wasn't the first time I'd noted that as gruff as he was, he had an old-world beauty to him. "We could have chosen to visit the library at any time. What I found most interesting was the way he greeted us at the manor. It was almost as if he'd been waiting for us before rushing to be on his way."

"Was he hoping we'd come here after meeting with him? Does he want us to know he's here for some reason, or is this all just a coincidence?"

He turned his expressionless gaze on me. "Do you know what I like about your constant barrage of questions?"

This was one of those no-answers-are-safe kind of questions. Everyone in the manor was aware of my inability to control my constant need to know everything. It had become somewhat of a joke at my expense, and I'd learned to live with it. They weren't entirely wrong.

"You're going to tell me regardless."

Another rare smile. "They're starting to make sense."

This was the moment, and far from the first time, where I had to decide whether to focus on the part where he appreciated my questions or become irritated over the fact he shared compliments in a way that reflected how stupid I'd been before. Since we'd be traveling together for a few days, I decided to be a grownup and kept my mouth shut.

He took a last look at the limo before the car made a slow turn as he took us back to a closer parking spot.

The entry to the library was met by a custodian with the same friendly disposition as the one in L.A.—and, yes, I was being facetious. After the "Welcome to the Renaud Museum of Vampirology & Knowledge" spiel, we were handed a map that was a replica of the one I picked up in SoCal. The only exception was the list of events on the back page. I stuffed the map in my pocket to review later.

I was surprised Sergi didn't ask about Philipe Renaud or ask for a manager at the front desk. Instead, he led me down to the third sub-basement floor and the rare book collection. The same place Simone and I had searched for the *De første dage*—the elusive book that might or might not share secrets to the origin of vampires. We perused the books as if we had an interest. I could barely read the covers since most were in other languages, or a form of English so old it might as well be a foreign language.

After twenty painful minutes, a custodian appeared from around a suit of armor that, based on the sign at the base of the stand, placed the artifact from the fifteen hundreds. I had a hard time imagining Devon wearing something similar.

"Can I be of assistance, sir?" The custodian, a thin woman with rimmed glasses, frizzed hair, and a bland expression blinked up at Sergi, completely ignoring me.

"Yes, you might be." Sergi put away the book he'd been perusing and gave the custodian as pleasant an expression as he could muster. "I'm in town for a short time and had to stop by to gather some information for a research project." He waved a hand. "You wouldn't be interested in that. But I thought while I was here I'd check in on an old friend. He's usually in town this time of year."

"Certainly. Does he work at the museum?"

"I believe he's still the curator. Philipe Renaud."

I sidestepped to the left to catch the custodian's expression when the Renaud name was mentioned. She was good. If I hadn't been watching for it, the change in her pupils and the quick glance to her left told me she was cooking up a lie.

"I'm sorry. Mr. Renaud retired from that position some time ago. He moved his residence and, from my understanding, does a lot of traveling."

"Ah. I thought it might be for naught, but I had to ask."

If I wasn't in the room, staring at the man, I would never have thought this was Sergi. He could actually act like a normal person. It must be killing him.

"It's quite all right. I'd ask if you'd like to see Lynette Renaud, the current curator, but I'm afraid the monthly trustee meeting is this week."

Once the custodian was out of earshot, Sergi hustled me to the car.

"What's the rush?" I stood on tiptoes before I got into the car to see if Lafitte's limo was still there.

"He's still here. Get in."

"The custodian was lying about something."

"It was more that she was manipulating the truth. She knows I'd sense if she was lying, but I agree she's hiding something."

"You could have pushed more."

"Yes, but I wouldn't have gotten anything more than suspicion. If the trustees are in town, there's someone else we can speak with, but they won't be available until later. We'll go back to the hotel room. You could use more sleep; we'll most likely be up late tonight. And I have several things to check on."

"And Colantha?"

"It's not even noon yet. They'll make their play to meet with you this evening."

"Great." I stared out the window. Back to the waiting game.

When we reached the valet at the hotel, Sergi took my arm as we walked through the foyer. When the elevator doors opened, he released me but didn't follow me in.

"Meet me at four-o-clock in the executive lounge. And wear something appropriate for an exclusive tea house."

*Chapter Eleven*

IF ANYONE HAD BEEN UP at the early predawn hour, they might have taken a second look at the large scruffy dog running down the street, sticking to the shadows, pausing every few feet to lift its nose to the air. They might have turned and run if they'd recognized the creature as a wolf and not a dog.

The wolf circled the block, trotting into vacant buildings then moving on until it found another building it liked. On and on it went for almost an hour before it turned and headed for the outskirts of town, which was a mere half-mile away from the industrial area of Santiga Bay.

The city streets quickly disappeared into a forest wilderness, and after several hundred yards, the wolf stopped in a clearing. Birds that had just begun to wake, quieted until silence descended over the area. The wolf laid down in the soft fir-needle bedding and whined. It was a long and soulful song as the wolf began to morph from beast to man. The process took ten minutes, and the man's face was scrunched in pain as the last of the transfiguration completed.

He rolled to his back and stared through the trees to witness the morning twilight. There wasn't much time. He stood and brushed away the forest debris. His tall frame still carried lean muscle, but time and heartache had taken its toll. He wasn't as fast as he used to be, and he tired quicker, but purpose spurred him on. After another quarter mile through the thickest part of the forest, he fell to his knees within sight of the massive cedar and caught his breath.

He lifted his nose, sniffed the air, and listened. After a full five minutes, aware of how close he was cutting it, he rushed to a grouping of three fir trees and found his duffel. He dressed quickly and quietly, swung the duffel over his shoulder, and approached the backside of the cedar where the land met a rock formation. Next to the rocks was a large hole—the entrance to the den.

He squatted and peered in. Seeing nothing but smelling his prey, he knelt and crawled a few feet until an icy-blue glow stared back at him.

"Hey, Devon. It's time to move." Decker backed out until he was a few feet from the entrance and stayed in a squat position while he waited.

He'd tracked down Devon's first den the day before along with the discarded deer carcass he'd been feeding from. One that had been laced with Magic Poppy. He'd burned it, then threw fresh meat into the den.

Once a vampire's beast took over, blood alone wasn't enough to survive. Many turned to fresh meat to feed the beast and keep it happy. Whoever had dosed Devon had followed him to his den and was prepared to keep him doped. Vampires were decent trackers, but not as good as shifters.

Having been hunted for centuries by vampires, shifters had adapted. They became stealthy at hiding their tracks and scent. And right now, he was the only one capable of saving Devon from further decline into the Poppy while evading the Eliminators. They weren't supposed to be hunting him yet, but Decker had spotted a couple of them spending time in the alley where Devon kept returning to.

Decker's plan was simple. Move Devon to a new location but keep Devon's scent fresh in the alley. Urine and a bit of blood was all it took, and after the first six attempts at getting Devon's beast to understand and comply, he got what he needed and used it sparingly. That tussle had left Decker with a slice to his thigh so deep, Sabrina had stitched it in the back room of The Den to speed up the healing shifter magic.

After a few minutes, the icy-blue glow grew closer as the beast moved to the entrance and stared out at the breaking dawn. He studied Decker, who held his position until he was sure Devon, or what was left of him, showed recognition. The beast crawled out of the den and stood, his full height reduced by the slight hunch in his shoulders.

The beast lifted his nose, and Decker threw him a piece of meat. He'd wrapped it the night before until he could no longer smell it, satisfied it would be safe in the duffel he'd hidden. The beast devoured it in seconds, then stared at Decker—waiting.

Decker took that as the sign he needed. "I found a place in the city where no one should find you."

When the beast shook its head, Decker shook his. "The cadre needs you close."

When the beast didn't move, Decker took that as another good sign. "The two shifters on the Council have refused the vampire's request for trackers." He chuckled. "I guess Lorenzo's success at keeping shifters off the Eliminator squads has backfired on him. When the shifters were told it was their duty, they advised the Council they weren't the vampire's cleaners. If they'd wanted their expertise, they should have allowed shifters to join the Eliminators. While the Council is upset, they seemed to have discovered the error of their ways."

What might have passed for a chuckle erupted from the beast. So far, so good.

"I have a plan. You need to trust me. Trust your cadre."

The beast howled, and even for a shifter, the sound made the hair on the back of his neck stand at attention. But the beast squatted, and the glow in its eyes receded to their normal eerie blue.

"Stick close, stay in the shadows. It's about three miles from here, most of it running through the city streets."

The beast grunted, and Decker took off. In his human shape, he could outrun a human, but he wasn't a young man, and the last few years had ravaged more than his spirit. But ever since Devon came back into his life, he had a new reason for living. Revenge. Absolution. Whichever it was, it gave him something to live for. Devon gave him that opportunity. So, he'd gladly taken the assignment to track and keep Devon safe. He would have done it even if Simone hadn't asked.

Though the fast-approaching dawn lightened the sky, Decker took his time, stopping when needed to lift his nose, the beast lifting his as well. When they both nodded, he continued on. They passed the alley where the team had tried to capture Devon, and several blocks farther, he ducked past a half-boarded window into an abandoned department store. The beast followed him as he weaved through the empty rooms and dusty remains of metal shelving and broken mannequins. When they came upon dressing rooms, Decker turned toward them and ran into the farthest one, and the beast followed.

"Did you smell him?" Decker whispered to the beast.

The beast grunted.

"I recognized the scent. I think it's the same vampire that was leaving you the tainted meat. Probably the one who dosed you in the first place."

When the beast appeared ready to howl, Decker grabbed his arm, hoping Devon was present enough to not rip it from his body. Fortunately, the touch had a calming effect, and the beast dropped his head.

"Trust us, Devon."

It took a moment for the beast to control his anger, then it nodded.

Decker rummaged in his duffel and pulled out a small vial. "We'll go out the back." He opened the vial and let two drops fall to the ground. When the beast tilted his head, Decker laughed. "It's a blended mix of scents that will disguise our own. Let's move out."

Every block, Decker released a few drops and continued the pattern for another six, moving toward the river that ran through town to the sea. When they reached the old paper mill, they worked their way through a cut in the chain-link fence that surrounded the facility.

The mill had shut down decades before, and the multi-building complex made an excellent hiding place. He led the beast up stairs and down hallways until he found the old bunk room that had two exits. He pulled a smaller duffel from his bag and tossed it on a sturdy metal cot.

"It's time you started living like a man again and not your beast." He turned to Devon. "Sleep on the bed, not the floor. There's a down blanket in the duffel, along with two more of these vials." He held up the one he used to block their scent. When the beast nodded, he continued. "There is also an ice pack with a couple vials of blood."

When the beast growled, Decker shook his head. "I know cold isn't the best, but the nutrients you need last longer when the blood is cold. Drink one tonight and the other tomorrow night. Look at me, Devon."

It took a minute before the beast turned to him.

"This is your best chance to pull out of the beast form. There's a deer in the next room to take care of the hunger. It should last a couple of days. It's in one of the lockers so the scent doesn't draw a vampire. You understand?"

The beast nodded.

"This room has two exits. Spend the next couple of days getting to know the facility and all its exits. If the Eliminators suspect you might be here, they'll blanket the complex. You'll need several ways to escape if I can't get to you first." He waited for beast to nod, and when he did, Decker continued. "Don't leave the facility. Do you understand? I'll be back in a couple of days. There are security cameras at the gates, and I'll keep an eye on the feed. We can't risk you leaving a scent trail. Learning the complex and planning exits will keep you occupied."

The beast grunted then slammed his fists on the walls. The sound echoed through the small chamber.

"I know you're scared and frustrated. Everyone is working to find out who did this to you and how to clear your name. The House is safe now. The Council will soon remove the sanction order."

Some of his words seemed to work, but he probably shouldn't have mentioned getting him back to normal. Even in beast form, Devon understood the improbability with how far he'd progressed before Decker discovered the tainted meat.

The beast fell onto the bed and curled into a fetal position, his growls turning into mewling sounds that made Decker want to cry himself.

Once he'd backed out of the room, he ran. Careful to not let anyone see him as he exited the facility, he raced along the river's edge and splashed through some of the water to throw off his scent. After everything Devon had done for him, Decker wasn't sure he'd ever see his old friend again.

*Chapter Twelve*

SIMONE STEPPED out of the limo and straightened her blood-red caftan. Her spiked hair had been dyed white, but streaks of red had been added. In any other environment, the streaks gave off pink highlights, was daring and vogue. In the chambers of the Council, where vampires reigned, it was a bold statement reminding the Council of who they were and who she was. Blood was their life force.

The cadre surrounded her—Lucas, Bella, and Jacques. She grunted. Jacques wouldn't normally be considered cadre, but he and Bella were perfect partners; it was impossible to include one without the other. And since Sergi was in New Orleans with Cressa, she required the extra security.

She turned when a black van pulled into the parking lot, and she cursed. The door slid open, and a dozen well-armed vampires jumped from the vehicle and created a second barrier around her.

If this happened at any other time, the entire group would be sent to discipline training. Lucas gave her a disapproving glance, and instead of irritating her further, she replaced her sneer with a conciliatory nod. The Council building wasn't safe territory.

It was a sanctuary at times, but when a House was being

threatened, it was a dangerous place. Even with the Council present, the halls were fair game for attack. The practice began centuries ago when war was an everyday occurrence. Battles were fought within the walls of the building as well as the fields. Many differences were settled before ever making it to the Council chambers.

In today's modern society, the halls were safer, but it wasn't unheard of that someone was attacked—even killed—without censure from the Council.

She'd felt safe enough yesterday when she argued for the House. But Lorenzo had assumed an easy victory so bloodshed wasn't required. With her request for a second meeting, the game had shifted. She might enter without a problem, but depending on the results of this hearing, the walk out might be a different story.

Still, she'd argued she didn't require such a show of force. The cadre was enough. But the cadre hadn't agreed. This was the exact time to show their might. That it wasn't just the cadre behind her, but the Family as well.

Her brief spout of anger had been tempered by a single glance from Lucas. This was what Devon preached. No matter how capable she was, or her need to prove what she could do, the Family only made her stronger. It continued to be a hard lesson to learn, and the reason Devon wanted her to wait another few years before achieving her own House. Her role at Oasis was the opportunity to develop and hone those final skills.

Though the cadre's disobedience might grate, she couldn't deny the power she felt as they strode as one through the front doors of the Council building, their boots echoing off the marble floor. When they reached the middle of the building where the Council chamber was in session, she noted the guards stationed around the anteroom. It was impossible to tell if they were from the House Venizi or from multiple Houses, and suddenly the number in her detail seemed razor thin.

A page waited for them, and Lucas broke away from the group

to meet with him. After several minutes of discussion, where at one point she thought Lucas might beat the man, the page lifted his hands in supplication then scurried into the chamber. Lucas remained where he stood, waiting for the page to speak with the Council. She suspected there was a change of heart in her request for a hearing.

Several long minutes passed before the page returned to discuss the Council's response. When they both seemed satisfied, the page returned to his position next to the door.

Lucas's features were expressionless as he returned to the group. The team tightened around them while Lucas explained. "The Council started their meetings two hours ago. It seems Lorenzo submitted another petition. They wanted to move us to tomorrow, but I argued precedent in the timing of our request. They'll fit us in."

"Lorenzo's trying to steamroll the Council," Bella sneered. Simone studied the young vampire. The female was a hundred years old, still untested in many ways. She was the youngest of the cadre, and a hundred years the junior of her partner, but there was something uncanny about her. She was quiet, excellent with developing distractions and last-minute battle scenarios, and hid an expansive knowledge of vampire law. But the most surprising was her gift at court intrigue. Her abilities with that particular skill were learned at her previous House where Devon met her and coerced her to join his Family.

Simone smiled at her and felt her fangs drop, but Bella didn't flinch. "Let's show Lorenzo who has the larger steamroller."

Bella smiled and stood a bit straighter. "Yes, Mistress."

They waited another thirty minutes before the page opened the door and announced them. If Lorenzo had hoped to unsettle her, he'd be disappointed. She'd faced that form of intimidation many times, and all it did was stoke her anger.

The slight brush of Lucas's hand against hers was enough to return her focus and settle her beast.

This was their best opportunity at preserving the House regardless of the eventual outcome of Devon's situation. Besides, she loved surprises, especially when she was the one delivering them.

~

SIMONE TOOK her place on the petitioner's dais. The cadre spaced themselves in a semicircle around her. The other guards remained in the anteroom. She'd wanted to bring Anna, who excelled in succession law, but the risk of attack would make her and, by association, the rest of them vulnerable. Anna had reviewed the pertinent laws and precedents with Lucas, but she hoped the discussion wouldn't go that far.

Isabella Stanton called the session to order and started the clock. Simone would have a half hour to state her initial case. More time would be allotted for questions, assuming they wouldn't summarily dismiss the request. Her one advantage: Lorenzo was easier to goad than people thought. If you poked in the right place.

"House Trelane, what is your new petition?" Isabella's tone was neutral, but her expression was warm.

The Council bench was full with the twenty-one members minus two. One was Devon's censured seat, the other was Boretsky's, the recently deceased member. Simone was surprised the seat hadn't been filled by his son, and she wasn't sure how to read that.

Her gaze fixed on each Council member as she surveyed the curved stone bench. This wasn't the Council's normal meeting room. They had an elaborately carved oak conference table down the hall. This room was used solely to hear House petitions and criminal proceedings. There was an adjoining room should a sentence require swift justice. And the Council wasn't squeamish to make those decisions when necessary.

"Council members, I am Simone of the House Trelane. I have new information to present in the matter of leader for the House."

"Enough of this," Lorenzo interrupted. "We've been through this just yesterday. What could possibly have changed in that time period?" His irritation focused solely on Simone.

Isabella slammed her hand on the clock. "Member Venizi. This is not the time for rebuttal or questions. This time belongs to the petitioner. If you can't maintain Council decorum, you will be excused for this session." Her gaze pierced him, and Simone assumed the previous two hours of Council business had strained her typically composed nature.

"The clock will be reset." She slammed her hand on the clock again. "House Trelane, please proceed."

Simone, who hadn't flinched during Lorenzo's bluster, nodded with respect to Isabella. "When the House Trelane met with Council yesterday, emotions were understandably high, considering the loss of an endeared member, and implications that a House leader might be involved."

Lorenzo snorted, but she ignored him.

"The decision at that time gave the cadre temporary leadership until Devon Trelane's capture and pending sanction of the House."

Lorenzo leaned forward as if ready to interrupt. Isabella glared at him, and he settled back, his brows furrowed, and his lips thinned in growing anger.

"In our haste to review our Father's succession plans, we overlooked the inherent succession laws."

Lorenzo leaned forward again, as did several other members. Isabella's brow lifted. Apparently, the Council hadn't given the succession laws any consideration, or perhaps they simply weren't given all the facts.

"According to those laws," she continued, "should anything happen to a House leader, whether by death, killed by an enemy outside of war, or convicted of a crime, then the heir of the leader," she paused for a brief instant, "or if one isn't available, an heir of the House is next in line."

The Council began to stir with mumbles and side conversations. Lorenzo stood and appeared ready to jump over the table. She sensed the cadre taking a step closer.

Isabella slammed the clock to a stop. "Council members will remember this is the petitioner's time." She turned her gaze to Simone. "Please explain." She didn't restart the clock.

"There's nothing to explain." Lorenzo couldn't seem to restrain himself. "Everyone knows Lyra Trelane has been catatonic and locked in an asylum for decades."

Simone shook her head. "According to the succession law as I understand it, the mental stability of the heir is not a factor to becoming a House leader as long as they have a strong cadre." She turned her gaze to Lorenzo. "And I can assure you, the House Trelane has a stellar cadre."

Isabella broke in before Lorenzo had the opportunity. "I think we can all agree the cadre of the House Trelane is more than sound to guide a successor." She glanced around the table at the other Council members, who all nodded in agreement.

Lorenzo, after clenching his jaw several times, had no choice but to agree or provide evidence to the contrary. He nodded with a quick jerk of his head, then he smiled. "There's the matter of the Council seat. For that, mental stability is required. Is House Trelane abdicating their seat on the Council?"

"No." Simone's tone left no doubt that she was prepared for this.

Isabella gave Lorenzo a warning glare, but he'd already slouched in his seat, apparently satisfied the matter was now up for discussion.

"It's imperative that a seat is filled with someone of sound mind." Council member Bertrand scratched his head. He was one of the younger members and had been an ally to House Trelane. "This heir would have to undergo testing to be approved to fill the Council seat."

Testing. Simone let the word roll around as she considered the

Lyra she'd met this afternoon. So different from the person she'd known to this point. Not that she'd known Lyra well, but she'd always made time for the girl when at Oasis. The option wasn't without merit, and she was grateful Bertrand had mentioned it. She gave a slight nod in his direction.

"The House Trelane requests the members put the question of the Council seat in abeyance until the final judgment in the case of Devon Trelane."

The mumbling of the Council members began again, but this time Isabella let them murmur while she studied Simone. She knew there was a game afoot, and instead of admonishment in that steely gaze, there was respect. It gave Simone the jolt she required to remain stoic.

When the members quieted on their own, Isabella steepled her fingers, tapping them ever so lightly on her chin.

"Madame Chairperson." Lorenzo's hands raised in supplication. "We're losing sight of the original issue, of why we're even having this discussion. Their leader is mad on Magic Poppy, and it's quite possible the entire House is responsible for the drug being back in circulation."

Lucas took a step, but he froze at Simone's glare and dropped fangs.

"Those are serious charges. Do you have evidence to present?" Isabella's irritation was clear.

"Not at this time." Lorenzo bowed his head.

"This isn't the first time you've brought an accusation to this Council without provocation. The Council doesn't care about your personal feud with the House Trelane. You know quite well that spreading rumors could bring charges against you, and you've just given their House two dozen witnesses that can be used as evidence."

Lorenzo clenched his jaw but said nothing.

"Perhaps we should table the entire matter of House leader until after the resolution of Devon Trelane's case." Council member Jacova relaxed in his chair as if he was lord of the chamber, ignoring Simone. There was no love lost between him and Devon. He and Lorenzo were thick as thieves.

"Before the Council rules, may I present a witness?" Simone held her breath. This was the moment it all came down to.

"We've already spent too much time on this." Lorenzo's murmur rolled across the chamber, but most of the Council appeared curious, including Isabella.

"You can assure this witness is material to your request?" Isabella appeared more than hopeful. It was almost as if the woman knew who waited in the hall.

"Most assuredly," she responded.

"Please proceed."

Simone nodded to Bella, who turned and strode to the door, the sound of her boots echoing off the ceiling. She stuck her head out the door, waited several seconds, then nodded back to Simone.

Simone waited for the door to open again, then turned back to the Council. "I'd like to present Lyra Trelane."

For the third time, the Council erupted in loud whispers, but once Lyra began her stroll to the dais, the members watched in silent awe, obviously confused by Lorenzo's earlier comment that she'd been in a catatonic state.

Lyra strode in as regal as any queen with her head held high, her shoulders back, and her rose-colored tunic and flowing pants giving her a youthful appearance. Her House medallion draped around her neck, reflecting the lights from the chamber. Her hair, pulled back into a chignon, gave her the touch of maturity the Council needed to see.

Simone glanced at Lorenzo, who appeared shell-shocked, and it took every ounce of strength to not laugh out loud. It was difficult enough to hold in a self-satisfied grin. She stepped down to let Lyra take the dais. This was where their hopes lay, at the feet of a woman who, up until two days ago, seemed nothing more than an adult child requiring diligent supervision.

Isabella smiled at Lyra. "Welcome to Council chambers, Miss Trelane."

"Thank you, Mistress Stanton." Lyra's voice was lyrical but strong, and her smile ethereal.

"Did you wish to address the members?"

Lyra nodded. "If I may. Just a few words." She smiled at the members, and when her gaze fell on Lorenzo, her expression changed. "Hello, Lorenzo. It's good to see you again." Her stony countenance belied her words, but she didn't dwell on him long.

For just a moment, Simone wondered what would happen if she left Lyra and Lorenzo in a room together with just one dagger. Though he towered over her, Simone would easily put her money on Lyra.

"As an heir to the House Trelane, I wanted to make my intentions clear. I have full faith in my brother and know well the kind of vampire he is. And while he may have faults, he is not capable of the assertions that have been raised against him." She paused, seeming to catch her breath, or god forbid, remember why she was there. Simone breathed slowly, not wanting anyone to hear her accelerated heart rate.

Then Lyra shrugged. "I've discussed our options with the cadre. It is my duty, not as Devon's sister, but as the daughter of Guildford Trelane, to take the role as leader of the House Trelane. However, once my brother is exonerated, the role will return to him." She paused and looked down at her hands, which she'd been wringing. She dropped them to her side. "Should he be convicted of a high crime and put to death, then I will retain the role."

"Just like that, you'll assume leadership." Lorenzo chuckled. "I'm curious as to where you've been all this time. I'm sure my fellow members would like to know as well before we decide if our previous judgment should be vacated."

This time her glare was icy. "Master Venizi. The Council has no other option than to vacate the previous judgment. Our succession laws are quite clear in this matter." Her smile was sickly sweet as she turned her gaze to the rest of the Council. "Unless, of course, the Council was going to readdress succession rights. I'm sure there wouldn't be any problem gathering the Houses for deliberation on the topic."

The members dropped their gazes, busying themselves with taking notes, jostling paper, or picking at the tapestry weaves on their robes.

"That won't be necessary, Miss Trelane." Isabel wrote something in a journal then closed the book. "The previous judgment against House Trelane has been vacated, and the Council recognizes Lyra Trelane as the new leader. However, the matter of Devon Trelane and the charges brought against him remain. Since the matter of sanction has been set aside, you have one week to bring him in, or the Eliminators will be sent."

She hit a gong with a small, bronze baton. Then she rose, followed by the rest of the members as she left the chamber through the back doors.

Once they were alone, Lyra stumbled, and in a flash, Lucas grabbed her around the waist. "Are you all right?"

Lucas's worried expression told Simone all she needed to know. "Let's move. Keep it tight, but we need to show decorum, people." She leaned toward Lyra. "What's happened?"

Lyra shook her head. "Sometimes the voices require more energy than I have." She tapped Lucas's arm. "Get me to the limo as quickly as you can."

Simone froze for an instant and glanced at Bella. "I didn't just hear that, did I?"

"At least she didn't mention the voices to the Council."

"Small favors." Simone glanced around at the tapestry-filled walls and painted ceilings. "I hope I don't have to look at this place anytime soon."

She strode out, Bella at her heels. She was going to have to have a long talk with Sergi when he returned from New Orleans.

*Chapter Thirteen*

I WAKE to a dark room and an acidic scent I can't place. It's cold, and I tug the puffy blanket closer. My body aches, and there's a hunger that nothing satisfies. I unfold my limbs and stand, the cover dropping to the floor.

My eyes adjust, and the room comes into focus. Alone. Hungry. I move to the next room, tripping over something on the floor but catching myself before I fall. A bank of lockers is against one wall. They're large, and I yank one open. Empty. I try the next. Empty. I continue until the fourth attempt. A deer hangs upside down. I slice it open with my long fingernails. And I feast.

"Devon!"

~

I SPRANG UP, my joints aching and a fierce hunger gripping me. It took a few minutes to remember I was in a hotel room, the afternoon light seeping through the edges of the heavy drapes. I stumbled from bed and managed to slam my toe against the dresser. A curse word flew from my lips, and tears filled my eyes. I didn't know if they were from the pain in my foot or something residual from the dream.

The bathroom was comfortably dark, and I felt for the tub, reaching up to turn on the shower. I ripped off my tank top and undies then climbed in. The icy water pricked my skin, instantly forming goosebumps. When the fog left my brain, I turned the water to hot and stood quietly until my skin changed from blue to red. When I couldn't take it anymore, I shut off the water and dropped to my ass, holding my knees to my chest.

Was this what the earlier headaches were trying to tell me? Devon, the beast, or some strange combination of them had been trying to reach me in their dreams.

At some point, I crawled out of the tub and stripped the towels from the rack, wrapping my body and hair before lumbering back to the bed, where I pulled myself into a fetal position. I didn't want to face the dream again, but I had no choice. This was why I was in New Orleans.

The dream was eerily reminiscent of the one where Devon had killed Sorrento. Except this time, I was in Devon's head, or more accurately, the beast's. I couldn't know for sure. Since I'd never dreamwalked with anyone else, it was my best guess. That and the deer carcass.

I grimaced and raced for the bathroom, the towel around my body falling, and I almost tripped, catching myself on the wall. I squeezed way too much yet not enough toothpaste on a brush and scrubbed for five minutes until the last taste of dead deer was gone.

I moped back to bed and tugged the covers over my head, crying myself back to sleep until the muffled sound of my cell phone woke me.

I blinked and glanced at the clock on the nightstand. Three p.m. I winced at my stiff limbs and fumbled for the phone, grabbing it on the third attempt.

I didn't bother checking the caller ID. I didn't have the strength.

"Hello." My voice crackled, hoarse and thirsty.

"Cressa?"

I almost cried with relief when I heard Ginger's voice. "It's me."

"You sound awful. Have you been out drinking?"

"I wish." I leaned against the pillows. "At least I'd have an excuse for this headache."

"A migraine? You've never gotten them before. Are you eating and drinking water?"

"No, and yes, and stop mothering me." I was fairly certain the dead deer didn't count as a meal.

"Touchy. I woke you from a nap."

"Sorry. We got in really late, then got up too early for no reason. I'm hungover from no sleep."

"Is that all it is?"

I was far from understanding the dream and nowhere near ready to talk about it. "I haven't eaten since this morning."

"That explains it." Her tone didn't sound like she bought my story, and I could have hugged her for not pressing. "Has Sergi told you the news?"

"Something about Devon?" Maybe that would explain the dream.

"I'm sorry. No." Her voice had dropped to a whisper then brightened. "The Council agreed with the succession law. Lyra's our temporary House leader. Word from Lucas is that Lorenzo was completely shocked to see her and was raging pissed at the Council's decision, though even he couldn't argue against it. House Trelane will live another day."

"That's good." Mustering up enthusiasm wasn't in the cards. "What about Devon?"

Ginger's delayed response told me everything I needed to know. "The Council gave us one week to bring him in before they send the Eliminators to find him."

A shortened deadline and almost a full day spent here with

nothing to show for it. "Thanks for letting me know. I need to meet Sergi in an hour. Let me catch up with you tomorrow."

"I suggest something from room service before meeting Sergi with that mood."

I snorted. "You're not wrong."

After hanging up, I called room service for a pot of coffee and a beignet. If sugar and coffee didn't pull me out of my fugue state, nothing would.

An hour later, fully caffeinated and the plate licked clean of every sprinkle of powdered sugar, I was dressed to kill. Hopefully, that wasn't a premonition of tonight's events. I went with black flowing pants with deep pockets and a sleeveless turquoise crop top. I added simple diamond studs Devon had given me and the House Trelane bracelet.

Sergi waited at the bar, and when I approached, he noticed the bracelet. His smile was warm and genuine.

"A nice touch." He kissed my cheek. "Shall we sit for a minute? I have news from home."

My cheeks felt warm from his attention, and I shook my head. "I spoke with Ginger an hour ago, so unless there's something new, I'm already caught up."

He studied me with the same eye as if I'd just finished a training session, assuring I was in one piece and didn't require any medical treatment.

"I'm fine. At least for now."

"Then let's meet Romero."

I'd assumed Sergi had set up a meeting with the vamp, but when we got to the tea house tastefully set along Lake Pontchartrain, we were directed to a table for two in one of back rooms with tall windows that overlooked the water. Along the opposite side of the room was a private table that sat six. Sergi gave a slight nod toward it after we sat.

"I thought you had a meeting set up with Romero." I spread a napkin over my lap as the server placed an appetizer on the table accompanied with a tea that hinted of mint.

"We have one when he's ready." Sergi took a bite of crab roll. "This is the house specialty. They're served immediately and best eaten warm."

"I feel like we're waiting to meet the godfather."

He stared at me for a moment. "You're talking about the book?"

"Or the movie."

He shrugged. "You're not too far off. Romero is the middle child in a small but prosperous House. There are two siblings that separate him from being the successor, so he branched out early, finding his own niche in business and special connections. He's committed to his Father and the House, but his business dealings are his own. It's through him that I first met Lucas."

"I thought Lucas worked for the House Lafitte?"

Sergi nodded. "That was the first House he went to after leaving home. He met Romero during his service with the House. Romero's family and Lafitte's are quite close, and Lucas ended up as one of Romero's bodyguards."

"And then Devon snatched him up. How did that happen?"

"It's a long story, but Romero knew Lucas wouldn't stay long. He's too talented to be a simple bodyguard. When Devon offered Lucas a spot in the House with the promise of one day being part of his cadre, Romero agreed to release him."

"Please tell me there weren't any hard feelings."

He chuckled. "Don't worry. Devon is still on very good terms with Romero. But I will ask, do you have your dagger?"

"You have to ask?"

He just smiled. After four more courses, I sat back with a pleasant grin. The cuisine in New Orleans was everything I'd heard about and more. We'd barely finished the dessert when Sergi stood and waited for me to rise.

I hadn't seen the signal, but I hadn't been looking for one. I should have known better. A couple who'd been sitting with Romero stood, bowed, then exited stage left as we approached from the right.

Romero, with creamy brown skin and eyes the color of midnight, was the epitome of a storybook vampire. Handsome, dangerous, and when he smiled the tips of his fangs showed. But rather than coldness in his coal-black eyes, they were filled with warmth and mirth.

"Sergi, I couldn't believe it when I heard you were in town." His voice was a rich baritone with a light French accent that could melt a woman's panties, and if I didn't have Devon in my life, I'd probably be drooling.

"A business trip, but how could I not take time to say hello." The two men kissed cheeks before Romero stepped back and took in every inch of me. Slowly. He wasn't the first man to undress me with his perusal, and I took the opportunity to give him a good once over, and his lips twitched.

"So, this is Devon's Blood Ward I've heard so much about. Cressa, is it?"

I didn't dare glance at Sergi and wondered if there was some underground vampire gossip mill. "Yes. It's nice to meet you."

He pulled me in and kissed both cheeks. "Only nice?" He chuckled. "I'll let that slide since we just met, but from what Lucas tells me, you're a force not to be taken lightly." When I did sneak a glance at Sergi, Romero gave my hand a squeeze and pulled out a chair for me. "Lucas and I talk on a regular basis. We keep each other up to date on events." When he sat, he shook his head, and his expression became somber. "I wish all the best for Devon and that his recovery is quick. As Sergi and Lucas both know, my Father is in support of House Trelane." Once he made his position clear, his mood instantly changed. "Now, tell me the current news and what can I do for you."

The two vamps spent thirty minutes getting caught up on

Lyra's temporary succession to House leader and the incident with the rogue shifters in SoCal.

"What brought you to our doorstep?" Romero poured a cup of spicy-scented tea, then sipped it.

"We're trying to locate Philipe Renaud."

Sergi's statement was answered with a blank expression and long stare. I almost rolled my eyes. Sergi was a master at waiting the other person out, but I had a feeling this wasn't the first time these two had played this game.

Romero thrummed his fingers on the table as he considered his words. When he smiled broadly, I couldn't take my eyes from him. He had magnetism before, but now it was off the charts. If his father and brothers had half an ounce of Romero's looks and charm, it was a wonder they weren't a more influential House. "It seems you're not the only one."

I shot a glance to Sergi. Had Venizi beat us to him?

"Can you tell me who else is asking?" Sergi glanced around the room, and I followed his gaze. The only customers who paid us any attention were a couple of tables away and were probably waiting their turn with Romero.

"It's nothing but whispers on the wind. No one can put a name to them."

"Do you know where he is?"

Romero shook his head. "No one knows or is talking. Either one amounts to the same answer."

"There was a trustee meeting at the Library this morning."

Romero's eyes narrowed just before a loud laugh erupted, and he took a bite of bread pudding that he must have been nursing all night. He took his time savoring it. "Barely a day in town and you already know more than most. Yes. The old man..." He looked at me. "That's what the locals call the Father of the House Renaud." He turned back to Sergi. "He called the meeting yesterday. It's rare for such short notice. Even with my connections, no one is sharing.

Though the timing seems suspicious, considering everything else going on."

Sergi seemed to be lost in thought, and after a long moment asked, "Do you know how long Philipe has been traveling?"

Romero shrugged, which gave no indication whether he considered Philipe might be on the run. It seemed, after I found a travel itinerary in the man's office at the L.A. library, Devon suspected the man was in hiding. When Romero didn't respond to the question, I had to question if there wasn't some truth to Sergi's fishing. He finally shrugged. "I'll give you this one promise because we're such old friends. If I should hear something I believe to be of value, I'll reach out."

Sergi didn't hesitate in his response. "It's always good to see you, old friend." He stood and held out his arm for me.

"Tell me, Sergi." Romero's gaze turned curious. "Does this have anything to do with Devon's current troubles?"

Sergi rapped his knuckles on the table and gave him a measured look. "Not his current one."

# Chapter Fourteen

JACQUES DROVE the group back to the manor. Lyra had fallen asleep before they left the Council grounds, and the rest of the team remained quiet until the limo pulled up to the front door. A black Escalade was parked in front of the steps.

"Have they sent Sentinels?" Bella asked.

At first, Simone didn't see any of the posted guards, then spotted one off to the far left, next to a tree. He was diligent but didn't appear to be on alert. Another guard came from the right, most likely patrolling the manor. She met them at the bottom of the steps, just as the group exited the limo.

"All is well, Simone. The visitors arrived about fifteen minutes ago. I would have sent you a text, but they asked for no communications." She lowered her gaze when Simone's own turned heated. "I think you'll understand once you meet them. Ginger is entertaining them in Devon's...your office."

"Ginger is entertaining them?" Her voice turned sultry, a sign her beast was upset, and the guard took a step backward. The cadre, used to Simone's quick mood shifts, spread out, eyes focused on the landscape and front door, watching for possible threats.

Lyra placed a hand on Simone's arm. "I'm sorry. I knew they'd be waiting for us. The Council meeting took more out of me than I anticipated."

Then Lucas was there, helping Lyra up the steps. Simone shook her head. In a matter of two days, the world had turned upside down.

Lyra and the cadre waited for Simone before entering the office. Simone hesitated, not sure of protocol, but with Lyra accepting the role of heir, she had no choice but to step aside. She opened the door and stepped back, waiting for Lyra.

When Lyra stepped next to her, she said, "Walk with me," and the two entered together.

Ginger popped up from the chair next to the sofa. "Oh, hi. You're back." She was all smiles but couldn't seem to stop bouncing on her tiptoes. "I hope you don't mind, the room was a bit chilly, so I started a fire. Then we started talking about a recent trip they made to Napa Valley, and well, Devon keeps a few bottles of wine stocked in here, or so Lucas told me." She stopped bouncing, but her right hand kept brushing back her hair, though it never seemed to be in the way.

Simone sighed. Ginger was teetering between nerves and terror. "We appreciate you entertaining our guests until our return. Would you mind letting Anna know I'll need to see her in a half hour?"

"Oh. Absolutely." She took a step then turned to the man and woman on the sofa, who Simone tried to place but was coming up blank. "It was a pleasure meeting you both." She half curtsied then all but ran from the room.

"I'm sorry for that. Ginger isn't part of the staff." Simone wasn't sure how to explain who she was. She wasn't even sure. *The best friend of my leader's thief and lover?*

The cadre spread out, performing the routine by rote—one by the door, one by the desk, and one by the coffee bar. Simone stood next to the chair Ginger had vacated. Once again, she wasn't sure the correct protocol for unexpected visitors. That never happened at Oasis.

Before she had a moment to think, Lyra swept around the couch and held out a hand to each of them, which they immediately took. "I'm glad you felt comfortable enough to come." Lyra released their hands and sat in the chair across from where Simone stood. She glanced up and nodded to the empty chair.

Simone, still a bit confused, donned a welcoming smile of her own.

"This is Asher and Maya Boretsky." Lyra lifted the wine bottle sitting on the coffee table and refilled the Boretskys' glasses before pouring one for Simone and a small glass for herself.

Simone took the time to consider the implication of members of the Boretsky House, the leader that Devon was supposed to have killed, sitting in this office. And again, she came up blank.

"This is Simone. She's first in Devon's cadre." Lyra hesitated, then shook her head with a soft, tinkling laugh. "I suppose my cadre for now." Then she introduced the rest of the cadre. "Sergi, our security expert, is on another assignment. Simone is leading our investigation into your father's murder."

The woman, Maya, held a hand to her chest. "I'm so grateful." She looked to the man next to her. "My brother is the eldest and now the leader of House Boretsky."

"But you haven't taken the Council seat yet." Simone still couldn't put the pieces together, then realized she'd spoken out of turn and glanced to Lyra, but she'd already turned back to their guests.

"And I won't until the matter of our Father's murder has been resolved." Asher gave his sister's arm a gentle squeeze. "We don't believe the Council is interested in investigating. They've been handed their perpetrator without questioning how easy it all was."

"Why would you believe Devon to be guiltless in this?" Simone asked and nodded to Lucas, who moved closer to the conversation. He was better than most at sussing out a lie.

Asher glanced at his sister, who seemed to have withdrawn from the conversation, but she gave his arm a reassuring return squeeze. "I need to give you a bit of background first. The House Boretsky has always been a divided House. Our Father's younger brother is considered a rebel. A risk taker. He believed in the future and what we could make of it rather than grasp for the past. Our Father, of course, felt different, wanting to hold onto the old ways, which is why he typically sided with the House Venizi."

"But not in all things from what little I've heard of the Council meetings." Lucas leaned against the bar, his arms folded, appearing indifferent to Boretsky's response.

"No." Maya spoke this time. Her smile was endearing, as if she was remembering a favored memory. "Father loved Uncle Noah. While they differed on many topics, there were one or two areas where they found common ground. When the Council's oversight involved one of those areas, Father always listened to Noah's recommendation."

"But over the last ten years or so," Asher took over, "Father had become enamored by Venizi. None of us were happy with how it looked to our old allies, and quite frankly, most of the Family disagreed with his alignment with Venizi." He stopped to take a long drink of wine then closed his eyes for a moment before running a hand through his hair. His gaze appeared haunted. "A week ago, Father came home terrified. I'm two hundred years old, and not once in all that time have I seen fear in his eyes as I did that day. He wouldn't tell me what happened other than he'd been duped. They'd all been duped."

"He never said what scared him?" Lucas looked to Simone, but she didn't have anything better to ask. His thoughts were her own.

Asher fell back against the sofa, almost caving in upon himself. A vampire who was feeling the weight of the Family on his back, trying to make sense of his Father's murder while balancing the good of the House. Simone understood quiet well. So did Lyra.

"Perhaps someone can make espresso for our friends." Lyra reached out a hand to Asher, who took it. "Take your time."

The hum of the espresso machine made the Boretskys jump, and Bella yelled, "Sorry for the noise."

Maya held a hand to her throat and laughed. "Father keeps a machine in his office as well." She shifted in her seat and pulled on an earlobe. "All Father would say was that he'd overheard something. A conversation he wished he could forget, but others needed to know. But he wasn't sure who to trust. He wanted to protect us. His cadre suggested reaching out to someone who wouldn't be observed by other Council members. That's why he reached out to Devon. Long ago, Father had been good friends with Guildford, but after his death and then Devon's censure, he began listening to Venizi, who wasn't as influential at the time."

"We believe someone had been following Father." Asher took the cup of espresso, savoring the first sip, and perhaps it helped clear his head. "The cadre suggested a private meeting in a neutral place. When we learned what happened and that Devon was the prime suspect—that Magic Poppy was involved—" He set down the cup, and his sister rubbed his shoulder.

Maya glanced around the room. Simone didn't have to follow her gaze to know the woman held everyone's rapt attention. "We immediately suspected foul play. Oh, we were aware of Devon's issue with the Poppy. Everyone on the Council would have known the reason for Devon's censure, although we guessed it wasn't the only reason. But we know Devon." She turned away.

"Wait." Lucas stepped closer. "You don't mean you knew him from long ago, you mean recently."

Simone wasn't expecting that. When her gaze shot to Lyra, she lifted a shoulder. This was news to her as well.

Asher nodded. "I ran into him a few years ago at my Father's club. He'd been there for a meeting with one of the shifters. Not The Wolf, maybe it was his second. I'm afraid I don't know the shifters well. Devon noticed me before he left and came over to say hello. I asked him about the shifters, not meaning anything more than general conversation. But then Devon explained the meeting, or more accurately the business dealings he had with the shifters. When I appeared interested, one thing led to another."

"When Asher told me, it was opposite of everything Father had been preaching. Vile from Venizi about the shifters being a lesser species. They weren't intelligent enough, were only good for labor. You know the stories as well as I."

"Devon introduced me to one of the smaller packs over in Chico." Asher drained the last of the espresso and stared into the empty cup. His brow wrinkled as he recalled the event. "He said the pack might be small, but they had a solid business network. We've been in business with that pack since our first meeting. Father never knew."

"And this is why you don't believe Devon would be on the Poppy?" Simone kept her tone even, but it seemed a stretch. It was impossible to know everything about a business partner, no matter how friendly they became.

Both siblings nodded. If they picked up on Simone's doubt, they didn't show it. Asher set down the cup, the espresso seeming to spur him on. "I suppose none of us truly knows another vampire—what they're going through, what secrets they hold. We were at the first Council meeting yesterday and were shocked by the immediacy of the sanction. We knew through Father of Venizi's hatred for everything House Trelane. Then to watch him sway the Council to make such unprecedented rulings." He shook his head. His faced reddened, and he clenched his fists. "After we discussed the meeting with the cadre, we suspected foul play. We were deciding what to do when we heard another Council meeting had been called. We weren't invited, since we haven't officially taken the House seat, but we wanted to see who showed up. When Lyra spotted us, she came over to offer her condolences and one thing led to another."

"We appreciate your support of the House, but what can we

do for you?" Simone found the information interesting but not much to go on. They already knew Venizi was most likely pulling the strings in Boretsky's murder, but without anything more substantial, it didn't move the needle on the investigation.

Maya opened her purse and pulled out a leather-covered book. She ran her hand over it. "This is Father's most recent journal. He didn't write every day, and it's mostly musings of an elder, but it's possible something in here might help you."

Lyra took the journal and held it to her chest. "We'll take good care of it while it's in our possession and will return it as soon as possible."

"Do you need extra security?" Simone asked.

"Father's businesses are scattered, as is most of our security." Asher held his sister's hand. "We have the cadre."

Simone glanced at Lucas, and he left the room. "We'll arrange for additional security. I don't believe the majority of your Family resides at the estate."

"That's right. Only the immediate family and the cadre. Everyone else is spread throughout Santa Rosa."

"I suggest you centralize as many of your family as seems appropriate. Just until this is over."

The brother stood, then helped his sister up before taking Lyra's hand. "I can't thank you enough for reaching out." He chuckled, but it sounded cold. "We haven't heard a word from Venizi. I hope you find enough to take him down."

Simone responded with a wide smile. "One step at a time."

*Chapter Fifteen*

After the tea house, Sergi drove me around the city. The sultry, twilight air was perfect for the scenic drive through the Garden District and past cemeteries with their above-ground tombs. I'd heard of New Orleans jazz funerals and found them interesting. If we ran across one, I'd force Sergi to stop so I could watch and learn.

The route eventually took us back to the French Quarter. We parked at the hotel and walked to Bourbon Street. Sergi was unusually relaxed, and he let me wander through the tourist shops and listen to music. After a dinner of appetizers at a corner bar where we people-watched, Sergi led me down a side street to a cubbyhole of a jazz club that probably attracted more locals than tourists.

The music was smooth and bluesy, and we found a half-circle booth toward the back where it was easier to talk, assuming I could get the quiet vamp in the right mood. The band was into their second set, Sergi was three scotches in, and I managed to get him to share campaign battles from four hundred years earlier. Great stories if you didn't mind the gory details that Sergi seemed to relish.

I twirled the umbrella in my Hurricane. I knew the drink was cliche, but I figured when in Rome. The first one I'd drunk was like drinking gasoline. The second one was from a takeout window and was more fruity, less rocket fuel. Since I was still able to walk into the jazz club without stumbling, I figured I could sip the next one, and it was either the tastiest one of the night or I was getting used to their potency. I was on my way to being a handful for Sergi to get home, so I might not have been the best judge.

There I was, twirling the pink and lime umbrella, a dozen subtle ways to broach the subject running through my booze-soaked brain when I blurted out, "So, how did Devon get hooked on Magic Poppy the first time?"

I could have died. I blamed the Hurricanes.

I hung my head, almost poking my eye out on the umbrella. And the day had started out so well. The minutes ticked by, and I racked my brain for another topic.

"He didn't tell me much about that first time." Sergi's voice was difficult to hear above the music.

I inched closer to him, keeping my head down, not wanting to meet his gaze and give him a reason to stop.

"He told me who the supplier was and..." He stopped, and I thought he changed his mind about telling me, but he kept going. "Let me start at the beginning. This isn't something I ever thought I'd share, but considering the circumstances, I think it's best if you understand the full scope of the situation."

Was it too late to tell him never mind?

"His parents had been killed in an accident while he'd been overseas. A few years later, he ran across someone by pure coincidence that suggested their deaths hadn't been an accident. He never told me who gave him the information. Who knows if it was true, but Devon was obsessed with finding the answer. During that time, Lyra had moved from her catatonic state into a manic one. She spoke of voices that only she could hear and would be awake for days, fighting the blood donors, until collapsing from fatigue.

"Lorenzo's influence on the Council had grown, and he pushed Devon as often as he could, knowing he was adding pressure on a new House leader. At the same time, Devon created animosity with his Father's cadre when he brought in his own guards. Even with the more-than-generous options Devon had given the old cadre, most of them left without a second glance."

I heard the ice clink against the glass in his drink, and I lifted my head to give him my full attention.

He met my gaze. "I think Devon still feels guilty about that. A rookie mistake, but those tend to be the ones that stick with a vampire." He sipped the scotch. "The bottom line, he was under intense scrutiny and stress. One day, he left the manor and never returned. It didn't take long for the rumors to start. Someone from Venizi's family had seen Devon in the Hollows.

"He'd rented a room at some cheap motel, and by the time I'd found him, he'd already taken his first dose. He wouldn't tell me about it, but he let it slip he'd purchased a second dose. I turned the room upside down and never found it, but he relented and told me the name of his supplier. When I tracked the guy down, he swore he'd only sold Devon the one sample. At the time, I assumed Devon had run across someone else with the Poppy and thought he could control it. But now?"

He stared at the stage. The band was on a break, and the club was playing a jazz mix over the speakers. Sergi didn't have what poker players called a tell. No affectation or habitual behavior that gave away his thoughts or moods, but I'd been in enough training scenarios with him to know when he was pissed. A blood vessel on his left temple pulsed when he was ready to punch something. I trusted he was under enough control to not act out in public.

"I've been asking myself if maybe Devon had been passed the Poppy without his knowing." He finished his scotch and waved an arm for the server. "It only takes one dose to become highly addicted." His hand clenched. "He always said he couldn't remember taking it, and I never believed him. When he found another supplier, I told him he was on his own. Before I walked away, I relented and said the House would be waiting when he was ready to lead again."

I wanted to say something, but there wasn't anything that would fix the past. He wouldn't want to hear platitudes or that there was nothing he could have done. So I said nothing.

His gaze returned to mine, and it was the first time I saw true pain in his eyes. "It was decades before he returned completely sober and full of contrition. It took several more years before he proved himself as leader of the House."

"How did the House survive without a leader?" If they hadn't considered Lyra for succession this time, it was doubtful they'd thought of it the first time.

"The cadre took care of House business as best we could. Devon was still the House leader in name."

"But he can't be now?"

"He hadn't committed any crime the first time. The Poppy was illegal, but there were no criminal penalties for being addicted. There were fines, but the criminal charges only applied to the suppliers, who conveniently disappeared once the Eliminators were aware of the Poppy supply."

"Will it take decades for him to get clean this time?" I'd be old and gray by then.

"It didn't take decades to get clean. It took a few weeks to break the addiction. It took decades for him to decide whether he wanted to come back. Decker helped him through that." When I perked up, he shook his head and swallowed a third of his drink. "That's a story for Devon to share."

He said it like it might be a possibility someday. Then he squelched my hopes just as quickly. "I need you to understand something. The beast never took control of him back then." His eyes glowed red, and I didn't think he was aware of it. "Do you understand what that means?"

I did, but I didn't. This was my worst nightmare, and I didn't want to think about it. But now that he put it out there, I couldn't deny it. The beast had control. Even if they weaned Devon off the Poppy, it was highly probable that what made Devon who he was would be lost. Most likely forever. Would that mean he'd have to be put down anyway, whether he was guilty of Boretsky's death or not?

"It's just been too long with too high a dose."

It was my turn to tear my gaze away, and I focused on the band, who'd returned from their break. Their first number was timely—a saxophone solo. Its soulful sounds attempted to rip my heart out. I took a deep breath and waded in.

"No."

"What?"

I felt a bit sorry for him. Except for Devon, he wasn't used to anyone telling him no. He should know me by now. I was probably way too deep in the soft cradle of a Hurricane overdose, but the truth was, I wasn't willing to give up until I could look at the beast and not see Devon. Because I had seen the beast in the alley, but the eyes were still Devon. Eyes that begged for help. I wasn't going to walk away from that.

"I don't know how yet, but we're not giving up on Devon." I stood and might have swayed. "And if you think otherwise, then you're not worthy to be in his cadre. Now, I have to pee." I stumbled my way to the restroom. Not the most suave of exits, but the twitch on Sergi's lips before I turned away told me all I needed to know. The asshole had been testing me.

I might have taken a short nap while sitting on the toilet. One minute, maybe five. I should have stopped at two Hurricanes, but I didn't stagger as much after splashing cold water on my face. I'd only taken a couple steps into the hallway when a hand snaked out and grabbed my upper arm.

I would have screamed for help if I wasn't grimacing in pain. The skeleton-thin man had the grip of a bruiser. It was a vamp that could snap my bones like kindling.

"Let me go." I threw my other hand out in attempt to slow our momentum, but I was nothing more than a Chihuahua being dragged away by a Doberman.

The sticky night air hit me as the whoosh of cool air from the club ushered me out the back door. The alley was narrow, and I spotted the limo two buildings down. I cursed my luck. My dagger was in my right pocket, but the vamp held me by my right arm. Note to self, carry a weapon in both pockets. Scratch that. Learn how to use a weapon with my left hand, then carry a second weapon. I was considering other options when the vamp came to an abrupt stop, and I bumped into him, which was similar to walking into a brick wall.

Sergi stood in our path. I should stop being surprised by his abilities. "I was anticipating buying you a drink. I have to admit, I feel slighted."

The vamp merely stared. Sergi stared back. I was sorry I'd worn the heels because this showdown could go on for a while. Vamps were nothing if not stubborn.

The front passenger door of the limo opened. Sergi must have heard it, but he didn't show any signs of it. He was either nuts or really brave, and it really wasn't much of a guess which.

Another overly thin vamp stepped out, and he opened the back door. His smooth, honeyed voice was meant to soothe. "We're sorry for our poor manners, but secrecy is of the utmost importance. If both you and Miss Langtry would come with us." He raised his arm toward the open door of the limo. "Miss Dupré has requested an audience."

Chapter Sixteen

SERGI GLANCED into the opened back door of the limo, then stepped aside to let me enter. I barely noticed him slide in next to me. My attention was on the woman who sat in one of the plush jump seats across from the soft leather bench where we sat.

I wasn't sure what I expected. Maybe a grandmotherly type with a plate of cookies or some scary voodoo hair ornament. I scratched my chin, ensuring myself my jaw wasn't hanging open.

When we'd walked into the jazz club earlier that evening, there was an enormous painting of Josephine Baker hanging in the entrance foyer. I had to take a double take because this woman was the perfect doppelganger for her.

She studied me, ignoring Sergi. That might have something to do with the vamp who sat across from him in the other jump seat. He stared at a point somewhere between Sergi and me.

"I'm not her." Her voice was deep, with a slight French accent. Or perhaps it was Creole. I wasn't knowledgeable enough to know the difference.

"You mean Colantha or Josephine?"

Her laugh was evocative, and I smiled. It was impossible not to. "Josephine was an amazing woman, and we enjoyed using our likeness to fool friends and fans alike. Although most of the time it was simply to give her peace whenever she was in the States."

A trickster. That was good to know.

When I just nodded, she turned her perusal to Sergi, giving him a quick once-over before her gaze landed back on me. Her eyes narrowed. "You don't talk much."

Sergi snorted, which made her chuckle.

"It's your meeting." A headache hit me, and I doubled over. Sergi reached out a hand, but the other vamp blocked it. I managed to hold out an arm to Sergi. "I'm all right." Then I squinted again. Maybe not. Then I wasn't in the limo anymore.

I stood on a cliff, the ocean waves—a hundred feet down—crashed against the rocks. I spun around. A dense jungle was a mere twenty-five yards away. Colantha sat in a raggedy, over-stuffed recliner with burnt-orange and lime-green stripes. The footrest was raised, and she stared out to sea as if she were watching a gigantic LCD display. All she needed was the bucket of popcorn.

There was an empty recliner near her, and she waved me over.

"I prefer to speak without your bodyguard listening." She glanced upward as if gathering strength to deal with a stubborn child. "Come sit. You've been waiting for this. I don't bite. That's why I have Frederick and Jamison."

Those must be her two vamps. I glanced around again, then sat in the recliner. My feet were immediately lifted as if the chair had a mind of its own, but I imagined it was her doing.

"Is this a dream?"

Her laugh floated away with the soft breeze I hadn't noticed before. "The easiest explanation is that we're in a dreamworld. One concocted from my own imagination, although this particular one is a mixture of several of my favorite places. This is my thinking place."

"And you come here whenever you want?"

"Of course."

I jumped when she patted my hand. She hadn't moved from the recliner, but we were now sitting side-by-side.

"But it's like a dream."

"In as much as we use our minds to create the worlds. But you're sitting in a real recliner. You walked across the rough surface of a real cliff. If you were to step off the ledge, you would fall to your death unless I stopped it."

That was good to know. "So gravity, or I guess, the normal rules apply."

She nodded. "For those that don't have the ability to modify the environment. If you were trained to use your skills, you could walk off that ledge and float down to the rocks." She leaned over. "With enough mental strength you could fly off that ledge."

I sat back. "You're serious?"

"Of course. I might create the constructs, but that doesn't mean you couldn't modify some elements. Take your chair, for example. Perhaps you prefer a different color fabric. You could make it a paisley design. Or perhaps make it leather."

"And how does one gain that power?"

This time her laugh sounded more like a cackle. "Right to the advanced course. You must be a Rasmussen."

That was like splashing ice water in my face. Any residual alcohol vanished. "You know my father?"

She glanced out to the sea, and she became motionless, like a robot waiting for its next command. A moment later, she patted my hand. "All in good time. For now, you must learn what it is to be a dreamwalker. You've lost valuable years that will delay the progress you should have been making by now, even without training."

"Why didn't you come for me before?" I could have been out of Christopher's influence before everything had turned bad.

"We knew you existed, but we had no way to find you. The only thing we could do was leave markers, a psychic imprint, if you will, that would notify us if anyone asked about Rasmussen. Then your bodyguard started poking around, and once we located you, your situation piqued my interest. I was waiting for the correct moment, but then you selected it instead."

That had been Devon's idea, not mine. "What happens now? Do you train me?"

"Tomorrow, we'll go to the sanctuary and give you a tour of where you'll be staying."

That made sense. I wouldn't lose time going back and forth from the hotel. "What time should we be there?"

She smiled. "Just you. And we'll pick you up from your hotel."

"Sergi has my utmost trust."

"I have no doubt of that. But he has responsibilities with his House. He can't leave them to stay with you. It's not necessary."

I should have known this was going too well. "I'm sorry. I'm not sure I understand."

"What part?"

"It sounded like you expect me to move here. How long do you expect this to take?" Yep, this was all too good to be true.

She clucked her tongue at me. "My dear, Cressa. It will take years."

"Yeah, well, I only have a couple of days and a friend to save, so we'll need to do the speed-reader's equivalent."

"You can't learn about dreamwalking in just a handful of days. Dreamwalkers spend years, decades learning their craft."

I pushed the footrest down and stood. "I think we might have gotten our signals crossed. I came here to find my father or some idea where he might be. I'd also hoped to get some basic training or maybe an instruction manual for my necklace."

I was suddenly in the middle of a raging forest fire. The flames whipped around us, and though the heat was bearable, my skin was slick with sweat. A dome barrier kept the fiery storm at bay, but it didn't make it any less nerve-racking.

While I was a hot mess, Colantha was dressed for a garden

party—a white summer dress, bright-pink platform sandals, and a face filled with anger. "Instruction manual? You are a neophyte."

I should be terrified, but name-calling was somewhat below my standards. Until she became Simone-scary, it was hard to waste the energy on getting worked up.

"Yes. I am." We had different expectations. I should have anticipated that, and I held up my hands in truce. "I have a debt I haven't repaid and a friend in trouble. I admit I know nothing of being a dreamwalker or how it will impact my life, but I'm not ready to commit years of my life to studying it. That doesn't mean I don't respect it, but for now, I just need to learn how to control it. The necklace was a disaster, but I have to know more about it."

She didn't respond, but the fire disappeared, replaced with a mountain lake, and we stood in a field of spring flowers. Intense emotions had created my shared dreams with Devon. Was it possible Colantha's emotions dictated these constructs as she called them? There'd only been one time where I'd had control over a dream, and I'd ended up in Devon's bed. If I could only remember how I'd done that. Somehow, I needed Colantha to teach me that much before I left.

"There's a matter of some urgency. Someone's life is in danger."

The scene changed again, and we were in an office or—I twisted around to take in the walls of books—perhaps a personal library. Colantha sat behind an immense desk. It almost dwarfed her, and she wasn't that small of a woman. My head spun from jumping so quickly between constructs.

"What did you have in mind?" She held my gaze and lifted a brow as she studied me.

Something had caught her interest. And while caution was in order, I jumped in with both feet.

"I have three days." I braced for another construct, but all the woman did was turn toward a portrait that hung between two bookcases. I squinted. I'd seen that flower before. "Isn't that the Blood Poppy?"

She swung back to me. "You know this flower?"

I shook my head and gave a half shrug, as if she was supposed to understand the conflicting gestures. "I've seen a larger portrait of it in the Renaud Library in L.A. I didn't know what it was until a vamp told me." My own gaze traveled off, a memory coming back. "I think there's an image of one on my medallion."

Colantha nodded and pulled a leather cord from beneath her dress. A medallion similar to mine hung from the end. "Yes. Along with an ibis and a dagger."

"You have one, too?"

"All dreamwalkers have one. An ordained metalworker creates one whenever a new dreamwalker is born into this world."

"Not handed down?" When Colantha gave me that cool gaze again, I added, "I just assumed my father passed his down to me."

She nodded in understanding. "It's been known to happen when a dreamwalker dies as a token of bond, but it doesn't always go to their first heir. Or any heir. However, I know that yours was made for you because I saw it made." She chuckled. "It's been rare over the last century for a dreamwalker to be born. We tend to take note of it."

I leaned back. This was too much. The Blood Poppy. Everyone having the similar necklace like some dysfunctional club. Mine being made for me. What was all of this information supposed to tell me? Nothing that solved my current dilemma.

"I'll make a bargain with you."

I frowned. If she pulled out a fiddle of gold, I'd run screaming. Although, where would I run if I was in someone else's construct? Could I wake myself up, or would I end up in another psychic coma?

Her expression turned stern, and her tone reminded me of my mother when she was in a mood. "Don't pout. I understand your situation. I would have been surprised and disappointed if you hadn't fought back. Very few would be willing to spend years in training with us. The ones that do are either very weak, or they're here for refuge. Others stay not out of motivation to learn our link with the environment, but to seize more power. That is not the true path of the dreamwalker. We are the instruments of nature, not its ruler.

She leaned over her desk, the silver medallion tucked back under her dress. "Three days now in exchange for three months when your debt is paid."

I could only stare. She was giving me my three days, but I couldn't help think there was a catch.

She clucked her tongue. "Is three months so much to ask for understanding your true nature? For certain, you won't discover it in three days."

She had a point. And what was three months? I wouldn't have to worry about it until the debt was paid, which meant I'd be able to help Devon and his mission once we got him back. And I refused to consider any other outcome.

I nodded. "Three days of training now in exchange for three months later."

She nodded as the construct faded back to the limo. Her smile made me think of the cat who ate the canary. I almost felt the feathers sprouting.

## *Chapter Seventeen*

AFTER THE BORETSKYS LEFT, Simone needed time to think. They'd been rushing to respond to the Council's orders, preparing the House and the family for a siege and possible sanction. Now that the House was safe, their priorities had shifted.

Lyra required rest, as did the cadre, and she shooed everyone out of the office. She missed Sergi, for no other reason than his quiet demeanor and steady presence. She picked up the journal the Boretskys had left, and after stirring the fire and adding another log, she leaned back on the sofa with a fresh cup of espresso.

She ran a hand over the journal as Maya Boretsky had done. The leather cover had been softened with age and heavy use. It was scarred in many places, and she lifted it to her nose, breathing in the scent of paper, leather, and something unfamiliar that she considered before storing the scent away in memory.

She opened the journal and began to read.

A gentle knock jarred her, and she blinked.

"Come."

The door opened, and Bella stuck her head in. "Cook says dinner will be ready in half hour. Lyra wanted to keep to a schedule."

Simone nodded. "I'll be there."

Once the door closed, she glanced at the fire, which was nothing more than embers, and returned to the journal. If they were sticking with their normal dinner hour, then she'd been reading for several hours. She finished the last pages in fifteen minutes and reviewed the notes she'd taken. She'd have Anna make copies and Lucas could return the journal in the morning. It would be a perfect time for him to review their security and determine if additional guards were required. It was imperative the Boretsky family was kept safe.

The journal hadn't provided any great insight, but two things came to mind for her immediate action—speak to Boretsky's younger brother, Noah, and find the man Cressa had pointed out after their visit to a tea house. The same man Cressa had seen conspiring with Gruber against Devon at a tea party.

It might be a dead end, but after weeks of training by her side and completing a couple of missions together, she knew one thing with certainty. Cressa paid attention, and if she thought the man was up to no good, it was worth checking out.

THE FOLLOWING MORNING, Simone considered the condominium high-rise with the lovely spring-green awning that covered the front entrance. It wasn't unusual for the siblings of a House leader to move away from the family manor, especially if there was animosity between them.

From what Asher had told her after a quick phone conversation, Noah, the council member's younger brother, had moved out ten years ago when the two brothers argued over Venizi's growing influence over their House. While the brothers had remained close, they found it easier to communicate with physical distance between them.

Asher had also mentioned that Noah didn't receive any financial aid from the Family, and based on the neighborhood where he'd moved, he was doing just fine. He hadn't wanted anything that had been tainted with what he considered Venizi's blood money. This would be an interesting meeting indeed.

After a friendlier-than-expected visit from Asher and Maya, she wasn't surprised that Noah was more than willing to meet. She sighed as she used her keypad to lock the sedan. The more eager someone was to spill the beans, as the humans said, the less information the person typically had, but she wasn't willing to let a sliver of a lead slip through her grasp.

Noah's condo took up half the top floor. Though it was almost eleven when he opened the door, he was in a silk bathrobe over sweats and a white T-shirt, his hair looked like it had been through a blender, and an oversized mug was gripped in his hands.

"It's Simone, right? Sorry, but I haven't been sleeping well since Hiram's murder." He walked back into the condo, leaving the door open.

She shut it behind her as she followed him past expensive artwork, leather-and-chrome furniture, and a state-of-the-art entertainment center before settling on a stool on the counter facing the kitchen.

Noah lifted a full pot of coffee. "Want a mug? Just made it." She nodded, and he set the coffee in front of her. "The second pot of the day." He glanced at the retro clock against a far wall and shook his head. "I've always been a night owl, but I just can't seem to get my shit together after..." His eyes teared up, and he busied himself with gathering sugar and cream while he controlled his emotions.

Simone dropped a few drops of cream into the coffee. "I'm sorry for your loss. From what Asher and Maya said, he was a well-loved leader."

He leaned against the counter. "He was, for the most part." He blew out a breath. "Even in these later years, after falling completely under Venizi's control, he was always fair to the Family, considering how many disagreed with the direction the House had taken. To be honest, I'm not sure he saw it."

"Did your brother have any enemies that would have acted out in revenge?"

Noah chortled. "Hardly. He was one of the quieter Council members. We argued all the time, but around others, he was considered the peacemaker. How ironic is that?"

"How so?"

He gave her a look that said how could she not know, then shook his head. "I'm sorry. With Devon's censure, he wouldn't have known unless he heard it from someone else. Hiram was always concerned about the future of our race, especially with the decline in our fertility rates and the rapid growth of humanity. He bought into the conspiracy."

"You don't believe humans are the cause of our dwindling numbers?"

"Hardly. I mean, the vast majority of them don't even know we exist. That we walk among them." He chuckled. "Even their best scientists couldn't be the cause of our decreased fertility. At least, the one virologist I know doesn't think it possible."

When she lifted a brow, he took that as the sign to continue.

"He's a friend I met through another House. He's human with more degrees than I can remember. I once gave him a sample of my blood, and he was fascinated. But without having a sample from before the fertility rates dropped, it's impossible to determine if there's a factor in the blood that might be causing it. Even then, with the chemical makeup of our blood being so different..." He shrugged. "He made it sound like it would be a lifelong pursuit in understanding what makes us vampire."

This was an area that Devon had been interested in as well. Was it a coincidence Hiram reached out to Devon, or did he know Devon had his own suspicions? She would need to call Sergi and get his take.

"Hiram's cadre didn't believe Devon was responsible."

Noah started pacing back and forth, drinking gulps of coffee with each turn, stopping to refill when necessary. "Why would he be? They hadn't spoken in years as far as I know. I was aware of the cadre recommendation. Hiram asked me, and I told him he was a fool for not reaching out sooner." He stumbled and landed in a chair, his mug hitting the elegant dinette table. He bent over, holding his head. "I should have gone with him."

"You would most likely be dead as well."

"Is Devon really hooked on the Poppy?"

"He wasn't the day of the murder."

His laugh was bitter. "That just shows how corrupt the Council has become."

"Why do you say that?"

"I called the Sentinel commander to see where they were in the investigation. Do you know what he told me? They're waiting for the Council to issue the warrant. They're not even bothering to investigate." His voice had become shrill, and it took a moment before he calmed down. "Wouldn't anyone sane find it odd that a vampire, who hadn't touched the stuff in decades and had been sober hours before the meet, would take the Poppy just before meeting a Council member who was seeking help?"

She didn't bother answering. They all knew there was something odd about the entire situation. Even with Devon's censure, the Council knew he was well regarded among the Houses and shifters.

"Did Hiram give you any clue what he was meeting Devon about?"

"No. He didn't want anyone in the Family to know. He was worried that just him knowing might bring retaliation to the Family." He ran his hands back and forth over his black-as-night hair, and she understood why it had been so disheveled. "Thank you for sending security to the manor. Asher is asking several Family members to move in until this all blows over."

"That's what allies do."

He barked out a laugh. "Yet it was the House Trelane who came, not Venizi."

There wasn't anything to say to that. "Maya shared your brother's last journal with us. Other than seeing his gradual concern with his private meetings with Venizi, there's no real lead to go on."

"He was good at keeping secrets. Sometimes he'd leave cryptic notes, but I haven't found any, and god knows I read that damn thing ten times after hearing the news."

Simone sat back and sipped the cooling coffee that was surprisingly good. She hadn't expected much from the visit, though it made her question again the Council's decisive move against Devon. She'd suspected there weren't any other investigations taking place. But why not? Had they simply gotten lazy over the decades, was the Sentinel commander not up to snuff, or was the Council truly corrupt?

One of her other suspicions came to mind that was worth a try. "There's a vampire who seems to follow Venizi around as though he works for him, but I don't think he's part of the Family."

Noah lifted his head, curiosity and maybe hope filling his jade-colored eyes. She wondered what color they glowed when the beast rose. "Do you have a name?"

"No. But your brother mentioned Venizi's shadow. Do you know who that might be?"

"His shadow?" He considered it. "You mean his assassin?"

She shrugged. "The term has been used to mean many things. A cleaner, an assassin, a fixer."

"Venizi has many followers that aren't part of his family. Most of them half-breeds."

"This one has an Eastern European accent. He's large, six-foot-six or taller, with brown hair and a thick neck."

He sneered. "You must mean Boris Gheata."

The name rang a bell, but she couldn't remember from where. "He's close to Venizi?"

"He's been at the manor a few times. When I was there, he never seemed to have an appointment, but Hiram always stopped everything to meet with him. I asked once who he was, and Hiram simply said he was one of Venizi's business associates."

"Maybe that's all he is."

He laughed. "Right. Okay, maybe so. But if I considered all the business associates Venizi has sent to Hiram's door, he stands out. And if I was a Sentinel, he's the first one I'd check out."

"Why?"

"Hiram was beyond distressed. If Venizi had the slightest concern that Hiram knew something he shouldn't, what better vampire to send a message than one of his closest business associates."

Simone let Noah talk for another thirty minutes, mostly reminiscing about the common interests he shared with his brother. She listened. Mostly because some of them were interesting and even humorous, and Noah seemed to need it. And the talent to soothe and comfort were common traits among the best House leaders. The skill didn't come easy to her, yet Devon believed in her and gave her the time and space to hone the ability.

When she was back in the car, she called Lucas.

"Was the meeting useful?" Ginger was speaking with someone in the background, and her voice became distant as Lucas found a quiet spot to talk.

"I have a name I want you to run down. Boris Gheata. And send it to Sergi in case he knows of him. He seems to be a business associate of Venizi's."

"Hmm. I haven't heard the name before, but we'll check it out."

"One more thing. Noah says he won't be leaving his condo for the next week. The building seems to be exclusive to vampires, and there's a security person stationed on his floor. I'd like one of ours to watch."

"I'll take care of it. Are you on your way back?"

"I need to run out to Oasis. Any word on Devon?"

"Decker said the move went as planned. He'll keep watch."

"And Lyra?"

"She's in her room, but she'll be down for lunch."

When Simone hung up, she leaned back in her seat. She wasn't sure what to make of Lyra and wished Sergi was there to give her guidance. For now, she was grateful Lyra had been at each meal and appeared stable. But the number of hours she spent in her room and her mention of voices made Simone's skin itch. Lyra's renaissance seemed too quick.

Sergi and Cressa would be back in a couple of days. With any luck, Lyra would be fine until then. She closed her eyes and considered her options. She chuckled. If she hadn't come to know Cressa as well as she had, the thought would never have occurred to her. Maybe a human was the answer she sought, and her laughter increased as she pulled out of the parking space. Who better to deal with Lyra than Ginger?

*Chapter Eighteen*

I GLANCED around the hotel room as Sergi pushed the door open and entered.

He picked up my bag and followed my gaze. "It appears you have everything." He held out his hand. My necklace laid in his palm. "I hope when I pick you up in three days, this will lie safely around your neck."

I gingerly picked it up, still nervous about its powers. "I just want to stop being terrified of it."

"No one likes to be out of control. Some of us more than others. It's something you and I have in common. In fact, you have it in common with all the cadre."

I slipped the necklace in my back pocket and rummaged through my backpack, not looking for anything, but not wanting Sergi see me tear up.

"We have another thing in common." I swung the pack over my shoulder. When he gave me that raised brow look, I gave him my sincerest promise. "I will find something that can help save Devon, or all of this was for nothing." I pushed past him and didn't say another word as he followed me through the hotel to the revolving doors and out to the valet area.

Colantha's pet vamp was standing at the front corner of the limo. Sergi walked to the trunk where the driver waited to take my bag. Then he stepped next to me, his head close to mine to keep his words private.

"Three days. I will be waiting here for you. You have your cell and my number. Call if you need me. I'll text with any updates, but your focus is to learn as much as possible. Keep your eyes and ears open. You can learn much by your surroundings and other people, not just with the instruction. You know this."

I nodded. It was one of the sole reasons I was so good as a thief. "Don't worry. I understand the stakes."

He nodded, gave the vamp a wicked stare, and when he glared at the back passenger window, I could swear he could see through the dark-tinted glass. Then he turned and walked back to the hotel without a backward glance.

The vamp opened the back door, and I slid in, placing my backpack at my feet. Colantha sat in her jump seat, her fingers tapping a glass of orange juice. "Would you like one?"

I shrugged. "Sure. I didn't eat much this morning." I drank mug after mug of coffee but barely managed to swallow a piece of toast. I wasn't sure if I was excited or terrified and decided it was a two-for-one emotion.

The evening before, or more correctly, way early this morning, I'd collapsed into bed exhausted, assuming I'd sleep until the sun woke me, but after two solid hours of deep sleep, I tossed the rest of the night. I was up before the sun lightened the sky, waited a half hour after my shower for room service to open, then sat the table, staring out the window at nothing until the clock slowly ticked its way to nine.

The vamp, who sat in other jump seat as before, pulled a small pitcher from the compact fridge and poured a glass. I took it and noted with some relief that he poured more juice into Colantha's glass. At least we were drinking the same thing. The juice was refreshing, and I drank it all in a few gulps. I wiped my mouth with the back of my hand like an uncouth street urchin. "Sorry."

Colantha's eyes twinkled. "It's good, isn't it? Frederick," she nodded toward the vamp, "only allows me two each morning." When I looked confused, she said, "It has a high sugar content, and I'm borderline diabetic."

I nodded in understanding. Then looked at the pitcher as Frederick put it away. I could probably drink that whole pitcher without batting an eye. Which was odd. I hardly ever drank juice.

"We have a bit of a drive. Relax and watch the beautiful landscape of our city."

I leaned back and turned my head to do exactly as she suggested. But as the city faded away and the lush rural setting took over, a tingle of fear ran down my back. I was being driven to the middle of nowhere with a stranger and two vamps. Yet, Sergi let me go. It brought more comfort than I realized.

We'd only been driving for twenty minutes when everything appeared sharper in focus with bright, rich colors that seemed more substantive than anywhere else. I held up my hand and clearly saw each pore in my skin. My light-pink nail polish glowed. Something wasn't right, but instead of turning to Colantha, my head dropped back and rolled to the right, providing the best way to view the passing landscape.

Unsure how much time had passed, I blinked and managed to turn my head toward Colantha. Her smile didn't seem right. "You drugged me."

She shrugged. "In a way. The first glass effects people differently. For some, they can't stop fidgeting. Others take a nap. By the way you're viewing your hands and the things around you tells me you might be having a psychedelic experience, or perhaps you're visioning everything around you in slow motion. It depends on the type of psychic power energizing your dreamwalks. Either way, the effect will fade by the time we arrive at the sanctuary." The twinkle was back in her gaze. "I suggest you enjoy it. You won't have many breaks during your three days."

I took her for her word and stared out the window at the colors and details until the movement of the car lulled me to sleep.

"Wake, child. We're here."

I expected a headache or nausea, the typical hangover penalties for being drugged, but my head was clear. The amazing colors and sharpness had receded, but I felt energized. "What did you give me?"

"An herb that promotes the correct chemicals in your brain to strengthen your psychic resilience."

"Resilience?"

"It helps to keep others from entering your dreams unless you allow them."

I considered that. "You mean like the time someone took control when I wore the necklace."

She nodded. "I would have preferred you built up the strength on your own, but with only three days, you required a bit of an advantage."

"Didn't you say you drink that twice a day?"

She laughed as Frederick gave her a discouraging shake of his head. "He's worried I give away too much too soon." She patted his knee. "We have others like you, new to this world of dreamwalkers and what can be achieved. They are constantly prac-ticing. Most days, their attempts don't bother me. But those in more advanced training attempt to touch the mind of the masters that live here. One or two can be handled without a problem. But more than that, day after day, it becomes tiring to fight the psychic pull. The herb helps to block them without draining our own energy. Otherwise, I'd be in bed most days."

I nodded and rubbed my arms in a weak attempt to prevent everything she said from making me want to bolt. Not quite ready for the next step, I glanced out the window to survey my surround-ings. If I was expecting a large structure that housed dozens of trainees, I was disappointed. There were three bungalows, built in a semi-circle around a large fire pit. Tall totems, six that I could see, were positioned at various points—one in front of each bungalow, one close to the fire, and two others on the outer perimeter.

Flashes of pitch-dark evenings with people in painted faces, dancing around a blazing fire, chanting unintelligible words, made me shiver. Voodoo. Maybe my overly imaginative mind was in overdrive, or it was the residual effects of the juice.

The driver opened the door, and Frederick got out. The two stood and surveyed the location. I didn't see another soul in sight. He ducked low and looked inside the limo, motioning for me to get out, and Colantha followed behind me.

I turned in a circle, taking it all in. We were in the backcountry of Louisiana. The fishy scent of a slow-moving river assailed my nose, birds twittered, and I checked the foliage for an alligator snout. I didn't think long walks were in my near future.

Colantha confirmed my fears. "We rarely see a gator this far up the river, but it's not unheard of. I suggest sticking to the main trails and keep your dagger with you at all times. Otherwise, as long as you stay within the boundaries of the sanctuary, you shouldn't have any trouble."

"The boundaries?"

She nodded to my left, and at first I didn't see anything, but when I searched farther out, the tips of a fence were visible over the dense shrubs. Razor wire ran along the top.

"This isn't a prison. The fence isn't to keep people in, but to keep people away. The main complex is farther in, unseen from any fence line. You won't have time to visit on this trip. There are small living quarters all over the property. We have a thousand acres; most of it is swamp or river. Security is controlled by our own vampires. In all the centuries we've been here, we've never had a breach. As you'll soon learn, security, secrecy, and solidarity are required and enforced. Now, enough of that."

She spread out an arm to the bungalows. "You'll stay in the

cabin to the right. All the normal amenities are within each one—bedroom, bathroom, a kitchenette, and training room. I'll be in the one on the left. Frederick and Jamison will stay in the middle one, which is also considered a community center where the main meals will be served. That's also where we'll meet for our training sessions. You have thirty minutes to get settled in, then meet us there. Wear something comfortable. You'll be sitting or lying down for long intervals."

She turned and strode with the same stealthy prowl as Simone. Jamison entered my assigned bungalow with my duffel. I swung my pack over my shoulder, gave the camp and fence a long look, then followed.

The inside was small but clean. The main living space was the size of a hotel room and panels separated the kitchen, similar to my old apartment. When I peered around the screen, I was surprised to find a modern setup including a coffee pot—thank the heavens —and a microwave. No stove or oven, but there was a toaster oven and small fridge. It would work. A kitchen table with four chairs sat to the right, in plain view of the living space.

Jamison opened a door to my right, and I followed him in. It was a decent-sized room, larger than the room in my apartment but smaller than my room in the manor. A large window could be opened to the night air, but the room was temperature controlled. At least I wouldn't sweat to death in the humid heat, and when I glimpsed the mosquito netting around the bed, decided keeping the window closed was probably a better idea. There was no television, but that wasn't a surprise. No radio or clock, either. No distractions.

"Are all the living quarters so sparse?"

"No."

So, Jamison was a talker. How would I ever get a word in? I snorted, and he lifted a brow before dropping the duffel on the bed and walking out. A moment later, I heard the front door shut. At least they wouldn't hover.

Another door was on the far side of the bed, and when I checked, discovered a closet on the left and the sink, toilet, and shower complete with tub on the right. Overall, a nice hotel suite.

I spent the short time I had unpacking and pulling out my training outfit. Fortunately, I'd brought a second set. It appeared I'd be living in them most of the time I was here. With ten minutes to spare, I sat on the couch and considered everything Colantha had shared. Security, secrecy, and solidarity. I expected to see the motto stamped on some wall hanging or embroidered on a pillow.

Something told me to prepare for condensed training sessions similar to Anna's. If that was true, these would be three very long days.

*Chapter Nineteen*

SIMONE SLAMMED the sedan in park and strolled up the steps of the manor. It appeared an afternoon of solace at Oasis was too much to ask for. When she entered Devon's office, Ginger and Lucas were already there, sitting by the hearth, the embers from the morning still glowing.

She strode past them and sat at the desk, opening the laptop and scrolling through emails. A new one from Sergi made her pause. They'd found Colantha Dupré, and Cressa was in training. Unable to conceive what that might consist of, she made notes of her meeting with Noah and sent a reply to Sergi.

After a quick review of the remaining emails, she pushed the laptop aside and leaned back, staring at her guests.

"Did everything go all right with Noah?" Lucas stood and held out a hand to Ginger.

She'd seen Ginger intimidated, irritated, but mostly happily oblivious of House matters except where her and Cressa's safety were concerned. Bella considered her brave beyond her ability to protect herself, and she held a fierce loyalty to Cressa. Her devotion to her friend might explain why she appeared pale and scared. Before they returned their focus back to Lorenzo, the humans in the House would need defensive training. Those that showed potential and expressed interest would be battle trained. It would make the House even stronger.

Ginger fidgeted while Lucas settled into the chair next to her. He'd matured since she'd arrived. It was no secret among the cadre and many within the family that the two had grown close. He didn't go to a club without her, and he'd increased his duties, taking on more leadership responsibilities. She was curious what brought them together, and any other time, she'd spend more time analyzing the relationship.

She turned her attention back to business. "Noah is grieving, but he didn't know any more than Asher and Maya. Except for the name Boris Gheata."

Lucas shook his head. "I've checked my list of contacts, but it's like I said earlier. His name means nothing to me. Sergi didn't recognize it either, but he's working his connections."

"It probably won't amount to much if we can't locate him."

"Lorenzo tends to keep his Family out of his more questionable activities, preferring to use outside contractors. If this man is close to Lorenzo, he's most likely got his fingers in unsavory activities."

She nodded. "We'll see how it plays out." She smiled at Ginger and wasn't surprised when she seemed to grow smaller in the chair. "But we're here on another matter."

Lucas nudged Ginger, who shot him a look before her eyes grew wide.

"Oh, sorry. I was just thinking if I'd seen anyone like the vamp..." She blushed. "Sorry, vampire Lucas has described, but nothing comes to mind." She lowered her head, and Simone waited, studying her as she wrapped her fingers in a long rainbow-colored scarf. It was the only touch of color she wore. Her leggings and long sweatshirt were both black. Even her earrings were black onyx. "I know I was told to get rid of my old cellphone, but I have tons of contacts on it, and I didn't want to lose them. It didn't even occur to me to download them to a flash drive, but I asked a friend to remove the GPS tracker." Her voice, which had started strong, softened to almost a whisper.

Simone turned to Lucas, and instead of appearing chagrined at not keeping better track of Ginger, he glared at her. For a moment, she didn't understand. Humans. Always so sensitive. She forced her facial features to relax, and taking a deep breath, attempted a more congenial expression rather than the irritation that Ginger hadn't followed instructions.

"Who is this friend?" She kept her tone light so she didn't spook the woman again.

Instead of being timid, Ginger straightened and looked her in the eyes. "His name is Bulldog. He's the muscle for our old neighborhood."

"A street thug?"

She lifted a shoulder. "In a sense. He runs security for Greco, and Greco owns the neighborhood."

Simone nodded. "Continue."

"Anyway, Greco has his fingers in a lot of businesses. One of them is a laundromat where he also runs a room of safety deposit boxes. Bulldog oversees the operation."

Simone nodded. "So Bulldog helped you remove the GPS, then you put the phone in one of these boxes?"

Ginger nodded and seemed impressed by her ability to follow along. It almost made her smile that a human would be so impressed by a vampire keeping up.

"Lucas takes me by there once a week so I can check messages." Her fingers twisted the scarf into a tight knot. "We stopped by earlier today. I had five messages from the Santiga Bay cops. Some detective. They say it's urgent I get in touch with them. They want to know where Cressa is."

"They said that."

She shook her head. "No. But why else would they be contacting me? All five messages were from the last two days."

Simone had to agree. "They must have traced Cressa back to her apartment. Are you also on the rental agreement?"

Ginger nodded.

"With all the activity at the apartment, even if the neighbors didn't say anything to the cops, something would have leaked." Lucas took Ginger's hand, and she wondered if it was his way to comfort her, or he simply wanted to save her scarf that continued to twist. "I've met Bulldog. The detectives won't have any luck with him. All he knows is that Cressa and Ginger haven't been around their apartment for over a month."

"Which was well before Underwood's murder." Simone tapped her fingers on the desk. "Devon should have dumped that apartment."

"Perhaps. But who could have guessed Lorenzo would have gotten rid of Underwood so quickly."

"How long can we put off this detective?" Simone asked.

Lucas shrugged. "A few days at least. They might have found the apartment, but there's nothing to link either Cressa or Ginger to us. They also don't know that Cressa is Pandora, so I don't believe they'll be able to trace her from that persona. As far as they can tell, Ginger and Cressa are ghosts."

"April spoke to Cressa the day after Underwood's murder," Ginger added. "She would have told the detective, but I don't think her mother said anything. From what Cressa said, her mom wouldn't tell them about her meeting with Devon. She doesn't even know his name."

"But she is the weakest link if April suspects anything," Lucas said.

"Maybe." Ginger released the scarf and absently straightened it. "But Cressa was sincerely touched by her mother's support. She knows Cressa didn't kill Christopher. If she was going to, she would have done it long before now." When Lucas shot her a glance, she shrugged. "She wouldn't have done it herself, but she knows people."

"Sergi and Cressa will be back in two days." Simone considered her own timetable. Her focus had already turned to Boris Gheata and what she could discover in that time period. "Will the police wait that long?"

"If they have other leads, they might hold off putting out an APB on Cressa. I don't think they'd go that far in locating Ginger. They probably found her old employer, but all they can say is that Ginger quit."

"I told them I was heading to Seattle. Maybe they'll think I moved up there and that Cressa went with me."

Simone sat back. "That would take some pressure off." She glanced at Lucas, who nodded his confirmation.

"It might not hurt to give the police someone else to follow," Lucas suggested.

"Not a vampire."

"No. Of course, not. Sergi started an investigation of Underwood's other shady businesses. There must be one or two humans that lost money with him."

Simone nodded. "Continue with that idea. Maybe you can find more possibilities. I believe Decker mentioned Underwood having a vampire girlfriend. My guess is he's had a few human ones as well. Maybe we can sow a seed in that direction."

Lucas nodded and made a note in his tablet. "If we're wrong about Lorenzo, maybe the cops will trip over the real killer."

Simone clucked her tongue. "If we could be so lucky."

# Chapter Twenty

"I WANT you to think about someone you've met in a dreamwalk. Someone you can use for focus." Colantha sat on a tall stool, the room dimly lit. Her forest-green empress-style dress flowed around her, showing off her dainty ankles and fashionable Mary Janes.

I stood in front of her, barefoot and in my workout clothes. When I'd entered the center bungalow, she'd been waiting for me, primly seated at one of the three dining tables, each seating four. The community room was as drab as my room, but it had the basics. Two sitting areas were complete with couches, chairs, and low tables covered with magazines. The bedrooms were down a hall to the left, and a door in the back led to a kitchen, or so I was told. The training room was through the door on the right. And it didn't get any simpler. It was a fair-sized, empty room with a cold stone floor and pit in the middle. The only furniture was the stool where Colantha sat.

I considered her statement, and the only one who came to mind was Devon. And when I thought of him, the only image it stirred was the beast. "Does it have to be someone I've seen in a dream?"

She gave me an odd look. "It will be difficult to accomplish what you want in three days by using someone you've never linked with. This isn't meant to be a dreamwalking experience with someone. This person is only meant to be a focal point to establish a construct of your own making. It's easier if it's someone who's already been in your dreamworld."

"All right. I'll use Devon."

Her brow rose, but she didn't look at me. It wasn't like I had several people to choose from, there'd only been Devon in my dreams. But...that wasn't true. Lyra had been in one of them, and she knew about the dreams. Before I could give it any further consideration, Colantha pointed to the circular pit in the middle of the floor. It was made of shiny, black tiles similar to those found in a hot tub or pool.

Frederick laid a blanket at the bottom of the pit, which was about three feet below the floor. A step on each side allowed for easy in-and-out access.

"Step inside and sit."

I complied, finding the blanket soft and comforting. When I glanced up, I was eye level to the flame of a pillar candle that had been set on the floor. It was made of black wax with a mixed scent of sage and citrus. Within the dim room, it was now the brightest object.

"A dreamwalker's primary ability is to make a construct. A place many visit to remove themselves from stress or perhaps to visit a favorite place. But without the basic training, you don't have the ability to create a construct of your own making."

"That's not entirely true."

She frowned. "I was under the impression the constructs you visited were places you hadn't been before. Prescient dreamwalking is a different topic."

"There was one time where I created the dream with Devon. It was, uh, intimate." My face heated at the admission. I was barely able to discuss intimate stuff with Ginger.

Colantha's knowing grin made me fidget. "And you controlled the construct?"

"I was in his room when I began the construct, which was the library of the manor. During the dream, I took his hand, and we moved to his bedroom."

She paced. "That makes sense. If this was your first time in control of the environment, you would automatically create something you were already familiar with. Were you wearing the necklace?"

"No. I told you I've only worn it once."

"Ah. Yes. When another entity took control." She held her hands behind her back, her head bent in thought. "If you think about it, up to that point of wearing the necklace, you didn't completely believe what this vampire told you. Isn't it easier to believe that once you accepted who you were, some modicum of control—or the appearance of it—was granted to you? And now that you've done it once, perhaps this next attempt will come more naturally."

She turned and stopped at the door. "Empty your mind of everything except where you wish to meet Devon. Focus on creating the construct. Nothing more. I'll return in an hour to check your progress."

She was gone before I could think to ask anything.

Unsure if Devon was the best idea, I considered Lyra again. But when it came to thinking of a location, I'd been more places with Devon, so I pushed thoughts of Lyra away and considered the safest place for building a construct.

The first task was to clear my mind. That should be easy enough. But even with my well-practiced meditation routine and Simone's enhanced techniques, it took longer than normal to center myself. I washed away concerns about the dead Council member, the dead Christopher, the future of the House Trelane without Devon, and the impact it all had on my life. I pushed Devon away until the only thing in my mind was the single candle flame. If this was a normal meditation session, I'd think of a clear lake as my mentor taught me, or a single image like Simone prefers. Instead, I pictured places where I'd been with Devon, but each time I tried, the image jumped to the alley where Devon's beast had been trapped. And with it came his eyes—pain and fear in a pool of icy blue.

I fell back against the cool tile and rubbed my forehead. Irritated and feeling the pressure of time, I reorganized my thoughts and tried again. Each effort resulted in flashes of places we'd been: his office, the widow's walk, the grotto, the solarium at the manor, the library, his bedroom at Oasis, and his bedroom at the manor. After several attempts, I determined that places we'd physically been together held a stronger pull than places from a previous construct.

For a reason I didn't understand, it made sense. There would be more strength in using a place I was comfortable. One I'd physically touched rather than one only seen in a dreamworld. Yet, with each location I tried, the image lasted mere seconds only to be replaced by the alley.

I'd lost track of time. I was exhausted, disappointed, and my head hurt. Maybe a quick nap was all I needed, so I curled into a ball and closed my eyes. Five minutes of silence, and I'd start again.

It was twilight when I entered the alley. The only sound was the coastal breeze ruffling papers and other scraps of debris on the cracked asphalt. There was an occasional bang of something hitting the brick siding of an old warehouse whenever the wind increased, blowing hair into my face before settling down. I pushed my hands deeper into my pockets as I took each precarious step deeper into the dead-end lane.

Sergi and Lucas had positioned themselves at the front of the alley, one on each side of the entrance. They were to stay there until Decker called for them. They hadn't liked the plan, but I refused to let them participate unless they followed Decker's orders. I didn't know why I trusted Decker over Sergi and Lucas in this matter, but this wasn't the time to question it.

I walked past the spot where Decker had concealed himself, covered with the garbage of the alley to disguise his scent. I didn't glance down at his hiding spot but noted through my peripheral vision the old cardboard box leaning against the building, still damp from the morning dew.

I heard Devon before I saw him. It wasn't a growl but raspy breathing that carried a slight hitch as if he'd been running for hours. I crept a bit farther before I stopped.

"Devon?" I took another step. "It's me. Cressa."

When nothing happened, I did the exact thing Decker told me not to do. I continued on with slow, measured steps until I passed the marker of the safety nets, walking deeper into Devon's space.

"I'm not scared of you, Devon. I'm here to help ease your burden. To give you want you need."

I stopped when I was only ten yards from the end of the alley, turning in a slow circle, searching within the dark corners for any sign of him. Then I spotted him. More accurately, I caught the ice-blue glow of his vampire nature—of the beast.

I swallowed the lump, curious why I wasn't shaking with fear. But his gaze drew me in, and I knew without a doubt this was our last chance before the Eliminators were sent. He'd positioned himself toward the back of a dumpster that was pushed against a chain-link fence. While he might choose to climb over the top, I'd bet three days of Simone's advanced training there was a hole in the fence, which would explain how he kept disappearing so quickly.

I held up my hands then lifted my jacket so he could see I was unarmed. Another squabble I'd had with Sergi. A dagger, silver or otherwise, wasn't going to protect me against the beast. I had to believe Devon wouldn't hurt me, no matter how far his beast had risen. Sergi had said it himself days ago—Devon considered me his mate.

With each step I took, the beast whimpered, and the glow of his eyes faded as he lifted his chin and smelled the air.

I nodded. "See. It's just me. I know you've been searching for me. Looking for nourishment. I'm here, Devon. Please let me help you."

By the time I stood mere feet from the beast, his eyes had melted into the indigo blue of his passion. That was the most I could see beyond my blurred vision. I held out my arms.

"Come to me, Devon. Let me help you."

His movements were slower than I expected as he stood to his full height. Even with his slight hunch, he was a few inches taller than I remembered him being. His tattered clothes hung like rags from him, showing a bulkier muscled frame than was normal. His hands ended in long fingernails that appeared razor-sharp. *The better to gut you with, my pretty.*

I shook my head and focused on his eyes. Still blue, still warm, the pain easily seen, as was the fear.

"You have nothing to be afraid of."

Then he was on me before I had a chance to even consider my options. He wrapped his arms around me, the words nothing but guttural sounds. He stank of rotten meat, cedar, and damp earth. I breathed through my mouth rather than my nose, but it didn't make much difference, since I was being crushed against him.

"You're hurting me," I whispered. "I need to breathe."

It took a couple of seconds before his arms relaxed, but he didn't let go.

The beast lifted his head, scenting the air. I managed to squeeze an arm out of his hold, and I touched his cheek. He dropped his head and grunted. He'd lost the ability to speak. The tears that blurred my vision now fell. One of his claw-like fingers traced a tear down my cheek.

Then I did something the others didn't know I'd planned. They thought I was only going to talk with him. But when the beast held my gaze, I pushed my hair aside, and bent my head to the left, offering him my neck.

Ice-cold water splashed over me, and I woke, sputtering from the chill and the unexpected soaking. My arms and legs flapped around like a bug on its back. When I managed to pull myself into a sitting position, I stared up at the fiery gaze of Colantha. Frederick held the empty bucket, but I growled at her, knowing damn well she gave the order.

"What the hell, lady?" I got to my feet, drenched by the two inches of water filling the bottom of my pit, the blanket I'd been laying on nothing more than a sodden rag.

"You're supposed to be attempting a vision, not sleeping away the day." Her words were filled with vitriol. Where the hell was her rage coming from? It wasn't like she'd given me much direction. Maybe she just hated to have her day wasted, and I could understand that. Except, I hadn't been sleeping.

"You didn't give me any instructions other than think of a place I'd been with Devon. I tried staring into that damn flame." I pointed at the offending object the water seemed to have missed because it continued to glow with defiance at its ability to defeat me.

"I checked on you several times but didn't want to interrupt. You've been here for three hours with no success."

I glanced around the dark room as if a clock had magically appeared. It wasn't like there were any windows to tell me anything different.

I climbed out of the pit, pulling the sodden clothes away from my body to release any remaining water. Frederick tossed me a towel, which I caught one-handed and started drying my hair.

"And I wouldn't say it was without success."

Colantha had been on her way out the door when she stopped and turned. "Explain." She sat on her stool and waited.

Another stool had been brought in, and I dragged it away, so I wasn't too close to her. I continued to dry myself as I recalled what I'd thought was only an hour, not three.

"I cleared my head as I've been trained to do in the past." I gave her a rundown of all the locations I tried to maintain for a construct, and why I thought some were stronger than others. She nodded as I spoke but never interrupted. "Whenever I thought I had a location, the image was immediately replaced with an alley. The place I'd last seen Devon where he'd been in his beast form."

I almost missed the glance she gave Frederick before turning her attention to me. "Go on."

"I didn't want that to be the location for the construct, so I'd stop and start over."

She nodded.

"No matter what I tried, it didn't work, and I was giving myself a headache. I was so tired, I thought I'd take a quick nap." I glanced at Frederick then back at her. "I guess I could have used more of that juice."

She snorted but didn't say anything.

"I guess it was more than a nap because I was suddenly back in the alley, though it was different than when I was there before, outside the dream."

I explained the dream, including the others that had been there, though I never actually saw them, just sensed them. Then I detailed my interaction, as brief as it was, with the beast.

When I finished, her gaze moved to the flickering candle. After several long minutes, she asked, "Do you feel as if you were in control?"

I considered that. "I don't think I was in control of the construct, but I was in control, or at least I think I was, of my own actions and decisions."

"You've said the majority of your dreams have been prescient."

I nodded. "Besides the one I told you about earlier that I'd created, there was one where I was in Devon's head when he killed Sorrento, and then just yesterday when I was in the head of the beast when he chowed down on a dead deer." I shivered at the memory.

"I need time to consider this. There's food for you to take back to your room. I suggest rest. We'll meet again in two hours."

I barely made it to the room, took a bite of the sandwich, drained the glass of special juice, and fell onto the bed. The pounding at the door was the only thing that woke me. I didn't know if it was one of the vamps or Colantha beating on my door. Either way, they needed a better alarm system, but I stood, feeling better than I should, and slipped into my second set of workout clothes. I kept my mind blank, not wanting to consider what Colantha held in store for my second session.

## Chapter Twenty-One

After Lucas and Ginger left the office, it was too late to drive to Oasis, so Simone spent time in the training room and pool while considering how to track down Boris Gheata. Though Santiga Bay was one of the smaller hubs for vampires—not many wanted to live that close to Council members who congregated throughout the region—it was amazing how difficult it was to find one.

She joined everyone for dinner then made a quick escape to her room where she pulled out her tablet and sent messages she didn't want to send. Vampires who owed her favors. Favors so old she'd lost count. There had been several she'd wanted to keep tucked away for when she had her own House, but Devon's life was more important than all of them. Though if she were honest with herself, she hoped several wouldn't respond. Perhaps another two hundred years would make it easier to stomach them.

Her luck wasn't with her. By morning, there was only one email response. And it was from the last vampire she ever wanted to see again, even if his favor could grant her almost anything. Then he surprised her further. He was in San Francisco on a business trip and swore he had the information she sought.

She waited until noon, and when not a single additional response came, she had no choice. She'd run out of time.

She stared up at the hotel, her gut in turmoil. A cold sweat had broken out when she pulled into the parking lot across the street. She'd considered driving to the hotel's valet but wanted a quick escape if needed. The car she took was one available to the general staff, and like all the others, was registered to an alias. She was thankful she hadn't eaten lunch but was sorry she hadn't called for a blood donor.

The fact she was sitting there, her emotions as raw as the young blood she'd once been, ate at her. She was better than this. She was Simone of the House Trelane. Known through most of the Houses and aristocracy as the first to Devon Trelane. She wasn't the sniveling vampire she once was when she'd last seen Gaius.

She swallowed the bile threatening to rise as she crossed the street and entered the hotel, not pausing until she reached the bank of elevators, a car opening as she arrived. Two other people entered with her and reached their floors long before her slow ascent to the top floor. Penthouse suite. She would never have guessed it. Gaius had always preferred the dank, dark caves where he kept his young bloods.

When the doors opened and she stepped out into a large foyer, she glanced to her left and right. There was a guard at each of the two available doors. Two suites and apparently both occupied by vampires. If she knew Gaius—and assuming his habits hadn't changed in the centuries since she'd seen him—one of the apartments would be for his current mistress.

"Tanaquil?" the guard to the right asked.

In a flash, the guard hung against the wall four inches above the floor. Simone's right hand gripped his neck, her nails digging into this trachea. His hands grasped at hers, but he was still young, a half-breed, maybe twenty years made.

The second guard raced toward her, but when he tried to grab her arms, she yanked him to her while still holding the other vampire. She snarled as she tossed him toward the other door, smiling with satisfaction at the sound of breaking wood as he hit. She turned to the one still hanging on the wall.

"My name is Simone. It would be best you remember that, or the next time I'll rip out your throat." She leaned into him until she was only inches from his face. "Do you understand me?"

"I think he's learned his lesson."

Not changing her stance or the grip she had on the guard, she turned to the open door, her fangs fully extended.

Gaius. As breathtakingly handsome as he'd always been. His lips, not thinned in cruel anger, but full, luscious, and smiling, as if they were old friends.

"I'm afraid it's my mistake. Old habits with the name."

She didn't move, her breaths coming hard as the man continued to struggle for breath.

He nodded toward his guard. "If I promise to remind them of your new name, will you release him so he can breathe? Half-breeds don't have the stamina of a pure blood."

She growled, wanting to scream at him that her name wasn't new, he just never bothered using it before, preferring his own demeaning names for his creatures. But she took a step back, and like she was tossing out the trash, threw him toward the other guard, who was still shaking himself off when he toppled over again as the other guard smashed into him.

She pulled the shoulders of her crimson caftan back in place then ran a hand down it, noting his full perusal as she swept past him into the room. It was a typical penthouse suite with all the luxuries one would expect, but he'd added his own touches—his battle landscapes, the Dagger of Omar, and a sculpture of an Egyptian cat. Some things never changed, and not for the first time, she wondered how long he'd been in town and how long he'd planned on staying. He was a long way from his home in Greece.

She walked to the middle of the room then turned to face him.

"Ah, my Somalian queen, how good to see you after all this time."

"I'm not here for your games."

"And still as touchy as ever."

His slow perusal, which was too reminiscent of bad memories, unnerved her, and she turned her back on him as she strolled from one sitting area to the next. She stopped to stare at the entertainment center with six individual panels, all showing a different station—from the stock market to weather to sports to a black-and-white action movie. The last two screens were the only ones with sound. They displayed nature scenes, and with the flowing river and twittering birds, the combination was meditative. That was unexpected.

"You said you had information on Boris Gheata." Simone finally looked at him with her chin lifted, her gaze unblinking as she looked him in the eyes. Something she hadn't done for centuries, and even then, rarely.

"Right to business. Not a surprise from what I've heard."

She refused to consider who might be talking to him about her, then reasoned it might have just been words in passing. Small stories one vampire tells another about old campaigns. Still. Had he been checking up on her?

"Would you prefer small talk? Like how long do you plan on carting that dagger around? You've managed to make an inconsequential weapon a mystery sought by the very wealthy."

"On second thought, right to business is a marvelous suggestion."

"That would be best. I don't have much time."

He walked toward the windows that looked out over the bay. A table near the window had been set with a coffee service, small sandwiches, and pastries.

"I heard the House Trelane was in trouble before I received your message. I try to stay away from Council politics, and quite frankly, I find the current Council more corrupt than any before them."

She couldn't argue the sentiment. But the days he spoke of were filled with constant battles for power, land, and a throne. Corruption simply took a different form within court intrigue, blackmail, and betrayals.

"Come sit down. Have a cup of coffee if not food." When she simply stared at him, he shook his head and smiled before sitting down and pouring two cups. "I know how difficult it must have been for you to reach out to me. There must have been others you contacted, and I can only assume they either didn't have the information you needed or didn't respond."

If she was going to play the role of Devon's first, she had to play it all the way. Devon had sat with enemies many times and was always cordial—until he had no choice but to show his fangs. She heaved a sigh and strolled to the table, taking the chair opposite him. She'd expected him to jump up and pull out her chair, and the fact he didn't, that he saw her as an equal, made her question the man before her.

"You were always a wise one."

He seemed pleased by her compliment and perhaps a bit surprised. "Do you need cream or sugar?"

"Just a touch of cream would be fine."

She plucked a pastry from the tiered platters, her hunger returning with a vengeance. It wasn't that she was any safer than before. Even with her prowess, she'd be a fool to think the vampire across from her couldn't hold his own. He was older than Devon. Much older. Old enough to know the ancient Romans—Julius Caesar, Cleopatra, and Augustus.

"I have to ask." She took a bite of the cheese danish and washed it down with coffee as he did the same, never taking his eyes from her. "I was expecting you to be long dead."

His head fell back as he laughed. It was a warm laugh. A sincere one. "You and many others." He wiped his hands on a napkin, and she couldn't help but notice his long, elegant fingers and his House ring. "There are only one or two of us from those early days in Rome that are still sane enough to hold a House. Although that's not really a requirement these days when battles are nothing more than well-mannered business dealings that a cadre could run on their own. But the answer to longevity is keeping the mind busy. Always keep your fingers in the midst of something, whether political, personal, or philanthropic."

She couldn't help but smile. "The business of running a House is enough intrigue for me. I prefer to stay out of politics."

"No more battles?" He licked the cream filling from the end of a pastry. Had his movements always been so seductive? "You seem well-trained."

"You know we don't use courts to settle our differences. And I am cadre."

He nodded. "And Trelane has done well." When a silence descended, he seemed to understand her need to move the conversation along. "Down to business then. I don't know what surprised me more—receiving your message or seeing that you sought information on Boris. I haven't heard his name in decades, possibly longer. You know how ancients tend to forget what century we're in."

That brought a chuckle she couldn't help. Gaius had turned self-deprecating in his old age. Or was he trying to stay on her good side for a reason?

He returned her grin. "But then I heard he'd surfaced at this end of the world."

"This was recent?"

He lit a cigarette as he considered the question. "Perhaps six or seven months ago. Possibly a month or two more."

"How do you know him?"

"I used him once." When Simone gave him a quizzical look, he added, "He's a fixer."

All the pieces began to fall into place. Someone to clean up Lorenzo's messes. Or was she reaching? "He's a freelancer?"

"I hired him back in the early nineteen hundreds, and even then, he wasn't the type to tie himself to one person."

"Has he been known to take on long-term assignments?"

He shrugged and refilled their cups. "You should try the lobster sandwich. They're rather addictive." He heaved a sigh after biting into one.

When it appeared he wasn't going to continue until she tried one, she obliged if nothing more than to quiet her hunger and move the meeting along. The sandwich was amazing, and she pulled the bread back to see what was inside.

He chuckled with delight. "I thought you might enjoy them."

"There's saffron in it."

"Yes. It was your favorite spice once."

She took another bite, refusing to look at him, not sure what to make of the fact that he'd remember something so simple from so long ago. And without wanting to, she whispered, "It still is."

"Marvelous. I hear Trelane has one of the best chefs in the country. I'll have mine share the recipe with him if you'd like." When she nodded, trying to wrap her head around who this vampire was while staying on point with Boris, he thankfully switched back to business. "I don't know about Boris, but it wouldn't be unusual for a fixer to take on a long-term contract."

"Do you know who he works for now?"

"Only rumors, but I don't think I have to give you a name you already know."

She nodded. "And only rumors they will most likely remain."

"I will give you one bit of advice where Boris is concerned." He held her gaze, and that golden glow she remembered so well lit his eyes. If nothing else, she knew he never lied when he allowed the beast to rise. "Some vampires can't change, and I would say he is one of those."

"In what way?"

"Boris isn't someone to take lightly. He's deadly, shrewd, and sometimes nothing more than a ghost. But like many of his ilk, he likes souvenirs."

That was something she could work with. If they could find where Boris was staying, they might find the evidence they'd need for the Sentinels. Before she could ask where he could be found, the penthouse door flew open.

"Gaius, where are you?"

For the briefest of moments, a flash of irritation sparked his gaze, and he gave Simone a look of apology before he stood and faced the angry woman. A raven-haired beauty swept her heavy mane behind her as she took in the scene. Her ample breasts were on full display as she heaved, apparently having run full tilt from across the hall.

"What's going on? I thought you were in some kid of trouble." Her tone started out as fear but ended on an angry note when she took in the table, the coffee service, and finally, Simone.

"I told you I had a business meeting and wasn't to be interrupted." His own tone held a bit of anger, but not like she remembered it. Whether it was because he was speaking to his mistress or he'd actually toned down over the centuries, she couldn't tell.

"What else could it have been after my door was broken to bits?"

He heaved a sigh and shook his head, tossing the napkin he'd been holding, now twisted into a ball, onto the table. "The only thing wrong with your door is a tweaked frame, and if you were concerned for my safety, at least you had the presence of mind to fix your hair and put makeup on before coming to my rescue."

He turned his back on her and smiled down at Simone. "Apologies. She's a bit much this early in the day."

The woman heard him and did nothing more than huff as she trounced down the hall, most likely heading for his bedroom.

"Just the early hours?" Simone's question held a bit of teasing, and his warm smile made her question all over again who this vampire was.

"Some things never change."

She laid down her napkin, stood, and pressed the wrinkles out of her caftan. "Perhaps you should rethink your taste in women."

"Perhaps so."

He walked her to the door. "I apologize for the interruption."

"As I said earlier, I have a time issue."

"Then maybe this will help." He handed her a slip of paper. When their fingers touched, she felt a spark that she hoped he hadn't felt, but a quick glance told her otherwise.

She focused on the note, which she quickly scanned. It was an address.

"Thank you." She tucked the note into a small pocket in her one-piece suit. "You said vampires can't change. I'd say that's because most of us aren't built for that."

"I believe I said some vampires can't change." He took her hand and kissed it, which sent the wrong kind of shivers over her. Ones she hadn't felt in a very long time. And he was the last vampire on earth who should be creating them in her. "But you have. And perhaps you would consider that when you think of others."

"Perhaps." She walked through the door then turned. "After all, it's not like you're going to live forever."

His brow lifted and that golden glow sparked to life.

"Haven't you heard? Those cigarettes will kill you." She gave him a hint of a smile then strode away. His hearty laugh followed her as she descended in the elevator.

*Chapter Twenty-Two*

I BLINKED as I slowly came out of the dream. A long breath escaped as I stretched my neck from side to side, working out the kinks from another long session. It was somewhere around mid-morning, but as usual, with four solid walls, it was anyone's guess.

From what Colantha told me after the third middle-of-the-night session, they'd been running from thirty minutes to two hours. If I thought I'd have the evenings to sleep, I'd been living in a fantasy world. I was allowed an hour nap between sessions, and the only thing keeping me going and supplementing my psychic power were the glasses of Colantha's special juice. It didn't matter how long each session was, I was given food and an hour nap.

If I hadn't known it would only last for three days, and the condensed training had been my doing, I would have made a break for it. I'd probably get eaten by a gator before I got anywhere close to a town. At least I had a cell phone. I giggled at my sidetrack to crazy but straightened immediately when Colantha frowned.

"Well. Are you going to enlighten me today or sometime next week when you're back home?"

She'd been getting testier as each session went by with little to no success. She wasn't alone. I was feeling the stress.

"I managed to hold the construct this time. I even changed a couple of objects to see if I could. But I don't feel strong enough to reach out to anyone."

What I didn't want to tell her was that I'd been partially cheating. I wasn't supposed to build a construct from a previous dream. And while my first dreams had been of Oasis, I'd been there once and experienced the garden, lake, and oak tree from a very different perspective. And it was from that viewpoint I created my constructs.

I particularly loved the long arbor in the garden and created the flowers in an ever-changing kaleidoscope of colors. Not racing through the colors but taking time in between to appreciate the contrast with the foliage supporting the blooms. When I made the leaves a blend of pink and turquoise, the colors must have overwhelmed me. Or maybe it had been the shadow of a presence somewhere behind me. It brought back memories of using my necklace and someone possessing me. I didn't know if Colantha was strong enough to pull me out of a psychic coma, so I stepped away, collapsing the construct.

Colantha clucked at the minor progress. It was the closest to a satisfied sound she'd made since the training began. "I've been thinking about the construct during your very first session. I believe the dream in the alley was in fact prescient. I'm not sure that I can explain why it manifested, but it was the alley itself you'd been trying to avoid. It's possible that was enough to trigger a prescient dream in that particular location." She stood and strolled to the table in the corner of the room, her slower pace a sign she was thinking, and poured a glass of juice for both of us.

I was still sitting in the pit. If I could have slept there, I'd be a happy little dreamwalker. But Colantha insisted I return to my room each time. Something about laying on my back to clear my chakras. I thought they were just fine all curled up in a fetal position.

I sipped the juice and stretched my legs, one at a time. "Are we going straight into the next session? How long was the last one?"

She drained her glass then stood over me until I finished mine. "I had wanted to wait until you were faster at building constructs, but it's critical, as you said, that you learn to control the medallion." Once she had my glass, she held out her right hand.

My necklace.

"Where did you get that?" I stood, albeit a bit wobbly, and reached for it.

"You need to take better care of it."

I snatched it out of her hand and looked it over, searching for any damage. "It was in my room—safe and sound."

"Obviously not safe, since Jamison found it in less than a minute."

I stared at her. The woman had her vamp steal my necklace, and now she was irritated that I hadn't hidden it well enough? "I assumed my room was safe from thieves."

My own irritation didn't seem to fase her. In fact, her voice grew hard. "Never assume. Hide it well, carry it on you, or store it in a safe."

I snorted. "Safes aren't safe enough."

"Really?"

"I crack safes. Take my word for it."

It was the first smile I'd seen on her since training started. She was still shaking her head when she sauntered to the opposite side of the room and pressed a button on the wall. A spot light shined from the ceiling, revealing a table large enough for two.

"Come here so you can see the symbols etched into the medallion."

I stepped out of the pit, eager to learn more, but I was reluctant to let go of the necklace. It didn't make sense, but there wasn't any explanation for irrational students who'd had little sleep the last two days. I placed the medallion in the middle of the table and at down, staring at the symbols.

She pointed to the first one. "The poppy."

My head snapped up. "Blood Poppy?"

She nodded. "Some call it the flower of life, others the flower of knowledge." She shrugged. "It was a long time ago, and in spirit, they mean the same." Her finger moved to the second image. "This is the ibis."

I squinted to get a clear picture of the middle symbol. It was obviously a bird, and with the long legs it looked like a stork, except for the long, curved beak. "I've seen these before. In books, maybe TV."

She nodded. "The ibis has been around as long as dreamwalkers existed. Probably longer. It is revered by many cultures, including our own. It represents many things and is the one symbol of the three that carries the most conflict among the great scholars of our species. I suppose not just amongst the philosophers but all dreamwalkers."

"What do you mean?"

"It's in the interpretation. Some consider it a symbol of knowledge and wisdom. Some see it as a bridge between life and death, while others see it as a sign of rebirth."

"Like the phoenix?"

She tilted her head, her forefinger rubbing the medallion. "In a way, yes. Not in physical death, but death of the spirit and the birth of new beginnings. There's a fringe group who believe it's a sign of fertility and healing."

"And what do you believe?"

She laughed. "Always the curious one." She leaned back, her focus a laser beam drilling past my outer surface, seeking what laid inside to sense whether she could trust me with something. Whatever she decided was impossible to tell, so I wasn't sure if she might be holding something back. "In a way, all the theories are a piece of the whole truth—knowledge, rebirth, healing, fertility. They all play a role."

"And the third symbol. It's a dagger of some sort." I bent closer. "There seems to be a marking on the hilt."

She nodded. "Yes. The Dagger of Omar. The symbol on the hilt represents the connection between vampire and dreamwalker."

I bent down to get a better look at the hilt. The symbol appeared random in design until Colantha used her long, pointy fingernail to trace the letters *D* and *V* that had been superimposed over each other. I didn't have to be told what those initials stood for. Its symbolism of balance between the species was clear as a bell.

"It was at the Battle of Omar the dagger was forged. And that battle is something for another day as well. There are so many variations of tales, it is an injustice to not hear them all should you come to the wrong conclusion."

I sat back and crossed my arms.

"Don't pout. You have enough to learn in the time remaining. You'll learn in the order I choose, not the one you prefer."

I huffed out a breath, knowing any further resistance would waste time. "So why all three together? And I noticed they're in a different order on the back."

"This is considered the front of the medallion—the poppy, the ibis, and the dagger." She turned it over. "This is the back—the dagger, the ibis, and the poppy."

"Don't tell me. It's the circle of life."

Her lips twitched, but her stern countenance didn't slip. "In a way, that's exactly what it is. But more to the point, it represents a true symbiotic relationship between dreamwalker and vampire. A physical connection if you will."

"Wait. What?" I glanced at Frederick. Was there more to her keeping vamps around than mere bodyguards?

"There is a strong connection between the two species that has been lost over time. Some due to the ignorance of a species who preferred to hide truths, but most of it was due to power and greed."

"The age-old dilemma."

She nodded. "Some say we dreamed them into existence, but

it's just a fairy tale." While she shrugged it off, I wasn't so sure she didn't believe some part of the story was true. It was best not to follow that path.

Another thought came to mind. "Is that why Devon and I have a strong connection?"

She studied me for a long time. Her face glowed under the spotlight, showing how flawless her skin was, and I began to suspect that she was much older than she looked. Like centuries old. But how could that be?

"I believe part of your connection is in fact due to your species, but I don't believe that's all of it. I think the two of you are very important, but..."

I waved her off. "It's a discussion for another time."

She nodded and stood. "Let's put the medallion to practice and see what happens."

I hesitated. "Do you have a healer around here?"

She gave me an odd look. "We have several. Why?"

I hesitated, not wanting to remember the loss of control when someone else invaded my body, leaving me in a psychic coma.

"Ah, you're worried about your first experience." She nodded toward the medallion. "Put it on."

I blew out a breath, and with shaking hands, slipped the chain over my head.

She held out her hand, and I took it. It was the first time we'd touched. Her skin was soft and warm. "Come, child. Should another entity try to take over, I'll be there to keep them out."

She led me back to the pit but this time she stepped inside. The circle was barely large enough for us both, and we sat cross-legged, our knees touching. Fredrick placed three more candles around us so all four sat at north, south, east, and west points. Then he lit them.

"For protection."

Before I had the chance to ask what that meant, she took my hands, and the room slipped away.

<h1 style="text-align:center">Chapter Twenty-Three</h1>

THE FOLLOWING DAY, Simone entered Devon's office to find Lyra and the cadre reviewing perimeter defenses around the manor. She'd gotten home late after her meeting with Gaius, taking the scenic route while replaying the afternoon and trying to figure out who she'd just had a pleasant, and—if she was honest with herself—all too brief meeting.

What had happened to the monster she remembered? And how long had it been since he'd changed? Assuming the man she'd just met was truly different and hadn't learned the art of well-practiced facades.

It required three meditation sessions to quiet her mind long enough to sleep, and then she found it impossible to wake. She'd eaten breakfast in her room, and Lyra had been kind enough to push their meeting to before lunch.

Lyra had taken a seat in front of the hearth and was leaning over the coffee table to review a map of the manor. The cadre pointed out where existing guards patrolled and reviewed the updates they wanted to make. Simone had been apprised before she left for San Francisco and didn't have any additional changes other than what she'd already suggested. She trusted the cadre would lead Lyra to the correct decisions.

If she had to guess, Lyra was interested but had no intention of second-guessing them. When Simone inched closer, she reviewed the open seating. She wasn't in the mood to coddle Lyra and was relieved when Lyra smiled but didn't wave her over. Simone took a seat on one of the stools and propped an elbow on the bar, mostly so she could lean her head against her fist and wait for the pounding to stop.

Lucas snapped his fingers to get the attention of a man she hadn't noticed sitting in a cushioned chair on the other side of the room. He was human, and when he approached, she recognized him as one of the new blood donors from Oasis.

She was tempted to refuse. But when he neared she felt the beast rise. If she waited any longer, she would be putting a blood donor at risk. Her bite was swift, and he never flinched. When she took enough rejuvenating sips, she helped him to a chair. The amount of blood during a normal feeding was similar to what a human donated at a blood center, but the exchange was a powerful connection between the two and tended to zap a human's strength. The new blood immediately energized her.

She'd been weak. Maybe that explained why she'd been swayed by Gaius's attempt at an apology for years of pain and torture. Maybe she was spending too much time thinking about it.

"Are you feeling better now?" Lyra's musical voice was tinged with concern.

Simone nodded before facing her House leader. "Much."

"Sergi says they'll be home tomorrow evening. He'll contact us when they leave New Orleans. I thought we should put together an updated report for his return."

Lucas made a couple marks on the map then scratched one out before writing something else. "I reported three of Underwood's associates through the police's anonymous tip line. The finances for several projects look suspect, and though I don't think the men had anything to do with Underwood's death, it should keep the police occupied while untangling the transfers. The security team at Oasis is following police bands to see if any APBs go out on Cressa or Ginger, and Jacques checked in with Bulldog. The cops won't be bothering him anymore."

Lyra smiled. "And perhaps with the earlier information they received about Ginger going to Seattle, they'll turn their search northward."

"Sergi will want to contact his friend in the department," Simone offered.

Lyra sat back and sipped from her cup of tea. "I'll make it one of his first priorities. What of Devon's defense?"

"I've got an address for Gheata. I don't know where it will lead, but it feels right." Simone gave a recap of her meeting with Gaius, leaving out everything but the information he shared about Boris.

"Can you trust this vampire?" Lucas asked.

She didn't hesitate. "Yes. It's been some time since I've seen him." She considered her response then answered as honestly as she could. "While he's changed in some ways, the vampire I knew centuries ago remains. He would never align with Lorenzo. And it will be simple enough to know if I've been deceived."

Lyra glanced to Lucas and Bella.

"I think it's worth checking out." Bella, who'd been distracted by the perimeter map, sat back, her leg bouncing with pent-up energy. "A surveillance?"

"Yes," Simone answered. "But I'd like to discuss it with Cressa first. It was her observation that led me to Gheata. She might want to be involved in the plan."

"Do we have time?" Lucas asked.

"We need to confirm Gheata is still at the address."

"I can—" Before Bella had a chance to finish, the door to the office burst open.

Decker rushed in, slamming the door behind him. He wiped his brow. "Sorry, I'm late."

"Is Devon all right?" Lyra had risen when the door opened.

Decker looked sheepish. "Yeah. Well, he's safe. He's a bit more cognizant, but his physical condition hasn't changed."

"He's been off the Poppy for a couple of days now." Lucas walked to the espresso machine, making a cup as if by rote.

"I agree." Decker grabbed one of the barstools and turned to face the group. "From what I've been told by the other victims, even those that were dosed several times never had this severe of a reaction."

"Is it because he had a prior addiction?" Bella asked.

"Maybe. Though it doesn't match what we've seen before. He might have been given higher doses, or perhaps he was dosed by means other than drinking the tainted blood."

"What do you mean?" Simone didn't like where this was leading, and she waved to Lucas, who brought over the espresso before returning to make another one.

"Injection."

Someone swore.

"Direct to the blood?" Lucas shook his head. "That would explain a lot, but it makes a full recovery almost impossible."

Lyra had pulled into herself, her focus on some point on a far wall. Whether she was upset, considering options, or hearing her voices again, Simone had no idea.

"We don't know that for sure." Bella had the opposite reaction to Lyra's. She began pacing, her increased heartbeat more an indication of anger at not having an enemy to attack than fear.

"No, we don't." Decker's breathing had settled. "Maybe some fresh blood would help."

"We can't risk a donor in his condition." Simone could see it now. Devon's beast taking control and draining the donor dry.

"That doesn't give us much to work with." Decker reached across the bar and poured a whiskey.

"Is he safe where he is?" Simone asked.

Decker shrugged. "I haven't seen any prints around the perimeter. No scent trails other than some wild game—a couple deer, a fox, some rabbits. How long do we have before the Eliminators are set loose?"

"Three days."

"What if we take him to Oasis?" Lucas asked. "The Eliminators could look all they want. It would give us more time."

"If they find out we hid him there, it will be our necks on the block," Bella said. When the group turned to her, she added, "I'm not saying not to do it. It's just, if we don't find the real murderer, our association is enough for the Council. We need to be in agreement."

"Bella is correct." Simone stood, suddenly needing something to hit, and the training room was the best place to burn off her growing aggression. "It's Lyra's decision, but I think you should all consider whether you want to risk it. We can make that call when the deadline is upon us. For now, let's see what Boris Gheata can tell us." She turned to Bella. "Can you confirm the address today?"

"No problem."

"Take Jacques."

Bella shook her head. "It would be best if I was on my own. If this guy has been a fixer for centuries, we need to play this smart. I have more options for cover stories when I'm working alone. I'll have my cell, and you'll know when I arrive and when I leave."

"I want Jacques positioned no more than four blocks away."

Bella nodded. "Not a problem."

"Now we need something to keep Cressa busy. She'll want to see Devon." Simone touched Lyra's shoulder, and she gave a start until she glanced up, her eyes out of focus. After a moment, she smiled and patted Simone's hand.

"Ginger can keep her busy," Lucas offered. "And she's lost time in her training. She won't sit for Anna's lessons, but she won't say no to the training room."

"Excellent." Simone nodded to the team. "Let's meet again once Sergi and Cressa get home. Our one and only focus is finding who set Devon up, or at least, who murdered Boretsky. Second is keeping Cressa at home and too busy to get into trouble."

When everyone began leaving the office, Lyra reached out to Simone. "Thank you for taking care of this. I need a small nap, and then I'd like to review the perimeter changes I've discussed with Lucas and Bella. I'd like your opinion before I share it with Sergi."

Simone nodded, a bit eager to see what Lyra had put together. "That will give me time in the training room. How about a late lunch?"

"In the solarium?"

"I'll let Cook know."

Simone left the office, jogging up the stairs to her room to change. Lucas's suggestion of hiding Devon at Oasis was brilliant but very risky. She was betting all her chips on Gheata being the one behind the murder. And while it felt right, proving it would be another matter. But, if he ended up being the key to clearing Devon, it was worth the favor she'd traded with Gaius.

# Chapter Twenty-Four

It was my last day of training, and we'd been at it for an hour—assuming I had any correct sense of time. We jumped from one construct to another. Some I knew, others I didn't. The ones I knew weren't only of the Trelane manor, Oasis, or thankfully, the alley. One minute we were in my old apartment, the next my bedroom in Christopher's mansion. Then we went to locations that only Colantha would be familiar with: landscapes of snow, expensive parties, sandy beaches, inner cities, and long-forgotten subway tunnels. Places that evoked horror and awe.

When the merry-go-round stopped, we sat in a small coffeehouse in San Francisco. It took me a moment to recall why it was familiar. Then it hit. I'd scored a big job and had just gotten the payout. I'd given a portion to Sorrento then took Ginger to the city for the weekend.

We'd been window-shopping and found this little out-of-the-way coffeehouse and bookstore. It even had a room in the back with boardgames. The place was busy, and though people were talking, I couldn't hear their voices.

I stared at the cup of espresso sitting in front of me. "How did you know about this place?"

She sipped her espresso. "I didn't."

I'd expected that answer, but I'd been stalling for time to wrap my head around the idea that some of the constructs hadn't been from Colantha after all, but from me. "I'm a bit confused by the whirlwind tour."

She laughed and settled back in her chair. "I have to admit, it's been some time since I've found a dreamwalker as powerful as you."

I snorted. "Right."

Her brow rose as she studied me. "You don't take this seriously enough."

I rubbed my face. "It's hard keeping up with all of this when I don't know what's coming next. It's like being left behind while the other kids boarded buses for the zoo. Maybe not knowing what's happening back home has me distracted."

She clucked. "Most likely a bit of each. I wasn't prepared to battle for control, but it's happened once or twice before."

"Battle?" I considered what constructs I could remember. "I wasn't consciously aware of most of those places. I assumed they were yours. But if they were mine, I expected something more recent."

"That's where the control comes in. The constructs were yours, and it's quite common that past locations might burst forth, especially when moving so quickly. I took control, but each time I did, you wrestled it back. It took some time to tire your mind long enough to allow me to settle us. Otherwise, we'd still be location hopping to the point of doubling back to places that hold the highest emotions—good or bad."

I shivered at that. Caught in a dreamwalker's groundhog day. That was a first. "If I didn't have complete control, how did I override your constructs?"

She reached for her medallion, and I hadn't noticed it was of a different design, though the etchings appeared the same. It was larger than mine, made of bronze, and hung from a braided rope of similar colors.

"The medallion?"

She nodded. "It's channeling your power to support the constructs and allowing you to take temporary control."

I frowned. "Am I going to end up in another psychic coma?"

"What type of instructor do you think I am?" Her curt tone was enough to know I'd insulted her, but her gaze softened. "Whoever took control from you knew what they were doing, most likely understood the danger but didn't care. My fear is that it was a dreamwalker who was either hospitalized or under some other duress. She somehow picked up the power of your psyche. She took unfair advantage, but she might have done it for her own sanity. Or perhaps she was already mad."

My breath rushed out. I'd been afraid of putting the necklace back on. Even so, I thought the initial experience was behind me. Until now, I'd assumed someone took control because of simple animosity. It never crossed my mind it might be someone being held against their will, possibly terrorized, and simply looking for a small piece of freedom.

"You can't think of that person or their reasons. You have to think of yourself. You might never have come out of that coma."

I nodded and drank the espresso. The caffeine gave me a jolt, and I glanced at the customers. "Do these people even know we're here?"

"No. And you have enough to think about than to worry about the customers. Be patient." She fidgeted in her seat. "You could have considered more comfortable chairs."

"Next time."

She clucked. "Your medallion channels your power. Focuses it like a laser beam, allowing you to spend less energy on the construct so you have more power to call people from their dreams. Up to now, you've been doing it while you've been sleeping, your powers coming from strong emotions. Now comes the time for the constructs to come when you call them. Eventually, you'll know when it's safe to call others. In the more advanced stages, you'll be able to reach out to other dreamwalkers."

"Other dreamwalkers." The thought was interesting. "So, what? Do all the dreamwalkers get together a few times a year for backyard barbecues, tailgate parties, and the holidays?"

She ignored my sarcasm, but her eyes twinkled, making me think I wasn't far off. The thought delighted me.

"Is it possible for a non-dreamwalker to initiate a dreamwalk if they had the medallion?" I was thinking of Lyra. I thought the nightmare of the shifter massacre had been my doing, but what if it had been Lyra's?

"Why would you ask that?"

I shrugged. "Just curious."

She eyed me for some time, but when I returned my best poker face, the one that drove Devon mad, she relented. "It has been known on a couple of occasions that a non-dreamwalker, one who had been previously introduced to a construct, can create one if they have a medallion. But they can only call the dreamwalker with whom they've dreamwalked with."

It was an interesting concept but didn't answer how Lyra ended up in that dream. I hadn't even known who she was at the time.

"You must learn to block others from taking over your constructs. They can be invited in, but may never take control."

"How will I know I'm strong enough?"

"When you can block my attempts for control."

That deflated all my expectations for an easy lesson, and I drained the espresso. When I thought about having another, a fresh cup appeared. I picked it up, drew in the intoxicating scent of the brew, and smiled at Colantha.

She winked, and we were sitting on top of a mountain peak. The wind blew the snow around us, and, within a minute, we were covered in white powder. I glanced down to find my cup of espresso still in my hands—frozen. My teeth began to chatter, yet Colantha looked warm and toasty in Sherpa gear. Bitch.

Next, we were at the beach. A small cove just south of Santa Cruz. I'd driven down with a bunch of kids from high school, and we stayed until almost midnight, roasting marshmallows and getting drunk. I'd been grounded for a week when I climbed up the trellis to my room to find Christopher waiting for me. But that day had been one of the happiest in my life.

I wasn't holding the espresso anymore, and to my irritation, Colantha wasn't in her snow gear. She was dressed in a white summer dress, lying on a chaise lounge while I sat in the sand. She turned and gave me a shit-eating grin. There was a goddamn flower in her hair.

No doubt about it. This was war.

I woke with a splitting headache. The first session with the medallion lasted three hours. We would have still been going, burning ourselves out, if Frederick hadn't doused the flames before turning on the room lights until they were so intensely bright they snapped us out of the construct.

Colantha's irritation melted quickly, and when I glanced at Frederick, his face was etched with concern. It was my best guess considering this was the first time he'd ever shown any emotion. We broke for food, juice, and two hours of sleep. Jamison kicked my bed an undetermined number of times to wake me up. Two more glasses of juice and another two-hour session.

Even though Colantha continued to overpower my constructs, it wasn't all bad news. I couldn't figure out how she adapted so quickly to each new construct, but I was improving at a fast pace, changing wardrobe, chairs, colors. I even created an ice cream cone. Did they have the same caloric impact as the real deal? Colantha dashed my hopes on that one.

The one thing I couldn't do was take control of the construct. After two more sessions, I was carried to my room, where I slept like the dead. The only reason I'd woke now was the beam of light from the window stabbing me with its intensity. I sat up, looking for the juice Jamison always left on my nightstand, but nothing was there.

I stumbled to the bathroom and started to shake. It was mild, but enough to make me notice. When I made it to the coffeemaker, I found the note.

*Meet us in the common dining room.*

The headache and shivers stuck with me as I stumbled across the grassy path to the center bungalow. Each step was like dragging a twenty-pound weight. I heard voices when I entered the building.

Sergi was at the table with Colantha and Frederick. I was surprised to see him, but it probably came across as the pained grimace it was. He was at my side before I could register the movement. He helped me to the table, and I caught his glare at Colantha, which earned him a cluck.

"The next couple of days will be difficult. She'll need plenty of bed rest, hydration, and no dreamwalking."

"Why is she shaking?" He lifted my chin to look into my eyes, and when I couldn't tolerate the bright light, I pushed his hand away. Or tried. It was like pushing a snowplow out of the way. After another few seconds, he relented and let my chin drop. "She has a headache."

Colantha nodded. "Probably a doozy, and it will get worse over the next twenty-four hours. She's going through withdrawals."

"From the juice?" My throat was so raw it felt like I swallowed a quarter of the Sahara Desert then crunched on a few rocks for shit and giggles. Sergi handed me a glass of water but took it away from me after a couple of sips.

"Frederick lowered the additives sometime in the evening and has weaned you off of them."

"The juice didn't taste any different."

"No. It wouldn't."

Of course not. So much easier to drug a person when they couldn't taste it.

"Don't pout. It was nothing more than an herb to strengthen your psychic powers, as I said before. The extended training sessions required the herbs for stamina. You'll get to the point where you won't need it except for the intense training we've been through. It's also impacting your core body temperature, which explains the shivering. Try to eat something. You won't want to, but you'll improve faster with nourishment."

I picked at the beignet, wondering if there was any place in Santiga Bay that made them this good. Conversation was light as everyone ate lunch, and I picked at random pieces of food only to stop the glaring from Colantha and Sergi.

The shakes increased to the point I had to give up trying to eat anything, afraid the piece of food would end up flying across the room. I sensed Sergi's desire to leave.

"Is there anything the House Trelane can do for you to compensate you for your time?"

I shot a glance to Colantha, curious if she'd find the offer offensive. But she was already giving it some consideration.

"If you don't mind listening to an old woman weave a story." Interesting that she considered herself old since she didn't look a day over thirty-five. She took a long sip of coffee before settling back. "There was once a powerful dreamwalker. Strong enough that we believed he might be the one to mend the fracture between our species. But he moved too quickly, showed his hand too soon. He was meant to find another as powerful as he. One with whom their combined strength could shield us all. But he was young, rash, and fell in love with a vampire. Perhaps if he hadn't discovered the ancient text, things would have turned out different.

"It was prophesied the ancient text would one day be discovered and dreamwalkers would once again walk free across the earth.

As it turned out, he didn't have the experience, and he caught the eye of a powerful vampire who had much to lose if the truth was revealed to the Council and Houses. The text, his love for another, and his inexperience were a bad combination with no one to guide him. There are nights when I still hear him calling, but I can't reach him."

"What happened to him?" I could barely keep up with the story, but I'd come to know this woman, and she wouldn't be sharing it if it didn't mean something.

"He was believed to have burned in a fire."

I grimaced. A horrible way to die.

"It wasn't proven?" Sergi always picked up on those little details.

Her smile was grim. "No."

"The House Trelane appreciates the story and will heed its importance." Sergi stood and helped me up.

Before I could ask for help to pack, I noticed my duffel and backpack by the door. Jamison nodded at me, and I hoped he checked the room twice before closing up my bags. I reached for my necklace and found it safely hanging around my neck.

Colantha stood and took my arms. "You should put that away while you heal. Then you should be able to wear it when you want, but it should always remain hidden. Remember..."

"Security, secrecy, and solidarity. I remember." Why was I tearing up? I'd barely met this woman, and she'd put me through hell. But I'd learned a great deal during the lessons with no way to thank her. "I appreciate your time. I know I set difficult parameters."

"Don't forget your promise to me."

I nodded. "Once my mission is complete."

Colantha, along with Jamison and Frederick, followed us out to the car. Sergi helped me into the front seat then stowed my bags. I waved as he pulled away, but when I turned around the three of them had already disappeared into the building.

The heat was running with fans on full, but I couldn't stop shivering. I must have fallen asleep because the next thing I knew, I was being helped up the stairs to the plane and guided to one of the plush seats.

"You can lay down as soon as we're in the air." Sergi covered me with several blankets. Then he hovered over me until I drank a glass of orange juice and ate a hard-boiled egg. By then, we were in the air, and he helped me to the couch, ensuring the covers were back in place.

"What did Colantha mean by that story?" Between the headache and overall achy feeling, I wasn't sure I'd heard it all correctly.

"I'm not sure. It's something I'll need to think about."

"All right." Before the call to sleep took me down, I remembered something else. Colantha never said anything more about my father or my prescient abilities. I guess there was no question I'd have to go back.

I vaguely remembered being propped up for the landing, then a car ride wrapped in a blanket and leaning against Sergi. The shivers were back, and no amount of heat warmed me. I was carried upstairs, and then happily wrapped within the covers of my own bed, my body melting into its warmth from a fire blazing in the hearth.

Distant voices woke me. They sounded worried, then angered, then cooing as a warm cloth was settled over my forehead. Then nothing except the faint concern that I was forgetting something. Someone. A man with icy-blue eyes pleading for help.

# Chapter Twenty-Five

I STOOD next to a chain-link fence. It was late afternoon, and the shadows lengthened across the sand and rock landscape, framing the empty buildings sprawled like an abandoned city. The place didn't look familiar, but the complex appeared massive. I could either spend hours walking through the buildings or put my newly acquired skills to work.

I rubbed my necklace, and the construct changed. The buildings towered around me, and I placed myself somewhere in the middle of them. I leaned against a metal railing and waited.

The medallion was warm against my skin. This was the first time I'd put it on since leaving New Orleans, and I was comforted by being aware of what was around me without worrying about some unknown entity taking control.

It was all good—as long as I didn't focus too closely on the construct. If I did, I sensed something, far off in the distance, hammering to enter my dream.

I pushed the distraction away and focused on the vampire walking across the windswept tarmac. His clothes were ripped and torn, dirt and mud stained the exposed skin, and his long hair was matted. But he was Devon and not the beast.

His eyes glowed icy blue, and his expression wasn't so much menacing as it was stern. I sighed. He knew why I'd come, and he wasn't going to agree to my plan.

When he was an arm's reach away, he stopped and spent the first moments taking me in. His gaze took a slow path up my body, heating every part it touched. I licked my lips, and his eyes instantly locked on them. Then he shook his head.

"Who told you?" I'd wring their neck. But there could only be one. "It was Decker, wasn't it?"

He didn't respond. He didn't have to. Simone didn't want anyone knowing where Devon was, me included. Which was why it had taken me longer than planned to find him.

"I don't want to talk about that." His tone was pleading. "We don't have much time."

I took a step, and he raised his hand. I didn't stop. "I'm not scared of you. Decker says most of the Poppy is out of your system. But you wouldn't hurt me even if the beast was in control."

He smiled, and it was so unexpected, so endearing, I almost took a step back. It broke my heart to see it, uncertain if I'd ever see it again if the Eliminators caught up with him.

"You think you can sway the beast as easily as you did me?"

I took a step closer. Then another until only inches separated us. I gave him my best teasing smile. "The beast likes me."

I was expecting another argument or some flippant comment about how scary vamps were. He would be right, but after seeing Colantha with her loyal vamp guards, some primitive part of me said I was different than a human. That somehow, dreamwalkers and vamps were connected at the root of our being. She hadn't said anything specific, but she was much older than she appeared. Maybe her youthful appearance was aided with vamp blood. She claimed an herb had been added to the juice. But was something else added she hadn't mentioned?

Before I could ponder it any further, his lips were on mine as his arms wrapped around me. I melted, hungry for his taste, his strength, the sound of his heartbeat. It seemed like months rather than a week since we'd last touched. Everything around us disappeared until it was just the two of us, but when I attempted to change constructs and take us to the grotto, it didn't work.

Then fangs were at my neck, and it was no longer Devon but his beast.

I woke, staring at the ceiling with my hand on my neck. When I pulled it away, there was no blood and no pain. And I was more confident than ever in knowing how to fix Devon.

~

AFTER THE DREAM, I must have fallen asleep. Maybe I'd still been in a construct because whatever energy I'd had was zapped. I could barely open my eyes to the dying fire, which was the only light in the room. My body and head ached, and I was weak as a baby bird. Whatever Colantha put in her special juice packed a wallop. I managed to roll over and let sleep envelope me until I heard a tapping at the door.

This time, the embers were dead, and light peeked around the edges of the drawn drapes.

"Come in," I called out when the tapping came a second time. It took everything I had to repeat the command again before the door crept open.

"Are you awake?" Ginger whispered, her head poking from around the doorframe.

"Barely."

She slipped into the room, gently shutting the door behind her. "I didn't want to bother you, but I also wanted to make sure you were okay. You were pretty out of it last night." She glanced around and wrung her hands. "Should I start the fire?"

"Why are you walking on eggshells? I'm not broken. It's just the worst hangover ever."

She straightened. "Hangover? That's not what Sergi said."

I snorted. "He didn't drink the special juice." I held a hand to my head and pushed up to a sitting position. If I moved really slowly, the pain was like someone hammering nails into my head. It was a reprieve from the jackhammer.

Ginger strode to the windows and yanked the drapes open. The bright light slammed into me, and the jackhammer returned.

"Not the curtains."

"Yes, the curtains. You need sunshine." She poured a glass of water from a pitcher on the dresser. "Drink up. You're dehydrated. Good grief, don't vamps know anything about hangovers?" When I'd drained the glass, she refilled it. "I suppose not, since they can't get drunk. More's the pity."

I laughed, almost choking on the water. "God, I missed you."

She plopped onto the bed, no longer tiptoeing around me. In fact, she seemed to be going out of her way to make me miserable again. "I missed you, too. I only heard bits and pieces when Sergi and Lucas were hovering over you. I guess it was pretty taxing— mentally and physically."

I shared the highlights of the trip, including the vamps I'd met before Colantha found me. "I think the physical strain was sitting in that damn pit for so long."

Ginger pulled out her cell and made a call. "She's awake and could use some coffee. Uh-huh, that's perfect. Thank you."

"Who was that?"

She ignored me and disappeared into the bathroom. And a minute later, water was splashing into the tub. Then she rummaged through my dresser, pulling out underwear, leggings, and a large sweatshirt.

I'd fallen back to the pillow in a vain attempt to make the room stop spinning. Before I knew it, she grabbed my hands and pulled me out of bed.

"Come on. Time to face the music."

"Ow. My body isn't ready." I stumbled as she dragged me to

the bathroom. "And it wasn't like I was out partying for three days."

When she pushed me toward the tub, the scent of lavender and mint lured me to stick a toe in. The water was blessedly hot, and an hour later, we were sitting on the bed, eating Cook's blueberry scones, still warm from the oven, and guzzling coffee.

"What's the news on Devon?" I focused on my scone but glanced at Ginger, who seemed overly interested in her coffee as she stirred sugar in.

"I think it's best you discuss that with Simone."

"Are you kidding me?" My voice must have risen because she blanched. Or maybe she was feeling guilty. "So, you're falling along party lines."

Her head popped up, and the tears surprised me. "No," she snapped. "It's not like that."

I pushed away the plate, knocking the cup and sloshing coffee over the tray. "It's that bad? Is he still alive?"

"Oh my god. Yes. Of course." She nibbled her bottom lip. "I didn't mean…" She twisted her napkin. "I didn't want to be the one to tell you."

Now my tone was deathly quiet. "Tell me what?"

"Devon has become more aware since Decker took away the meat dosed with Magic Poppy."

"Isn't that good news?"

"Yes. But his physical condition isn't improving."

I let her words sink in. Devon couldn't shed his beast form. When I saw him as the beast, he couldn't even talk. Would my only interaction with him be in a construct? I couldn't look at Ginger, and I scrambled off the bed, stumbling to the windows. I couldn't breathe.

Ginger's arms wrapped around me. "I'm so sorry, honey. No one's given up, but the focus has shifted to a vamp who might be the killer. I think they're hoping Devon might show improvement in a couple of days." She lowered her voice. "I think they're considering taking him to Oasis."

"Hide him from the Eliminators?" I couldn't believe Simone or Sergi would approve of that. "Do you know who they suspect?"

Ginger stepped back, shaking her head. "Lucas is pretty tight-lipped about it, and I haven't pushed."

"Thank you for sharing what you did. I know it was hard."

We hugged, and it seemed like the weight of the world was on our shoulders. She pushed me back and stared at me, her mouth opening and closing. Then she spit out, "I forgot to tell you the cops are looking for you."

Chapter Twenty-Six

EVEN AFTER DEATH, Christopher continued to haunt me. It was different this time. My mom had my back. Who would have thought it? I'd have to reach out to her once Devon and the House were safe.

I climbed the stairs to the third floor, nodding to the vamp standing guard. That was new. Bodyguard or babysitter?

I'd barely knocked when Lyra called out, "Come in, Cressa."

I hated when she did that.

Her room was bright with midday light, and the air smelled of paint. She stood in front of an easel that faced the western windows. I stepped closer, surprised at the scene that was both similar and foreign to her other paintings. The primordial forested island wasn't in any of her other works—at least not the few I'd seen. But there was the familiar cove. On the white-sand beach, a single red umbrella shaded a blanket complete with picnic basket and a bottle of wine. A person sitting on the blanket was beginning to take shape, but it was too soon to tell if the figure was male or female.

Lyra finished a couple of strokes then set her brush aside,

turning and wiping her hands on her paint-stained apron. She removed it and tossed it on a nearby worktable.

"It must be nice to be painting again." I glanced at another landscape, the paint still wet. This scene I knew well. It was the gardens outside the manor with the old sycamore tree—another favorite object of Lyra's. It showed up in several of her paintings, each setting a different time of day, different colors or shading, but the same tree.

Lyra perched on the sofa that faced the same windows and patted the seat next to her. "Come sit."

She picked up a decanted bottle of wine and poured two glasses. Did she always take a break with wine, or was she expecting me? It wasn't far-fetched that I'd seek her out once I'd returned. She said we'd talk about the necklace after New Orleans.

I considered the chair next to the couch, but she was still patting the sofa.

"What's the matter, Cressa? Are you concerned about my dual personalities? Perhaps I'm still a bit crazy?" Lyra glanced out to the sea, the waves as wild as her heart. "Perhaps I am. And while there are two of me inside, there's little to fear from either one. What do they say? The only one in danger of getting hurt is me.

"My best friend Avery and I would sit here, staring at the ocean for hours and confessing all our sins." Her laughter sounded like a light spring rain. "If we only knew how silly our misdeeds were compared to the horrors of this world." She closed her eyes and lifted her chin, exposing her long graceful neck.

I sat next to her and touched her arm. It was a moment before she passed me the wineglass.

"For as long as I can remember, I've viewed myself as the before and the after. You first met the after, the child that rose from the accident. The day my whole world was stripped away from me. Of course, it was months before I spoke at all. Maybe it was years. I don't remember. They said I had some form of psychotic break, which seemed reasonable considering what I'd just been through."

She sipped her wine, and when she turned to me, her expression wasn't sad or regretful or angry. It was ethereally blank, as if she were telling someone else's story. "I know I've shared some of this before, but I wanted you to hear it all in context. Other than Devon and the cadre, no one else knows the story.

"It was two months after the accident that the first dream came. So real. Too real. I was in a place I didn't recognize, with people I didn't know. I thought it was a nightmare, but at the same time, I recognized the feel of the dreamworld. The one Hamilton had introduced me to." Her focus moved to a painting on the wall. "They came each night, all of them different, horrible, terrifying, and I began to experience the repercussions of continual beatings and starvation. The only way to avoid the dreams was to not sleep. Being vampire, it's possible to go long periods between sleeping, but few of us have the stamina anymore. I was surprised how quickly it came back."

"That's when you started walking the property at night?" I asked. The first night I'd come to the manor, I'd seen someone with a lantern standing in front of the gravestones. My curiosity had been piqued to discover who that mystery person had been.

"Yes, and when I became a child again, unwilling to face the responsibility of being an adult, no longer remembering who I'd been before. The dreams lessened but never went away."

She gripped my hand. "The dreams changed when you came here. Faces fell away as if pieces of broken glass. But the image behind the mirror is still elusive. I felt its presence when I put your necklace on."

"A woman?" I thought back to the malevolent presence the first time I'd worn the necklace.

"No. A male. But I can't see more than that." She scratched her head. "It's like an itch that won't go away. But I'm more lucid than I've been since..." Her hand dropped into her lap.

After several seconds, I touched her arm. "Lyra?"

"We had traveled to the city—San Francisco—and met with one of Father's oldest friends, Philipe Renaud."

I jerked at the name then gulped the wine. Philipe Renaud was the vamp we were searching for. The one who could lead them to the *De første dage*. I nodded to show I was listening, encouraging her to continue.

"Father had a private meeting with him while Mother had lunch with Hamilton and me." Her voice cracked, and she glanced again to the sketch of a young man, the same man that was in the majority of her paintings.

I studied the image, understanding why she painted him so often. He appeared the same physical age as Lyra, and his hair was cut in a style similar to the early nineteen hundreds. He was quite handsome, and it wasn't too wild of a guess to assume it was Hamilton.

She wiped at an eye and cleared her throat. "It was the first time Mother was civil to him." She gave me a curious glance. "He was human."

My eyes widened. "Oh. That's interesting."

She giggled, a sound reminiscent of the child she had been. "That's the first time I've heard that response."

"I'm sorry. That was rude."

"Not at all." Her smile was warm and reminded me of Devon. "The typical response was no words at all, only stares of nonacceptance and ridicule. Or the one that said my curiosity would eventually wane." She finished her wine and refilled both glasses. There was a slight tremor in her hand when she set the decanter down. And when she gripped her glass, her knuckles grew pale, and I cringed, waiting for the stem to snap. She released a soft breath before sipping, the crisis momentarily resolved.

"What Hamilton and I had was special." Her eyes glistened with emotion. "We understood each other on a level no one else could begin to understand. He was the love of my life. Nothing could touch us." She heaved a sigh. "Until the accident." Her gaze returned to the ocean, and her posture stiffened.

"We were almost home, but I wasn't paying attention to the drive. Hamilton and I were in the back seat, talking about the museum. Father had been off studying the book Philipe had reserved for him while we spent hours wandering through the stacks. We were laughing about something when the car swerved.

"At first, it didn't seem a problem—Father avoiding something in the road. Then there were bright lights, the car swerved again, then..." Her voice cracked, and her eyes closed. When they opened, she appeared calmer. "It felt like something might have hit us. I can still smell the gasoline, wildflowers, burning rubber, and a cigarette. Then I was pulled out of the car. My leg was broken, maybe my arm, but it was healed shortly after so I can't remember. Then the explosion." Her hands shook as she covered her face.

I gave her time to recover. There wasn't anything I could say. That I was sorry seemed so inadequate.

"I'm grateful I didn't see him after he'd been burned to death in the car. Both my parents perished, too. Everyone but me."

"It's normal to feel survivor's guilt."

She shook her head. "That's not something that happens with vampires. Although I'm sure what happened to me afterward doesn't happen to anyone, either. All I could think of, the only place I wanted to be, was back with Hamilton and the dreams we shared. Where he would hold me and kiss me and tell me everything would work out. But instead of those dreams, I only have nightmares. Fire and blood. Torture and death." She took in a shaky breath and released a nervous laugh.

"Now I'm the before once again. No. That's not quite true. It's impossible to be the before once the after existed. I'm something new that combines the before and the after to become the now." She giggled. "Perhaps it's the wine."

I smiled and glanced at our empty glasses. I didn't know her tolerance for alcohol, but I was already suffering the mother of all hangovers. "You're probably not wrong."

"But this isn't what you came to see me about."

I was still reeling from the bombshells she'd shared, but I couldn't leave without discussing the issue currently facing us. "I need to find Devon." I didn't have time to wait. We were down to two days, and I'd slept through most of the morning.

"Decker is keeping him safe."

"But he's not getting better."

She turned back to the window, her gaze unfocused. I was losing her. Then she grabbed my wrist. "He's too dangerous while he's in beast form."

"Not to me."

She shook her head, her grip on my arm tightening until I was blinking through tears. "Let me go, Lyra. You're hurting me."

She snapped her hand back but never turned away from the window. "I'm sorry. I'm doing everything I can to stay focused. It's too much."

"You need to lie down."

She nodded, and I stood, turning her so she could lay on the couch. I placed a sofa pillow under her head and glanced around the room, spotting a blanket folded across a chair. I covered her and felt her forehead. It was cool.

"Lyra? Can you hear me?"

No response. Not a flicker on her face to acknowledge my presence. I didn't know what was happening with the voices. Was she still half-crazed? Was this what it looked like when someone was in a construct?

I gave her a final glance before leaving. I nodded to the guard and raced down the stairs to the first floor. I had to speak to Simone about Devon, but I couldn't get my head to stop spinning. Had I heard what I thought I did? Had she just confided to me that Hamilton had been a dreamwalker?

# Chapter Twenty-Seven

SIMONE WASN'T at the manor. Convenient. She'd left first thing for Oasis and wouldn't be back until the following morning. I searched for Bella, but depending on which vamp I asked, she was either on a classified assignment or was handling security at the safe house.

My frustration reached a boiling point, and I detoured to the kitchen. Cook was stirring a pot when I stormed in.

"There's only soup for lunch," he shouted without turning around. Based on the chaos in the kitchen, he was a busy chef. "The bread is in the warmer, bowls are out. Don't ask for anything else."

I stopped at the long island where, on most days, the magic happened as he concocted spice combinations and hovered over cookbooks to create his masterpiece meals. Today, it was filled with dozens of cannisters and jars of various ingredients.

"I just wanted to thank you for the scones."

He swirled around, red sauce spattering the stove and countertops. "Ack!" He mopped up the mess with a nearby towel. "What a mess."

"I didn't mean to startle you." I did the best I could to hold back a grin, though I might have felt a wee bit guilty.

"I knew someone was there, but I wasn't expecting you." He set down the spoon then opened his arms. I hugged him tightly while he patted my back. "Everything will be all right. Our Father has been through worse."

I wasn't sure that was a true statement, but I knew he was trying to keep his own spirits up.

"What's with all the cooking?" There were several pots on the stove and something roasting in the oven. Fresh loaves of bread filled a separate counter.

"Lucas asked for quick meals to be prepared should there be a siege."

"Eliminators or Lorenzo?"

He shrugged. "Does it matter?"

I assumed it didn't, since he put it that way. "I've noticed a few more vamps in the house."

He nodded and went back to stirring what I could now smell was spaghetti sauce if the red splatter hadn't been enough of a clue. "Everyone is being moved to either the manor or Oasis." He shook his head. "The safe house up the road is already overflowing with security teams."

I looked around the kitchen and spotted the dining table. It was piled high with full food containers. Coolers and plastic storage bins were lined against the wall. I nodded toward them. "Food for the safe house?"

Cook nodded. "Most of it's ready. I'm finishing up a few items, then Jacques will get everything delivered."

"Is Sergi around?"

"Somewhere. He might be in his office, or Devon's, or marching around yelling orders." Cook didn't get irritated often, but apparently, the cadre had pushed him over the edge.

"Is there something I can help with?"

His tone softened. "No, child. You're supposed to be on bed rest."

I rolled my eyes, tired of always being the invalid. "I'm fine. I had a bit of a headache when I woke. Your scones are magical. Two of them and a boatload of coffee and I feel good as new. I just can't seem to find anyone to bring me up to speed on what's going on."

"Unfortunately, I can't help with this one. The cadre are very quiet about their plans. All I hear are the orders they shout."

I squeezed his arm. "It's normal for stress levels to increase the closer we get to the deadline."

He nodded and patted my hand. "Try his office. That's the most likely spot."

I found Sergi in Devon's office after checking his first. The door was open, and two vamps I might have recognized stood in front of the desk, staring at a map. Sergi was pointing to various spots when he lifted his head.

"Cressa. I thought you'd be resting."

"Yeah, I keep hearing that. The headache is gone, and I feel fine. What's going on?"

Sergi rolled up the map before I reached the desk and handed it to one of the vamps. "You have your orders."

They both nodded at me before striding out.

"What are they up to?"

"Simone wants you to remain at the manor until after the Council's deadline." He was really good at ignoring my questions. Games were more fun when two played.

"I hear Simone went to Oasis. Is she securing the perimeter there as well?"

Sergi opened and closed files, then stuffed them in a lockable storage container. They must expect the worst if they were clearing files.

"Where's Devon?"

He eyed me, and as much as I was hoping he was considering

how much to tell me, he was more likely deciding which answer would make me go away the fastest. "He's safe."

"What's his condition? Is he still crazed on the Poppy? I want to see him."

"Simone will be back in the morning. I'm sure she'll share what she can about Devon and our plans for the Council."

"So, it's like that. Where's Anna?"

"She went with Simone." He went back to packing files, then he stopped and gave me one of those glares that didn't scare me anymore. "The next couple of days are going to be difficult. And it will mostly likely be worse after the Council's deadline. I suggest you take this time to recuperate from your training. Find a good book or paint your toenails with Ginger."

Oh, yeah. Two could definitely play this game.

I stormed out, slamming the office door with a satisfaction I hadn't felt in a long time. I hadn't expected my request to be easy, but refusal to talk to me about anything, well—I thought we'd gotten past that. After all this time, they seemed to have forgotten who they were dealing with. Pandora didn't take shit from anyone. Besides, I had my own plan cooking.

I strode through the manor—a woman on a mission. There were plenty of vamps, just not the ones I needed. I went back to my room and changed into a pair of black jeans, a comfortable sweater of the same color, and sneakers. I stuffed a few items into a backpack and set it next to the door. The necklace was around my neck, my wallet in the backpack. I glanced around for my cell and spotted it on the nightstand next to my day planner. When I grabbed my cell, I knocked the planner to the floor, dumping several business cards and sticky notes. I was shoving everything back in when two cards caught my eye.

One was Harlow's card. I twirled it through my fingers then stuffed it back with the rest of the stack. The other was a silver business card I'd been given weeks ago. That one I stuffed in my back pocket before shoving my phone in the backpack.

When I opened my bedroom door, I was in for a surprise. A vamp was stationed outside my door. There was one in front of Ginger's as well.

The vamp turned to me when I stepped into the hall. "You're only allowed to visit your friend. You can go downstairs when called for dinner."

That asshole. Sergi did know who he was playing with. I crossed the hall and pounded on Ginger's door, doing my best to hide my sneer. If Sergi thought a vamp guard was going to stop me, he hadn't covered all his bases. At least, I hoped he hadn't.

Ginger's door flew open. When she noted the two guards, her expression changed from annoyance to sheer pleasure. "Oh, good. They just brought up two bottles of wine and a slew of DVDs. Let's get hammered."

She pulled me in, slammed the door behind us, then turned up the speakers on her TV. "I've already called Lucas, but he can't override Sergi's orders, which Simone approved."

"Damn it. It's because of me."

She nodded. "They consider you a flight risk."

I snorted. "Well, they're not wrong." I paced her room. As usual, it wasn't easy. A tornado had obviously come through here. "I'm pretty sure I can get out of the manor, but I don't know if I can snag a vehicle."

"Have you ever checked out the neighboring yard?"

"No. Why?"

"Remember when you told me there was a thin path where the perimeter wall meets the cliff?"

I grinned. "I do now. I've never had a reason to check it out."

"I did out of curiosity. The property next door looks as secure as this place, but what about the wall itself?"

"What do you mean?"

"There's no razor wire; it's just a wall. A tall wall, but the brick is eight to ten inches wide."

"I can walk across the top." I ran through what I remembered of the long wall. "You were thinking to climb up from where it ends at the cliff?"

She nodded and nibbled her bottom lip. "But it's a long walk to the front of the property."

Her plan wasn't much different than what I'd been thinking. "The arbor. I can climb to the top of the wall from there."

"The arbor doesn't extend to the wall. Nothing does."

"That's true for the most part. But I was thinking about its leaves, which will block a portion of the wall from most points on the property. Five minutes at most is all I need.

"They'll be watching for you."

"Maybe. But it's not like they're going to shoot me."

"Then what?"

"I'd planned on grabbing a staff car, but I'll never make it out the gate."

"It's a long walk to any bus stop."

Fate was on my side when I remembered the business cards. "Do you think they're tracing your calls?"

Ginger considered it. "I don't think they have the tech to do it live. They'd have to work with the phone company. I'm sure they have someone on the inside, but I doubt they're considering it. Not with everything else going on."

"I agree. And by then, this will all be over."

"Are you sure it's a good idea to go after Devon?"

"I didn't have to hear it from Decker to know he doesn't have much of a chance on his own. I can see it in every vamp I look at. Even Sergi." And the hours ticked away, reducing any chance I had of getting to him in time. "Let me use your phone."

She glanced around, snagged it off a dresser, and tossed it to me.

"Do you have Harlow's number on it?"

"I didn't. But after that little caper you did with him—you know, the night Christopher got killed in the same neighborhood —I thought it best to have his number handy."

"Smart thinking." I found his number in the contacts list, hit the button, and prayed he'd answer. It took four rings before I heard his gruff voice.

"Ginger, luv. Good to hear from you."

"It's me, luv. You busy tonight?"

"Cressa. Hey, Trudy, it's Cressa. What's up, luv?"

After five minutes of telling him my plan, him telling me I was nuts, and then both of us agreeing he was probably right but it didn't change what I needed, he agreed to meet me a few blocks from the manor.

"I need to make another call, but I'd rather do that in my room."

Ginger was already up, tossing DVDs and snacks onto a tray. She handed me the two bottles of wine and glasses before opening the door, holding the tray in one arm. The two vamps stared at us as we crossed to my room.

"We want a fire, and my room already has the wood." I nodded toward the door and lifted my full hands. My guard nodded and rushed to open the door.

Once inside, I sighed with relief. I opened the wine while Ginger loaded a DVD and turned up the volume. I grabbed the silver business card, my cell, and ducked into the bathroom, shutting the door behind me.

I sat on the toilet, the cell in my hand as I stared at the card. Was I making the right decision or getting in the way? If anyone had bothered to clue me in or take five minutes to listen to me, I might not have to make this decision. But they shut me out in the name of security and protection.

It all came down to one thing. Devon. What was his best chance?

With shaking hands, I dialed the number.

~

"What do you mean, she's gone?" Simone, hands braced on the desk, leaned toward the cadre standing before her. Each one could have been a statue—even Bella.

"We haven't been able to locate her anywhere in the manor or on the grounds." Lucas stared at the wall behind her.

"For god's sake, relax. Sit." She dropped into Devon's chair and turned to face the blinds covering the window. "When was she last seen?"

"Ginger was with her until almost eleven." Lucas continued to stand while he gave his report as if Simone hadn't said anything. "Then she went back to her room. Dimitri said she stumbled at the door, and I confirmed this morning they'd been drinking most of the night. We know they ordered dinner in. Dimitri also mentioned that he'd seen Cressa in her room when Ginger left. It looked like she was picking up the remains of their dinner."

"She's going to be looking for Devon." Sergi had been grumbling since his return from New Orleans. Cressa getting away from them only made it worse.

She had to hand it to the human. Dreamwalker. Whatever the hell species they were supposed to consider her. Two guards at her front door, a dozen working the perimeter. "Double the perimeter guards." Once this was all over, Devon would be wise to add Cressa to their security detail. If there was a hole in their defenses, she was obviously the one to find it.

"She didn't take a vehicle." Jacques reddened when everyone glared at him. "I know it seemed obvious since no one signed her out of the gate, but I thought it best to confirm."

"You were right to do that," Simone said. "Her bedroom windows were closed. Did she just walk out the front door?"

"Her windows were closed, but only one set was locked." Sergi flipped through screens on his tablet.

"So, she left here as Pandora." Bella perched on a barstool, one leg tapping furiously. "Out her window and then somehow off the property. Did she walk to wherever she went?"

"At this point it doesn't matter," Sergi said. "Maybe she'll tell us when we catch up to her. We know where she's going."

"How would she know where he is?" Simone didn't expect an answer, and she didn't get one. "Did you contact Decker?"

He nodded. "He was planning on going over in a couple of hours. He wanted to be prepared in case we decide to move Devon today. He agreed to head over early." Sergi checked his watch. "He should be there by now."

"Is Devon safe to be around if we send in a team to watch for Cressa?"

"I don't think Decker would feel comfortable with that. Devon became agitated when he sensed Cressa was near. The beast would consider anyone we send in a threat."

Lucas rubbed his face. "There's got to be something."

"The Eliminators are probably out on the streets searching for him already." Jacques moved to sit next to Bella.

"Already?" Lucas asked.

Bella nodded. "They won't move in until told, but they won't see any harm in pinning down his location."

"Too many people out there." Simone tapped her fingers on the desk. The rhythmic sound appeared to have a calming impact on the cadre. "Lucas and Sergi, I want you to head over there. Don't go in until you get clearance from Decker."

"Any news on Gheata?" Sergi asked. Until they heard from Cressa or someone who had spotted her, there wasn't anything more they could do for the moment.

"We know where he lives. Bella confirmed that last night. I haven't decided on the best way in. I was hoping Cressa could help us with that until she went off on her own." She wanted to snap off the corner of the desk, just to rein in her growing temper. "We have no choice. Move Devon to Oasis, and let's hope we find something on Gheata that will prevent the Council from punishing us all.

"Bella, I want you and Jacques to keep an eye on Gheata's house. Be discreet. Don't follow him. Just babysit."

They both nodded.

"I'll run the check-ins for the perimeter guards while you're out."

Sergi perked up, sitting straighter as he read something on his tablet. "Decker is on scene, but he can't get in to the mill."

"I thought there were several gates." Simone didn't need another problem with only two days left. "So, what's the issue?"

"There are six points of entry. And each one has two wolves guarding it."

*Chapter Twenty-Eight*

HARLOW and I waited on the service road, three hundred yards from the main gate of the old mill. It had been closed since I was a kid. I'd only been here once before with a group of rebellious teenagers, but we'd never breeched the fence line, preferring to take an old game trail down to the beach to light bonfires and drink. And that explained why I hadn't known where I was when I'd met Devon in my dream constructs.

In those few years since I'd been down here, it hadn't changed much, except for the increased weeds growing over the lumpy remnants of asphalt. The city council had spent years trying to convince businesses to repurpose the land. I vaguely remembered from Christopher's constant complaints during family dinners, there was a massive price tag for cleanup that went along with the purchase of the land and buildings. So the prime real estate lay bare and mostly forgotten.

It had been a smart decision of Decker's to move Devon here. The massive complex was close to the city, but with the way the land was positioned, the mill could only be seen from the ocean or after driving down the old service road where Harlow had parked.

The main road to the mill had grown over long ago and been rerouted to a more scenic drive along the coast.

"How much longer?" Harlow asked. He'd been a lifesaver and hadn't hesitated to meet me. Trudy had wanted to come, but we both thought it safer for her to stay home by the phone. We compromised, and she was parked a mile away at a diner that opened early for breakfast.

The call to The Wolf had been more difficult, if only for my nerves. He'd answered on the second ring. "Cressa?"

"Are you psychic?" I heard his laugh, deep and warm.

"The magic of cell phones, and honoring Devon's request to keep you on my contact list."

I was curious but needed to stick to my script. "You once gave me your card for when I needed help."

"I did."

"I'm not sure this qualifies, but I don't have anywhere else to turn."

"I've been monitoring the situation with Devon and the House Trelane. Does this have something to do with that? Do you need shelter?"

"Not exactly." When I hesitated, The Wolf remained silent, giving me the time to work up to my request. "If you know about Devon, then you probably know that even coming off the Poppy, he's still in beast form."

"I'm aware."

"I know this is going to sound crazy, and I know you don't have all the facts, but I believe I'm the only one that can put the beast to sleep."

The silence lengthened, and I gave him the same courtesy he'd given me. I waited patiently, staring at the bathroom door, positive someone would guess my actions and break it down.

"What are you asking of me?"

"The cadre won't listen to me and refuse to tell me where Devon is. They believe my plan is too risky."

"You need his location?"

"Yes."

Silence again, but only for a moment. "Are you sure you know what you're doing?"

"Yes." No hesitation. He needed to believe like I did.

"Can you get out of the manor?"

"I have it all worked out. I just need a location."

He chuckled. "It seems there's no stopping Pandora when she's on a mission."

I snorted. "Yeah. So most of the rumors are true."

"Do you know where the old paper mill is?"

I had to rack my brain before I remembered. "Yeah, down by Slawson Cove?"

"That's the one. There's an old service road. It can be difficult to find."

"I know exactly where it is."

"Meet me there at five am. Does that give you enough time."

"My friend Ginger will call you if I don't make it out of the manor."

"You know the police are searching for you."

"Just call me Miss Popular." When he didn't respond, I added, "They've been temporarily diverted away from my location."

That warm chuckle again. "See you at five."

Ginger left my room an hour before midnight. I watched the yard from my window until one a.m., counting and timing the guards movements around the perimeter. One stayed close to the weak point by the cliff that Ginger had mentioned. I assumed another would be across the yard at the other point where the wall ended. I could see a portion of the arbor and only saw one vamp walk along the stretch of wall every fifteen minutes. My guess was that they were sticking close to the front wall, the back, and around the manor. The guards at the manor worked a clockwise route every ten minutes. This would be the most difficult part of my plan, but if I was already outside with the window closed behind me, I would save time dropping and running toward the thicker landscaped part of the yard. The trellis on the far side of the window was a stretch to reach, but I clung to it while two guards walked by, stopping to check something on the ground before looking up. Their gazes were a few yards to the right of me, and I guessed they were looking at Lyra's windows, where a soft glow emanated. A minute later, they'd moved far enough away for me to start my descent, jumping to the ground halfway down.

From there it was more a rush and wait as I raced from one spot to another on my way to the arbor. I climbed a nearby tree to reach the wall, and always wondered why they never trimmed the branches away from it, until I reached the top and peered over the side. The landscaping would make it almost impossible for anyone to breach the wall from there. Vamps could do it, but other spots along the wall would be easier targets.

Once on the wall, I only had to time my movements against the vamps rotations. After thirty minutes, I was jogging down the road and cutting down side streets until I spotted Harlow's car. In our line of work, it wasn't unusual to stake out a mark, and he came prepared. Once we'd parked on the service road, he pulled out a large thermos of Trudy's wake-the-dead coffee and her sweet rolls.

"I hope you know what you're doing." He'd stuffed three sweet rolls down before I'd finished one. But I was ahead of him on cups of coffee. Between the caffeine and the sugar, my leg was bouncing to the steady beat of the ocean waves that could be heard through the slit of the open window.

"It's just a gut instinct."

He grunted. "I always listen to my gut."

Then we both laughed, breaking the tension.

When the limo pulled up next to us, Harlow gave me one of those papa-bear looks. I gave him an awkward and unexpected hug.

"Thanks for having my back."

"Anytime, luv. You know that." Then he couldn't help sliding a hand to my ass and giving it a squeeze. "I still have high hopes of scoring a big job with your boyfriend."

That deserved a punch in the arm, a quick kiss to his cheek, and I was out the door with my backpack.

When I slid into the limo where the door had been cracked open for me, I wasn't sure what to expect. "I'm sorry for all of this, especially so early in the morning."

"It's nice to see you, too." His smile was more endearing than I remembered, but I was somewhat freaked out the last time I'd seen him, when he'd traded me to Devon to square a debt.

I returned his smile, my cheeks warming. "Sorry. It is good to see you."

He gave me a long perusal, not seeming to miss anything. "You're being treated well."

"Some days like a princess, some days like a field soldier."

His laugh echoed through the limo. "And somehow that seems to fit you. When this is over, I need to invite you and Devon to my home."

"I'd like that."

"But first, why do you think you're the only one who can save him?"

I hadn't expected the question. I couldn't tell him about dreamwalkers, but I owed him something for the risk he was taking, especially if the Council ever found out. "All I can tell you is that there's something in my blood that can counteract the Poppy." I wasn't sure how I knew based solely on my dreams, and it was a huge risk trusting him.

That little gem of information took a moment to process. "Why would you think that?"

"Can you trust me enough to not ask?" I shook my head and glanced out my window. "I'm not sure I know. And I have no proof."

"If this is true, this isn't something you want exposed. Especially among other vampires."

I turned back to him. "I know. And Devon and the cadre will be pissed at me. But Devon has to be saved, and not just for me." I felt the heat on my cheeks, and though a brow rose, he didn't say anything. "The two of you have an important mission. One that will be impossible without him. We can't let Lorenzo win."

He settled back and studied me, both his brows now lowered in concentration. "You think Lorenzo is involved in this?"

I snorted. "We all do. There just isn't any proof."

He nodded. "Devon will owe me a very discreet discussion once he's put the beast and the Poppy behind him."

I sighed with relief.

"He's in the mill. Where exactly, I can't tell you, and I can't allow my wolves past the fence. However, no one, not even the Council, could object to a pack of wolves finding another predator in their territory and the need to investigate."

"You've known where he was the whole time? Even back in the city?"

He nodded. "And the trees where he denned."

I grimaced at the thought of him burrowing in a den.

"We smelled the tainted meat he'd been given, but it was too dangerous to get involved without knowing who was out there. Unfortunately, the smell of the meat was too overpowering for us to catch the scent of whoever delivered it. But we also knew Decker was caring for him."

"I'm not judging. I'm glad you were monitoring."

"There are six entry points that don't require scaling the fence or going over the barbed wire that runs along the top. Four are main gates, two are breaks in the fence. I have two wolves positioned at each of those entry points. They'll give you access in and stop anyone from following you. But if they're challenged, they have orders to abandon their posts. Do you understand?"

I reached out and squeezed his arm. "Thank you." It had been an unexpected move, but he grabbed my hand and kissed it.

I pulled his card from my pocket and offered it to him. "This should take care of the favor you promised."

He pushed my hand away. "You were right. What you do here today helps me as much as the House Trelane. Keep the card."

I didn't argue. He was definitely someone I wanted on my I've-tried-everything-else list.

"Now go. It won't be long before they discover you missing."

I nodded, stopped to give him a last look before exiting, and when he nodded with a smile, I returned it before shutting the door behind me. Harlow hadn't left yet, but as I sprinted down the road toward an entrance, I heard both cars start up.

Now it was me, twelve wolves I'd never met, and one recalcitrant vamp, who, if my dreams were truly prescient, would stonewall me for as long as he could hold out against my charms. I snorted. Easy-peasy.

*Chapter Twenty-Nine*

I JOGGED along the fence until I came to the first gate then slowed, searching for the two wolves that should be there. My nerves were already a jumble over my plan for Devon, and they amplified at meeting a pair of strange wolves.

I didn't know anything about shifters. Did the wolves have awareness of themselves, or were they driven by their animal nature? Would they recognize me? Maybe I should have asked The Wolf a few more questions. It wouldn't take long for two wolves to rip me apart if they didn't like the way I looked at them. I scanned the area, not seeing anything.

Then, as if forming out of shadows—they were there.

They blended into the brush in the pre-dawn light and were larger than I was expecting, St. Bernard-size on steroids, with broad shoulders and lean muscles. A gray one laid next to a bush, but it rose to sit on its haunches, its nose lifted into the air. The better to sniff my scent.

A second one, black as night, stepped from around a boulder. Big and bad. Its yellow eyes bore into mine as if it were trying to tell me something. I hoped it was something along the lines of "Don't worry, I won't eat you."

Saying something like "nice doggy" or "nice wolfie" didn't seem safe—or respectful—so I went with the idea they were more aware than the savage beasts they appeared to be and might understand me.

"Hi. I'm Cressa. I'm one of the good guys." I held my arms out to show I wasn't carrying a weapon. "I think you're here to show me a way through the fence?"

They both tilted their heads, just like a dog would do, and I had to hold back a grin.

"Look. I probably should have learned more about shifters before now, and I promise to get caught up after this current emergency is over."

They tilted their heads to the opposite side. Good grief. Thank the stars no one was recording this. Would they remember this conversation once they shifted back to human? It could be humiliating to run across them at a dinner party.

"Yeah. I'm being stupid. Can you just show me where I can get through the fence?"

The two gave each other a look that seemed to confirm they were fully aware, and I could already hear the story they'd share with other wolves at said dinner party. I was pretty sure my cheeks were turning red.

The black one trotted over, its head down, tongue lolling to one side, yellow eyes still trained on me. I stood my ground, though my body had tensed for defense—or running, which would be the worst thing I could do.

It whined, pawed the dirt, then turned and trotted off toward the fence, tail wagging. I took that as an invitation to follow, and keeping my eye on the gray one, hurried after Mr. Black. Somehow, giving them names sounded safer, though I'd feel bad if it was a female. Mr. Gray kept pace behind me, and each time I turned around, its gaze focused on our surroundings. A definite team effort.

Mr. Black stopped at the gate, left paw placed on the bottom corner of the post where the fence had been cut. From a few feet away, no one would notice unless looking for it. I bent down and pushed against the chain link. A three-foot gap opened up, which was large enough to squeeze through.

I shrugged off the backpack and slid it through the opening. When I crawled through, my hair caught on a piece of cut fence, but I managed to extricate myself without leaving strands behind. Once I stood and brushed off my pants, I looked for the wolves. They were five feet away, staring at me.

"Thank you. I appreciate you helping me out. I owe you one." It was tricky business giving a favor to a shifter or vamp, and doubly risky when I'd only seen the shifters in their wolf form. Nothing like having a shifter track me down after a couple of years and say, "Hey, I was that black wolf that helped you out back at that mill. Time for a favor." I grinned as I waved at them, then turned and considered my options.

It would be foolish to do anything other than follow my dream —to a point. I strode for the heart of the facility, glancing back once to see if the wolves were there. I didn't see them, but there was no doubt they were there, blending into nature.

The farther into the facility I walked, the more things looked familiar. And after another five minutes, I found the spot where I'd waited for Devon in our dream. It hadn't taken long for him to appear, but reality might work differently, and the full dawning hit me that this was the real deal. This would be a true test if my prescient dream would work as I expected. My fall through the second-story window had turned out real enough. But the dream of the wolf massacre had manifested in Los Angeles rather than at the Humboldt pack's birthday party. Or was there a second attack coming I could prevent?

I pulled out my phone and texted The Wolf. It was brief.

"Keep an eye out for other vamps on the Poppy. If celebrating a birthday, no parties until this is over."

It was vague and cryptic, but perhaps it was enough for now.

Either way, he was going to think I was nuts, but I'd rather have them prepare for the worst. If the dream had been prescient, and whoever was behind the Poppy wanted to make a bigger statement than killing a handful of rogues, who better to attack than an alpha near The Wolf's territory? Especially if they assumed Devon's beast was out of control.

Maybe I should have contacted Sergi before The Wolf. He'd been monitoring the Poppy situation, but with everything going on with Devon and the House, it was doubtful he was staying on top of it. Who was I kidding? The wolves wouldn't even be on his radar now. What a perfect opportunity for an ambush.

A noise made me spin around and reach for my dagger. No one was there. Another sound—the scraping of metal. He was coming. I stepped toward a spot of daylight and slowly turned, searching the shadows for movement.

On my second turn, he was there.

At the edge of the receding darkness, his large misshapen body lumbered toward me. It wasn't until he got within twenty feet of me that I could see the torment in his icy-blue gaze. Fear. Anger. Pain. Regret. When each emotion flickered by, I envisioned Devon in his true form. Fear for my safety. Anger at my disobedience. Pain from his physical torture. And regret. It was the last one that almost did me in.

I didn't know if it was regret for not seeking me out sooner, or regret for our future that would never be. The emotions washed over me, but my own sense of loss for something that might never be didn't make me sad. It made me spitting mad. No one was going to take away our future. I wasn't exactly sure what that future was, but what I knew, deep in my heart, was that this wasn't the end for us. It wasn't the end for Devon. Not like this.

Simone might never find the real killer. Devon might have to face the Council, but he'd do it in his true form—not the beast. That was the only thing I could guarantee.

I opened my arms wide and waited. His steps were tentative, as if I were a magnet drawing him in as he fought against the beast.

"Come to me. I've missed you." The tears fell without warning, and maybe they were the exact push needed to force Devon the rest of the way. By the time he reached me, he was shaking his head no, but he couldn't stop his momentum until he was directly in front of me.

His appearance hadn't changed. The ridged forehead was still prominent, and his face contorted as if caught between two forms. His fingers still ended in long, sharp nails, and the tips of his fangs showed.

He was a man stranded in the desert, and I was his oasis. The thought made me smile.

"I'm here to give you what you need."

When he took a step back, I reached up and caressed his face. "I'm not here for Devon. I'm here for his beast, and I'm not afraid." I stepped toward him and threw my arms around his waist, laying my head against his chest, listening to the quick staccato of his heartbeat. His arms hung by his side, and he refused to touch me.

"Listen to me, beast. I'm here for you. Push Devon aside. He won't help you. Only I can help."

He struggled, trying to push me away, but I locked my hands behind him and held on. It was like harnessing a tornado, and we danced across the debris-littered floor.

My foot caught the edge of something hard, and I let out a squeal but refused to let go. Devon wasn't expecting my legs to go out from under me, and it pulled him off balance. We crashed to the ground, and we rolled once before stopping with me on top. I took immediate advantage, pressing my lips to his, letting my weight go limp on top of him. I ran my tongue over the corners of his mouth, distorted, and somewhat ghastly. The taste was part Devon, part dead deer.

I closed my eyes and pushed back the bile. I refused to back down.

He responded.

Maybe it was Devon, maybe it was the beast. It was passionate and hungry. It had been five days since we'd been apart. It shouldn't have been that big of a deal. We'd never had a chance to talk about what was between us. Was it just the sex or the companionship? Perhaps it was something deeper that neither of us were ready to share. It didn't matter. The heat he exuded and the demanding kisses set my blood on fire.

I was so caught up in the moment, I almost forgot the reason behind this ploy. While my body said just go with it, my mind held on to the last thread of reasoning. I reluctantly pulled away from his kiss and moved my lips down his neck. Then I bent my head to the side, my neck exposed.

"Drink from me, my beast."

There was a tug of resistance, and I mentally cursed. "You gave me your blood when I needed it the most. Now it's time to return the favor. I'm not scared. I trust you."

His heart raced. It pounded against my chest as he held me locked in his embrace. I didn't move, my neck exposed. Waiting.

Then his fangs punched out, and with a growl, his tongue licked the vein seconds before his teeth broke skin. I jerked. It wasn't so much from the pinch of skin, but from the unexpected sensation of him drinking my blood.

There was a definite erotic feel to the intimacy of Devon—or rather, the beast—at my neck. My skin tingled, and I wondered if he was drinking too much. I didn't care. His tender sucking was intoxicating, and his occasional lick to clean the blood from my neck aroused me.

Then the chills began, and I knew he'd reached the danger point.

"Beast. That's enough."

I wasn't sure he heard me, or if I would need to fight him off. I didn't want to, and more importantly I wasn't sure I had the strength. But he only suckled twice more before pulling back his fangs. He licked my neck for any blood he'd missed, and I pictured a bloody pool on the floor. The fact he had enough restraint to stop after my only asking once made me question whether the beast was more than just irrational hunger, or if Devon was gaining more control over it.

He rolled over, his arms crossing over his stomach until he was in a fetal position. I wasn't sure what was happening and discovered I didn't have the strength to stand. Or crawl. I did manage to roll over and place a hand on his hip. His body shook, and for the first time since leaving New Orleans, I wondered if I'd been wrong.

Had my blood poisoned him instead of cured him? Several terrifying minutes passed, and after a volley of violent jerks that was like riding a bull, he fell still.

Had I killed him after all?

## *Chapter Thirty*

I GRIPPED the shreds of Devon's pants and pulled myself over to him, still weak from blood loss. I wasn't sure if I'd passed out or not, but if I had, it hadn't been long. Deep shadows permeated the surrounding structures except for the dawning light that circled us. My body shook, one more clue I'd lost too much blood. It hadn't seemed that he'd drank that long, but I might have been mildly distracted by the intimacy of the moment.

Devon hadn't moved, and I tucked myself behind him, my arm draped over him to grab his wrist. His pulse was weak, but it was difficult to be sure with my shakes. I inched higher and checked the pulse on his neck. Yes. He was still alive. That was something, but we weren't going anywhere anytime soon.

I was mulling over our non-existent options when I heard the soft tap of nails on concrete. It took a few seconds to place the sound, then I wasn't sure whether to be terrified or relieved. The sound came from behind me, and I rolled over to face the threat.

Mr. Black, its head lowered to meet my eyes, stood ten feet from me. It whined as it lifted its snout and gazed at Devon behind me. It stepped closer, its eyes back to me as it chuffed.

"We need help. Can you get us help?" I had no idea if it understood, but it wagged its tail, chuffed one more time, then ran off. All I could picture was Timmy asking Lassie to get help. I laughed. I couldn't stop, and still on my back, I began to choke. Then I saw stars and rolled over as gasps for air came between each hacking cough.

A hand gripped my shoulder and pulled me to my side as another hand slammed my chest. I wasn't sure that was necessary, but after a couple minor chuffs of my own, my breathing eased. Somehow, I was still grinning, and I rolled to my back. Devon's arm slid from me, having expended what little energy he'd had left.

Several minutes went by before the sounds of someone running echoed through the complex. Maybe two people.

"Cressa." Sergi laid a gentle hand on my shoulder and then my forehead. "What were you thinking?"

I must have still been grinning because his expression turned from concern to irritation in a single breath. At least, that was what it looked like. I was seeing double, so I couldn't swear to it.

"Sergi. Look." Lucas squatted between me and Devon, blocking my view. He didn't sound distressed, so I took that as a good sign.

I rose several inches until my head spun.

Sergi pushed me down. "Stay where you are." He stepped over me and went to Devon. He mumbled something to Lucas, and I cursed that I didn't have super hearing.

"Call for the van." Then Sergi was next to me. "Just relax."

"Devon?" I attempted sitting up, but my arms had no strength, and I fell back.

"He's fine. We'll talk about it later. We need to get the two of you out of here."

I closed my eyes, sleep overtaking me now that I knew we were safe. Sergi and Lucas were here.

∼

WHEN I OPENED MY EYES, I didn't recognize where I was. I remembered the mill, being lifted into a van, a poke in my arm, then nothing. I sat up, then grabbed my head. The ache wasn't as bad as coming off Colantha's special juice, but the bright light streaming in from the window made me squint and drop back down.

"The healer left something for the headache."

I turned my head to find Bella sitting sideways on a floral chair, her booted legs hanging over the arm. She held up a vial with a pink liquid. "It's the same medication she gave you after your coma." She tossed the vial, and it landed a foot to the right of my hip. "She says she added a peppermint flavor."

I struggled to sit up, thankful for the overly zealous number of pillows stuffed behind me. The potion the healer had given me the first time held two doses per vial. I assumed the same applied and drank half the liquid.

"Are you my babysitter?"

She laughed. "Yep. Just until you woke. Simone requests that you stay in your room."

Then everything slammed into me. I hadn't woken from a dream. It had all been real.

"Where's Devon?" I glanced around the room, and what little I could see through the window was enough to confirm I was at Oasis. That made sense. Their plan had been to bring Devon here.

"He's resting. The healer just left."

I swung my legs to the side of the bed then waited for the headache and my vision to stabilize.

"He's not taking any visitors. Simone is holding a meeting with the cadre to determine our next steps. She promised to come up and talk with you when it's over."

It was useless to argue. With the amount of energy it required to move my legs, I doubted I could follow Bella far without collapsing in a hallway.

"I could use some help to the bathroom." Once I had privacy, I worked each of my limbs, testing their strength. When I was satis-fied, I performed a few squats while holding onto the sink and managed to get back up easily enough.

A knock on the door preceded Bella's shout. "I'm heading to Simone's office. You'll stay here, right?"

I waited a heartbeat. "I'll probably drown in the tub while you're gone."

Once the outer door closed, I took a quick shower. I glanced around the bedroom, hoping the towel wrapped around my body wasn't the only choice of attire. I opened several drawers before I found a pair of sweats that fit well enough. The windows faced the back of the estate. With the oak tree to the right, and the edge of the private garden wall to the left, I wasn't far from Devon's room. The problem was the chaotic interior design. I'd have to traverse a few hallways without getting caught.

Devon's room would be easy enough to determine. I searched for rooms with double doors at the end of halls that faced the correct direction. If this didn't work, there was always another plan. Maybe there was a staff person who didn't know I wasn't allowed to see Devon. Or maybe the gate to his private garden was unlocked.

After checking two halls and running into a pair of humans who smiled as they passed, I found the double doors at the end of the third hallway. I was relieved there wasn't a guard. If the guard was inside, he'd block my entrance. More to the point—he could try. No one was stopping me from getting to Devon. Not after everything I'd gone through. I had to know if the beast was still with us, or if Devon had put it to rest.

I closed my eyes, counted to three, then tested the knob, which turned easily and quietly. The room was dark, the thick drapes pulled across the sliding glass doors that led to the balcony. A gas fire glowed on the left and the bed was to the right. I remembered this room from our shared dreams.

The lamp on the nightstand emanated a low, yellow light and

revealed a form in the bed. I crept over and was only a couple feet away before I could see his face.

I sucked in a breath. My dreams had given me the answer. I hadn't been sure, and it was more than I could have hoped for. Devon's facial features had returned to his normal beautiful visage. His skin appeared tinged with bruises, but with the physical transformation he'd undergone, it wasn't surprising. More blood would erase the last of the beast.

He looked so peaceful. After a bath, with his hair washed and dried—it was like the last week never happened.

When I stepped closer, I noticed three vials next to the lamp. The pink liquid was the headache remedy I had been given. The purple liquid was also familiar. Something about inducing deep sleep to prevent psychic dreams. Or, that was the case for me. There was no question he could use a solid night's sleep. The third vial was clear with bits of rainbow-colored fragments floating in something thicker than water. I'd be interested in knowing its purpose.

I slipped into a nearby chair and watched him sleep, then felt awkward, unsure that I should be here. We'd been so close a week ago, and now, even after giving him my blood in such an intimate moment, I felt like an outsider. Ginger would help put this all in perspective. Whether I was still weak from blood loss or recovering from my dreamwalker training, I was beginning to question my actions. I should find someone to take me back to the manor.

Now that I was assured Devon was safe, it was best to let the cadre take care of him and clear him of Boretsky's murder. Unable to stop myself, I moved a lock of hair from his forehead, my knuckles gently touching his skin and finding it cool to the touch. Another positive sign.

I leaned back to leave when his hand snaked out and grabbed my wrist. Rather than pull away, I moved closer and stared down into his warm blue gaze. All trace of the beast was gone.

"Don't leave." His voice was raspy from disuse and sleep. "Lay next to me."

"I don't want to make things worse." Though I'd be happy to slide in next to him.

"I'll heal faster if you do." Was that a smirk?

"Really? I didn't know I had such magical powers."

"You tamed the beast."

He wasn't wrong.

"Please." His soulful gaze and pouty lips played to my heart-strings, until a twitch developed at the corners of his mouth. He was up to something, but when he lifted the covers, revealing a good portion of his naked body, I didn't care if he had an ulterior motive. I licked my lips, and he pulled me down. I needed to hold him, so I slid in next to him.

The bed was warm, and his familiar scent washed over me. We held each other—no kissing, no roaming hands—only arms hugging each other close.

"Thank you," he whispered in my ear. "The beast thanks you."

"I'm glad you're both back to normal." I lifted my head to look at him. "You are okay, right?"

"I need blood, but the healer wanted to wait until her potions had time to settle. My head is clear if a bit achy, and I'm fully in control again. You'll need to tell me how you thought to do that, my brave little thief, but later. I think we could both use a little more sleep."

We slept peacefully in each other's arms, until his bedroom door burst open. Four vamps rushed the room before coming to an abrupt stop.

Devon swore and rolled over me in some protective gesture. When he saw who'd stormed in, he rose on an elbow so I could breathe again.

Lucas was the first to crack a grin before backing up to stand next to Bella, who gave me a sly smile, leaving Sergi and Simone out front.

"I'm sorry, Devon." Simone, who shot me a glance, had to be second-guessing her actions. "When we discovered Cressa wasn't in her room where I'd asked her to remain, we grew concerned."

"And what? After risking herself to save me, she decided to sneak in my room and stab me with her dagger?" Devon stood, uncaring about his nakedness in front of the cadre. He searched the room until he found a robe that had been tossed on a chair.

When no one responded to his question, he sighed and a ran a hand through his disheveled hair. "I understand your concern for my welfare. But there's no one at Oasis who doesn't have my trust. You know this."

"There are many things happening, and we haven't had time to debrief on Cressa's new skills." Sergi's decision to side with Simone was understandable. He and I might have gotten close during our trip to New Orleans, but I'd be a fool to think that anyone but Devon came first.

Devon nodded. "If I understand the situation, we only have until tomorrow before I turn myself over to the Council for the murder of Boretsky. If I don't, the Eliminators will be activated. I need to be brought up to speed on your plans, but we'll do it with Cressa's participation."

They nodded without hesitation. Simone turned her severe gaze on me, and while she was irritated with my disobedience, I saw the gratitude beneath her badass persona. I gave her a slight nod, and her expression softened.

"Will thirty minutes be sufficient?" Her tone had also eased.

"Yes, but we need coffee and something simple to eat. I also need a blood donor before we meet." Devon pulled back the drapes to reveal the mid-afternoon light.

"I'll send one up immediately." She backed away, but before she took more than a couple steps, a throat cleared in the hallway. "And you have a visitor." She stepped into the hallway and whispered to someone.

Lyra entered the room, and when she saw Devon, she rushed

into his welcoming arms. After a long hug, he pulled back to give her a thorough perusal. Her hair was woven into a single braid down her back, and she ran her hands down her rose-colored tunic and matching flowing pants. She was sophistication and class.

She laid a hand on his cheek. "I told you Cressa would save you." She gave me a warm smile then gave Devon another quick hug. "See you downstairs."

She took Sergi's arm, and the cadre followed, closing the door behind them.

Devon took my hand and led me outside to the balcony. Though the house was a single story, the backyard dipped in elevation, leaving the back of the house appearing to be a second story. The air had a bit of a nip to it, but it felt good as I sucked in the cool floral scent of the garden—roses and lilacs. He stepped behind me, drawing his arms around my middle and pulling me against him.

His whisper tickled my ear. "Was it because of what Lyra said that made you take such a risk for me?"

It took me a moment to understand his meaning. The evening I'd first met Lyra, prior to Devon being dosed with the Poppy, she'd told him I would save him. Neither of us had mentioned it, and I'd had no idea what it meant at the time. Our focus had been on the trip to New Orleans.

I hadn't recalled her words until she mentioned it again after Devon's beast had taken over. Was it possible that her words had spurred my dreams? I had no idea.

"Since returning from New Orleans, I haven't had much time to consider what I learned, what I can do. I remember Lyra's words, but so much was happening, I'm not sure when I recalled them. What I still don't know is why I have prescient dreams. But knowing that some had come true, I had to put my faith in that." I leaned my head against his chest. "Do you remember any dreams when the beast was in control?"

He rested his chin on top of my head. "I was going to say no, but I see fragments of you when I think back to when he slept and some small part of me woke. The first couple of days while strung out on the Poppy, I don't remember anything but hunger and pain." He stopped when I squeezed his hand. "That's behind us now. When they were hauling us back to Oasis, I listened to their recriminations about me going alone to meet Boretsky. It will be long time before I'll be allowed to go anywhere on my own." He sighed. "Sorry, my mind keeps jumping subjects. I'm hoping the blood donation will clear it and that it's not permanent." He gave a derisive chuckle. "I'm doing it again." He glanced into the distance. The edge of the lake was still visible through the encroaching darkness. "I caught glimpses of you at the mill, but whether they were real or dreams, I couldn't say."

"There were two dreams. One when I was in New Orleans. It was mostly fragments, and they might have been memories from when I saw the beast in the alley before I'd left. The second was the evening I returned to the manor. It was similar in feel to the one when I fell through the window. I offered myself to the beast against your wishes."

When I looked up, he held my gaze, searching my eyes, but for what I didn't know.

He kissed me. His lips were dry, a bit chapped, but warm. And it tasted of him. It was short and sweet, and he leaned his forehead against mine.

"For once, I'm thankful for your rebellious nature."

# Chapter Thirty-One

"So, your focus is on this Boris Gheata because he's been seen in the vicinity of Lorenzo and had provided Gruber the folder Cressa stole at the tea party?" Devon scanned the cadre, and they all nodded in agreement.

We were in Devon's office at Oasis. He was rarely there and it was more Simone's since she ran the estate for him. His office at the manor was as modern as the historical society would allow, and it held a certain charm. The office at Oasis followed in the same design style the rest of the house had been built—wood, stone, and glass. Half of the office reflected a sleek business decor including the desk, the floor-to-ceiling windows, and a seating area with stiff leather couches and chairs that faced a multi-screen entertainment center. The other side was what I considered comfortable chic. The focal point was the massive gas-powered stone hearth surrounded by leather couches you could sink your ass into and overstuffed chairs that provided a more relaxed setting.

Rather than sit at his desk, either because he didn't feel like treading on Simone's domain or he wasn't fully himself, he took a position on the couch on the business side of the room. I sat next to him with Simone to his left and Lyra to his right. The rest of the cadre filled out the remaining sofa and chairs. Decker had also joined them after cleanup at the mill.

Simone nodded at Devon's question. "We don't know if Gheata stole the information in the folder Cressa took or if he was simply the messenger, but the fact he keeps showing up in proximity to Lorenzo was enough for suspicion, especially since he isn't part of the Venizi family. When it was discovered he was a fixer and had been for centuries, it moved him to the front of our very slim list of candidates."

"And you're positive you don't know this vampire?" Sergi asked.

Devon shook his head. "The name isn't ringing any bells. I'll admit, my mind is still fuzzy. It's better with the additional blood, but I'm not a hundred percent."

"You'll feel better after a few more blood transfers. It's not unusual for the remnants of the Poppy to linger for a while." Decker glanced at me, and whether the others understood why, I got it. If my blood had a restorative effect on Devon's beast, Decker wanted me to give him more. The others appeared appalled at the suggestion while Devon was with his blood donor, but I'd already been thinking the same thing.

"Maybe Father had known him, though the name doesn't sound familiar," Lyra offered, and she smiled at her brother. The two of them needed quality time together, and I made it my mission to see it happen before the meeting with the Council.

"It's more likely he's a strong believer in the old ways." Lucas perched on a barstool, his elbows on the marble bar of the refreshment center. He kept an eye on Devon when he thought no one paid attention. "If he's as old as it sounds, and being a fixer, there's no doubt he'd be happier if vampires ruled over the humans. It makes sense he'd find a contract with Lorenzo to be lucrative in more than just money."

The rest nodded, and Devon stared at the screened windows. They had been dimmed from the bright light, and I considered opening them, knowing he enjoyed the sunshine, and it might improve his mood. He turned back to Simone. "And you trust your source on this?"

She grimaced but nodded. "I don't have the best history with him, but he's never been known to lie. His faults lay elsewhere."

"Since he's the only lead we have, what's the plan?" Devon tapped his fingers on the arm of the couch. He'd been running hot and cold with his strength and attention spans. It had only been an hour since receiving new blood, and he seemed energized with each new point of their investigation, but when he stared at the hearth, I expected him to leave the group to find a book to curl up with.

I placed a hand on his leg that began to bounce, and he quieted.

"He's currently renting a house on the west side." Sergi played with his tablet, and one of the screens of the entertainment center popped to life. The residential district looked to be a decade old. A red circle had been drawn around one of the homes. "According to Simone's source, he's similar to other fixers who like to keep souvenirs. We're hoping he likes to keep them close."

"You want Cressa to go in and snoop around." Devon didn't appear to like the idea, and I didn't think much of it, either. It wasn't that I wasn't game. It seemed a simple enough task, assuming the cadre could keep Gheata away from the house long enough, but it put me too close.

When Sergi nodded, Devon shook his head. "If anything goes wrong, she'll be connected to me. If she were to find anything in the house, it would be considered tainted evidence."

"Then we don't let anything go wrong." Simone rose and walked to the screen. She used a laser pointer as she spoke. "The entire block is mostly humans with a few shifters. Gheata is the only vampire that we know of. There are numerous entrance and exit locations, and we can have backup at each of them."

"Do you know Gheata's schedule?" I was intrigued as another thought came to mind. One that would require a lot of bargaining.

Simone nodded to Sergi, who replaced the map with a detailed time schedule complete with dates, times, and observations as she continued, "For the most part, his schedule is unpredictable. But that would be expected for a fixer, whose assignments vary." As the data slowly scrolled on the screen, it didn't take long to see what she was talking about. Sometimes he left early and came home as if he were working a standard eight-to-five shift. At other times, he came and went several times in the same day. While his movements continued to change during the day, similar events became apparent.

"We think we've found one weakness." The screen stopped, and Simone pointed to two entries. "These events occur between eleven p.m. and three a.m. and match surveillance videos outside a club called Vipers. And don't ask how we got the videos." She glanced at Bella. "It's trustworthy."

"That's a vampires only club." Lucas leaned back in his chair. "It makes sense he'd stick to that type of club based on what we know of him, but keeping to a routine seems out of character."

"I'm not sure he's thinking like that," I added. "It's not unheard of for cautious men to make idiotic mistakes. If I understand what a fixer is, they would be meticulous in planning and executing jobs." When I received nods, I warmed up to my premise. "And he's been doing this for centuries. Even the best get sloppy. After all this time and never getting caught." I shook my head. "I think he's the best when he's on a job, but when it's his personal time, he's gotten used to no one coming after him. Others are too scared of him to bother trying anymore."

"Overconfidence." Devon ran a hand through his hair and kept his focus on the screen. "Something even the most practical vampires could be accused of." His smile was self-deprecating and warranted in light of his recent actions. "It's a solid start, but I'm not comfortable with Cressa going in."

"I agree." I waited for my words to sink in. It took longer than expected, and something nagged about his slow response. I caught the moment my words registered, but it was Simone who spoke.

"You don't want to go in?" She was confused, and it made sense. I wasn't typically the shy one.

"I didn't say I didn't agree with your idea, but it shouldn't be me going in."

"Who do you suggest?" Her stance had become the one she used in the training room. The one that should intimidate me, and if it were just the two of us in the room, I might have backed down. Today, I felt the safety in numbers.

"This is something I wanted to bring up to Devon, but we were leaving for New Orleans, and then the Boretsky thing..." I shrugged, slipping a quick glance to Devon, whose brows had lowered, fine lines appearing on his forehead. "I visited my old crew." When Sergi and Devon both seemed ready to explode, I waved them down. "Just hear me out. My original reason was to see who sold me out to Sorrento. Once I learned who it was and what Harlow did to replace him, I realized the crew was a team we could use."

"Why would we hire human thieves when we already have one on the payroll?" Sergi would always be the toughest sell.

"I've already stolen two items associated with Devon's censure. Items snatched at parties that both he and I attended. We need to change things up because it won't take long for a vamp to notice the connection between what was taken and who was at the events. I'm not saying there won't be times I would be the best one for the job. I'm still your main thief. But there will be times, like this—" I nodded toward the screen, "—that a secondary crew would be better. His new hacker, Roxie, is a whiz with tech. If Gheata's place is rigged with security, which I'm sure it is, she can get the crew in and out without anyone being the wiser."

"How well does this human crew do with taking orders?" It wasn't surprising that Simone would be asking.

I snorted. "Harlow doesn't take orders from anyone. But here's the deal I worked out with him. He plans the mission, but it has to be approved by Devon and Lyra. I'll take lead, but Harlow has to call the shots once they're deployed." When Sergi and Simone got their hackles up, I shook my head. "This isn't negotiable. They're humans sneaking into vamp-controlled environments. The jobs will be high risk. He knows his crew, how they work under pressure, and has to be the one calling the shots during the mission."

I looked to Devon. His focus had returned to the window. His creased forehead hadn't changed, and though it was common for short delays in response as he considered his options, I was concerned the effects of the beast, or my blood, were still impacting him.

"I agree with Cressa." Everyone in the room turned to Lyra. "She's worked with this Harlow on many missions. As you stated, Simone, Cressa is our resident thief, and when a mission requires those skills, we should hold her recommendation in high regard. I also understand the security breach of her discussing the Family without our approval, but now she knows. It doesn't lessen the fact this solution might be the best we have."

All eyes turned to Devon, but I wasn't sure he was listening anymore.

"Cressa," Lyra's tone was cool and tempered. "Could you work up a plan with Harlow and Sergi?"

I nodded enthusiastically, but Sergi glanced to Devon and then Simone. Simone nodded her acceptance.

"Excellent." Lyra clapped her hands together as if she'd just won a prize. "Now, if you don't mind, I'd like Devon to take me for a walk through his garden. It's been a long time since brother and sister has found time to reminisce." She held her hand out to him. "Come walk with me, brother."

Devon turned away from the window, and his frown drained away. He squeezed my hand then rose, and taking Lyra's arm, walked out of the room without a backward glance.

Something had changed during the meeting. I wasn't sure if it was the discussion or Devon simply needing rest. It worried me. And when I glanced at the cadre, the uniform look of concern made my blood run cold.

# Chapter Thirty-Two

After a stilted late lunch, the cadre and I reconvened in a small conference room with floor-to-ceiling windows that displayed an atrium complete with koi pond and luscious vegetation. The lunch had been more than nourishment. It gave Harlow time to drop everything he was doing then drive to City Center for Jacques to pick him up and blindfold him for the drive to Oasis.

Now, we all glared at each other, and it wasn't lost on me that Harlow and I were on one side of the table and the cadre on the other. We'd run through numerous plans with little success. Regardless of their promise to Lyra that they'd give Harlow and me consideration for our expertise, it was impossible for Sergi and Simone to relinquish control. I had to talk Harlow off the ledge half a dozen times to prevent him from storming out and walking back to Santiga Bay.

After another round of useless suggestions, I slammed my fist on the table. "We're getting nowhere, and we're losing precious time. So, here's how we're going to do this. Harlow and I are going off by ourselves to come up with our best plan. The cadre can stay here and come up with your best plan. We meet back here in one hour. Devon and Lyra will make the final call." I stood, grabbed

Harlow by his arm, and dragged him out the door before anyone had time to protest.

We didn't get far before Harlow started complaining.

"That was quite the shit show, luv." He followed me through the house, and I cursed, hoping he didn't notice we'd passed the same wolf statue for a second time. When we reached the end of the hall, I took a left instead of the right I'd taken before. It wasn't my fault. I'd only been here once, and the house was a maze. Simone should leave maps at the front door for visitors.

"Everyone's a little stressed. We're running out of time." We passed a large library, which I remembered, sighing with relief that we were close to an exit.

"Which is why they shouldn't be leading the mission."

"They're not supposed to be. But sometimes they need a good slap to the head to realize they don't know everything about everything."

"Well, if they expect us to carry this out tonight, we need someone to get them off our backs."

I found the solarium and rushed us out of the house and down a path that led to the spot by the lake where Devon and I had danced during a shared dream.

"Won't your boyfriend worry about us in such a romantic setting by ourselves?"

"You heard about Sorrento, right?"

He gulped and held up his hands. "I'm only kidding."

I laughed. "Relax. He's protective, not jealous." I had no idea if that was true but decided to keep that part to myself.

"So, the vamps have a nice room with comfortable chairs and their fancy laser pointers, and we're out here in the woods."

I dropped down next to a tree and leaned against it. "This was more about getting away from them and giving us time to talk."

He sat cross-legged next to me, and we watched the ducks and geese float around the lake. We listened to the birds and the rustle of leaves in the soft breeze. I'd bet anything he was wishing Trudy were here. I could calm him to a point, but he was putty when she was close.

"Why do vamps have to have so many levels of fuckery?" He picked at the grass, placing a long stem between his teeth, his eyes squinting against the late-afternoon sunshine.

"It's that superior intellect."

We both snorted, but he was right. Their plans were usually elegant, but with every idea we explored, they had to top it. Now that Harlow mentioned it, it came down to ego. When I considered the jobs I'd worked for them, they'd always agreed with my plan, but was that only because Devon approved? At the evening reception at the Renaud Library in L.A., Simone and I had gone off script. But not until I pushed her buttons about whether she had what it took to be the leader of a House.

I sighed, then shook my head. "They've made it too difficult. This isn't anything more than a smash and grab."

"But instead of smash and grab, it's take pictures and get out."

"If we let the vamps run perimeter surveillance…"

"And let Roxie control the house security, we can use Jamal as a distraction…"

"He doesn't still do that?" I had to stop our normal back-and-forth planning. Jamal was the exit man. He wasn't just the driver; he kept watch to make sure we got out safely while also covering Roxie's van so she could focus on the tech stuff. In the early days, Jamal performed crazy stunts as a distraction if the job required it. Similar to what Bella was good at, except with more human hare-brained stunts. The nutty thing was, they typically worked.

"He doesn't do it often. But we had a job a couple of weeks ago where it came in handy. He looked like a hobo, limping around in clothes I don't think he's ever washed. He played one of those guys that tries to wash your car window for spare change." Harlow's deep chuckle scared away a finch that was pecking at the grass. "He walked around with a filthy rag and a dirt-streaked bottle of window cleaner. Most people sped up when they saw him coming. Gave us a good five minutes to clear out before the mark returned."

I laughed, picturing Jamal in the getup. "I think in his heart he's always wanted to be an actor."

When our chuckles died down, I brought us back to the plan. "The house is in a decent neighborhood."

"Average middle-class. I'm thinking an old shopping cart filled with miscellaneous crap and a couple trash bags of empty soda cans and water bottles."

I nodded. "Walking the streets picking up recyclables for change."

"He can keep the car close for our getaway if we can't get back to Roxie's van. It won't be the first time he's dumped a shopping cart in someone's driveway."

"At night?"

"What better time for a homeless person to go through a neighborhood without someone calling the cops?"

"And with the vamps on the perimeter, he should be safe."

"It would be best if we can get in and out without worrying about that."

"Call Roxie and have her start working on the security."

"What about the vamps?"

"Our plan divides the team into areas of specialty. We know how to break and enter, they know surveillance and manning the perimeter. Devon will go for it, so will Lyra."

"What about Simone? She seems to be the one in charge."

I shook my head. "She's used to driving to a solution. But make no mistake—Devon and Lyra will have the last word."

"And where will you be in this plan?"

"I'll be in the van with Roxie. While she keeps an eye on you and the security, I'll be the liaison with the vamps. If Gheata gets anywhere close, I'll let her know. It's best there's only one person in your ear."

"And what will your boyfriend think of that?"

I breathed in the scent of freshly mown grass. It reminded me of childhood days and building forts that Christopher made the gardeners break down the minute he got home. Well, partially memorable days. I pushed the thought of him aside, along with how hard the police were searching for me.

"I think Devon will be happy I'm not going in, and he won't be able to argue me playing intermediary."

"Intermediary for what?"

We both spun around to find Devon standing at the top of the path. Lyra, her arm still woven through his, smiled at us before turning her gaze to the lake.

I couldn't have planned it better, and quickly filled them in on our plan without the cadre there to interrupt. But I should have known, after we laid it all out, what Devon's first question would be.

"And what do Simone and Sergi think?"

"They want to send a vamp in with them."

"It makes sense."

I shook my head. "They think a vamp would be the only one capable of spotting evidence of Boretsky's murder or Magic Poppy. But this crew has seen it all. We've stolen from all kinds of people, most of them dirty of something. Even drug lords. Not often, but they make a good mark and don't live as securely as they think they do."

"We never mess with what we call the street lords," Harlow chimed in, the stem of grass hanging on his bottom lip. "They have a constant flow of thugs in and out twenty-four hours a day. The ones higher up in the food chain prefer a more quiet lifestyle, but they all go clubbing. Sometimes they don't leave anyone behind. I agree it's not smart considering the risk. Our goal is typically to retrieve a single item, not steal them blind. Most of the time, we're given enough information to know exactly where our target is. Every so often, there have been times we almost gave up the search. Fortunately, Trudy has a knack for finding hidden compartments."

"Still, it seems having more bodies to search makes sense." Devon's observations were valid and were the same arguments his cadre made, but he didn't seem as impassioned about them. I glanced up at him, then at Lyra. Whatever their stroll had been about, Lyra seemed uneasy.

I nodded. "Sometimes, that might be the case. But the cadre and Harlow's crew have never worked together before. It was easy to see from the planning session that no one is going to listen to Harlow. And when on a job, Harlow is the word. Not even I argue with him."

Devon gave us a skeptical glance.

"It's true." Harlow stuck his chest out and gave his tiny beer belly a good scratch. "Everyone has a voice during planning, but once I've made my decision, that's that. There can only be one leader on a mission."

After several moments, with his focus on the lake, once again either distracted or simply happy to be seeing things through his own eyes, he nodded. "I'll inform the cadre. When can you be ready?"

"Harlow needs to check in with Roxie to investigate Gheata's security system, assuming he has one. Then it's a wait and see what Gheata does this evening."

"You can be ready to move that quickly?"

Harlow nodded as he stood then stretched his back. "If the stars align, it will be a go. There's a hole-in-the-wall lounge called Leon's about six or seven blocks from the target. It's not our normal stomping grounds, so no one should be looking for us." He winked at me, knowing full well there was most likely an APB out on me. "If Roxie discovers a problem before then, I'll call. Otherwise, we just need to nail down a few items and wait for the word."

"I'll walk you out." I stood, feeling good about our plan. I took Devon's hand and kissed him on the cheek. His skin was cooler than normal, but I didn't say anything before walking Harlow to the foyer to find a ride back to his car.

Devon's reserved behavior was worrisome, and the possible reasons plagued me. I was so distracted by it, I barely noticed the buxom blonde leading Harlow away and the leering wink he gave me as he followed after her.

# Chapter Thirty-Three



ONCE HARLOW WAS SAFELY ENSCONCED in the car for his ride home, I turned to find Lyra, her hands clasped in front of her, waiting for me. When I reached her, she took my arm and walked us toward the back of the house.

"I feel like I've been on my feet for hours." Her words were lyrical, as if it was a normal spring day. "I could use something refreshing to drink. Would you join me?"

Her question, while earnest, was also code for "let's talk about Devon" in case vamp ears were too close.

"Yes, that would be great. I think I've overworked myself playing babysitter between the cadre and Harlow." I scanned the open doors, committing each room to memory. With Devon keeping the estate to a single level, the floor plan was massive, and while there was no doubt I'd get lost again, at least I'd know where the kitchen was.

Lyra's room was on the opposite side of the house from Devon's but also faced the backyard, with several wide windows that bathed the room in sunlight. Like the rest of the estate, the decor was light and airy with touches of wood and stone. The four-poster bed was adorned with silk drapes that had been tied back. A room fit for a queen. Or Devon's little sister.

Dozens of canvases leaned against a single wall while several hung from other walls and were similar to the paintings in her room at the manor. With how long she'd been shut away over the decades, there had to be a storage room filled with hundreds of others she'd painted.

She led me to the balcony where a tea service waited, along with a plate of cookies. I watched two hummingbirds fuss over a feeder as she prepared the cups of tea.

"Considering the tight timeframe we have, can we just cut to the chase? What's wrong with Devon?"

If she took offense to my tone or urgency, she didn't show it. She poured a touch of milk into both cups. "I know adding anything to tea is sacrosanct in tea houses, but I like the way the British drink it. If we had the time, as you say, there would be finger sandwiches and scones with clotted cream." Her laugh seemed to fit with the twittering of the birds.

She nibbled a cookie and took a sip of tea, her gaze roaming the yard, most likely putting her thoughts together. "Devon says his experience with the Poppy wasn't like the last time, the rise of the beast notwithstanding."

"The beast didn't emerge the first time?" That was news, though I had no clue what that meant. "Does that mean this strain of the drug is more potent?"

She lifted a shoulder. "That's his guess. Decker believes he wasn't dosed in the same manner, which would be to drink it. He believes the Poppy was injected into Devon's bloodstream. Fortunately, he was able to get a blood draw from the beast." When my brows rose, she laughed. "Decker wasn't sure he'd survive it, but he thinks the beast was too focused on his hunger to notice."

"I didn't think Decker could get that close."

"Even though the beast didn't rise the first time, he seemed to have recognized Decker and understood he'd helped him before.

But it's obviously speculation. We drew an additional sample once we got him home."

"To determine if there are any remnants of the Poppy left?" When she didn't respond, and I gave it more thought, my stomach twisted. "You're wondering if something different will show up in his blood. Something that came from my blood."

"We don't know. Do you?"

I had an immediate response ready, then felt stupid. Of course, something would be different with my blood. It was the whole reason I'd manipulated the beast into drinking it. But the honest truth was that I didn't know why or how it might be true. I'd had cuts and scrapes like any other kid, but I'd never been to the emergency room. Up until now, there hadn't been any reason to question my blood or to consider it different.

I shook my head. "I have no idea what, if anything, would show up in my blood. If my mother was concerned, she never mentioned it. Colantha didn't mention blood, but with the condensed schedule, we only focused on the dreams."

She nodded. "I wasn't sure and thought it best to ask."

"I get it. I'd also want to know if it showed something unique. But what if it does? Where did you send it?"

"Don't worry. Devon has connections."

"With who? And don't tell me it doesn't concern me." I wasn't sure I was successful at keeping the panic out of my voice. Labs and testing facilities kept records. Depending on how they secured the records could mean anyone could access them.

Lyra placed a hand on my arm. "I'm sorry. You're right. But I'm not sure you'll be settled by the information."

My laugh was a nervous one. "Probably less settled if I discovered it from some secret government agency when I'm snatched off the street."

Her laugh didn't make me any less concerned. "Nothing of the sort. It's just that Devon doesn't always trust vampires outside of the Family."

I snorted. "Nor should he." Half the Council was against him. What was the saying? You're not paranoid if people really are after you.

She took a deep breath. "He gave it to a shifter who has a private lab."

"Decker?"

She almost spit out her tea. "Heavens no. I mean, he does have connections, but you need a sizable financial infrastructure to support labs and facilities."

My brows rose. "The Wolf?"

She was as surprised as I had been earlier. "You know The Wolf?"

I grinned, curious whether she'd soon look at me in a different light. "Did no one ever tell you how Devon and I met?" When she shook her head, I told her everything. From being in debt with a loan shark, Sorrento capturing me, the first trade to The Wolf, and then Devon.

"You're working off a debt?"

I snapped a cookie in two, devouring one of the pieces and washing it down with the cold tea. "He and I have renegotiated the details of the original arrangement to both our satisfaction. I'm not a slave or anything."

"Of course not, and I didn't mean anything by the question. I simply never questioned how you came to the manor; I just knew it was right that you were here. I suppose there's always some reasonable explanation why things happen, but I believe you came to us because we needed you. That this was the place you could be who you were meant to be."

The sting of tears hit me, and I bent my head, stuffing the other half of the cookie in my mouth.

"So, you know The Wolf. Does it bother you that he has Devon's blood?"

Grateful she put us back on a less personal track, I shook my head, somewhat fascinated how this had come full circle. "When I couldn't get the cadre to tell me where Devon was, I called in my own marker with The Wolf."

Lyra dropped her teacup on the table where it rattled in the saucer as she released a deep belly laugh I'd never heard come from her before. She laughed so hard, doubling over in her chair, that I couldn't help but laugh with her. It was several minutes before we wiped our faces and were able to look at each other without starting over again.

I sobered when the press of time returned. We still hadn't gotten to the main point. "Tell me what's wrong with him."

She placed a fresh napkin over her lap and refilled the cups. Once the milk was poured, she sat back and sipped. "Physically, he's back to himself with no signs of the beast. He's a bit weak, but the healer has allowed low-level activity for him to regain his strength. But mentally..." She glanced away then seemed to pull on some of her own inner strength to meet my gaze. "He's obviously missing pieces of this last week, which makes sense if the beast was in control. But he can't focus on anything for a long period. He has a slight headache that he claims comes and goes, but I think it lingers longer than he's willing to admit. And he seems to have forgotten things he should know." Her hands trembled when she set down her cup. "He's never had to be reminded of anything. Ever."

If I was worried for him before, now I was terrified and understood the cadre's concerns. "What did the healer say?"

"She thinks it will just take time. She gave him a potion to help with the mental clarity."

"The clear liquid with rainbow sprinkles?"

She gave me a tired smile. "You make it sound like an ice cream treat." She rubbed her temples. "The healer wants him to get fresh blood every day for a week, which is when she'll return to check on him."

"Can we hide him from the Eliminators for that long? He

can't face the Council if his own confidence is lacking, even if we're lucky enough to find something on Gheata."

"That is now Devon and the cadre's concern." She set her napkin on the table, which she succeeded in twisting into a knot. "Have you met him in a dream since his recovery? I know there hasn't been much time."

"No. But I have a few ideas of my own." I finished my tea and placed a hand on Lyra's arm. "Thank you for keeping me updated. The cadre has closed me out."

"They get very protective of Devon. Even I have a hard time getting them to confide in me, and I'm the House leader."

I chuckled. "Somehow that makes me feel better." I stood, and when she made to get up, I shook my head. "I can see my own way out. Enjoy the beautiful day. I need to see if I can find my way back to my room. I need a nap before dark."

"That's hours away yet."

"I'm not sure that gives me enough time. This place is huge."

Her laughter followed me to the slider, but before leaving the balcony, I turned back to her. "It's good the cadre has his back, but they're not the ones that can cure him."

Lyra wanted me to dreamwalk with him. I wanted him to drink more of my blood. I wasn't sure either would fix what was wrong with him. But one thing was clear to me. Lyra's tea service was to let me know, one way or another, the time to act was now.

<h1 style="text-align:center">Chapter Thirty-Four</h1>

"I'M TELLING you Jamal can handle the alley." Harlow was as irritated as I'd ever seen him. If the payout for this job wasn't more than the crew made in a year, he would have walked after the first five minutes of their meeting.

The dark lounge stank of body odor and burnt popcorn. It was better than vomit, but it made me question what had been sticking to the bottom of my shoes on the walk to the back table.

I arrived with Devon and the cadre, and Harlow had been waiting for us. Jacques stayed in the limo, and Trudy had preferred sticking with Jamal, who was parked across the street and a block down from the lounge. Roxie's van was already in position near Gheata's house.

The first disagreement was Sergi's changing their original agreement to stay a minimum of two blocks away from the target location. Then he wanted to put a vamp in the alley with Jamal, and one across the street hidden in the dense-foliaged landscape.

Harlow wasn't going for it.

"If I had to guess, I'd say the lot of you haven't spent much time in an alley. Or if you did, did you actually look around, see who lived there, what they ate? When you're starving, you're not so picky. It doesn't take the smart ones long to know that people with money throw out food that's still edible. Sometimes they have to wipe the green mold aside, but hunger is hunger. Jamal knows what he's doing."

He glanced at each vamp before landing on Devon. "If Gheata is half as good as you keep telling me, then he'll know there are vamps close by. That's why he picked a nice human neighborhood to move into. I don't care what you're paying me. The risk to my crew is high. I have the last word, or we walk."

When Sergi opened his mouth, Devon placed a hand on his arm and gave Harlow his full attention. "We agree to your plan. The perimeter vampires will stay two blocks away. Our task is to monitor Gheata, and should he leave early, find ways to delay him." He gave Harlow a broad smile. "I do have one minor request of my own, and I won't take no for an answer."

Harlow lifted a brow, but he matched Devon's grin. "Let's hear it."

"I go in the van with Cressa."

"No." I hadn't planned to respond, but it popped out without a second thought, and my mouth couldn't seem to stop. "You also agreed that Harlow and I were the leads on this mission. I'm the liaison with the vamps." Simone and Sergi grimaced at my use of the word vamp, and though Devon said it didn't bother him, I should show more respect. Next time. When Devon wasn't aggravating me.

But he had his hands up. "You are in charge. I'm only there as an observer. But, based on the intel on Gheata, he can be unpredictable. You won't be able to focus on the mission without someone watching your backs. And Jamal will be in the alley. I can be your protection."

"It would be better if I performed that task," Sergi said.

Devon shook his head. "You're needed to orchestrate our teams. If Gheata leaves early, it will take an experienced maestro to keep all the musicians in sync."

"All right. Enough," Harlow growled. He was on edge, and I would need to talk him down before everyone was in place. "Cressa, Devon, and I will leave through the back door. The rest of you should leave in intervals, but do what you do. Just remember to stay two blocks away unless we call."

Then he was up, striding toward the exit sign. I was still watching him as Devon lifted me up by my elbow, steering me in the same direction with long, even strides. Once outside, we looked both ways before spotting him to the left, half a block ahead of us. He knew we followed. He had the vamps in a bind. This had to be done tonight if we hoped to find something, or the Eliminators would be after Devon.

Three blocks later, Harlow slowed enough for us to catch up. He didn't say anything, but at the next intersection, a gray Civic screeched to a stop, and Harlow opened the back door, waving his hand for us to get in. Devon pushed me in before diving in behind me. Harlow was already in the front passenger side as the car's tires squealed, and the vehicle accelerated faster than I thought a Civic could go.

"Hey, Jamal." I waved my hand in front of my nose. "It smells like you're already dressed for the part. At least, I hope that's what it is."

He laughed. "It's not easy getting ready for a job. I keep telling Harlow how much time's required to get a disguise well-seasoned."

"Well, I'd say you win an award for realism." I pushed the button to lower the window and gave it three more attempts, swearing under my breath, until the window crept down. I sucked in the fresh air before my eyes watered. Devon must be struggling with the stink, but he didn't show it. He seemed to be enjoying himself.

We weren't far from Gheata's place, and Jamal drove a two-block radius around the house, then again from one block away before pulling into a driveway next to a mom van. We got out quickly and quietly, following Jamal as he strolled down the street to where Roxie had parked her van. There were a mix of other vehicles parked along the sidewalk, so no one should second-guess it being there.

Harlow rapped twice, waited a beat, then knocked again. It wasn't needed. Roxie had a camera monitoring the back door, but she let him play his games. The door opened, and Trudy jumped out. The downside of the van was that there wasn't a lot of room inside with Roxie's modifications. On the other hand, even the FBI would be impressed by her gadgets.

"Hey, Pandora. It's been awhile." Trudy winked. It had been a week since Christopher was killed, the same night we'd run a quick job. I'd considered it a test to see what our new hacker Roxie could do, but in all honesty, it had felt great to use my skills again. It was killing me not to be going in on this one, but neither Devon nor I could be traced back to this.

"I can't believe you haven't traded up." I pointed my chin to Harlow.

"I think he puts something in my morning coffee," Trudy snickered, and Harlow thumped my ass, ignoring the glare Devon gave him.

Roxie stuck her head out. "What is this? A party? We have a job." When she noticed Devon, she smiled, and her eyes sparkled. "And who are you, handsome?"

Devon reached for her hand, and when Roxie complied, he kissed the top. "I'm Devon. I'll be an observer this evening."

She winked and waited a moment before drawing her hand back. "Then get your sweet ass in here. And everyone else, go away. Oh, except you, Pandora. You get in, too." She disappeared for a second then opened the door wider, tossing two phones to Harlow and Trudy. "Those are wired to a specific encrypted account in the cloud. Take pictures of everything of interest. Take as many as you want; there's unlimited storage. Once you're out, destroy then toss. Understand?"

They both nodded and tucked the phones in their cargo vests.

They pulled out earbuds, then, giving me half-ass salutes, turned and walked away hand-in-hand. I smiled. They looked like two mercenaries out for a midnight lover's stroll.

Then I was all alone. Devon had already climbed in the van. I gave a slow perusal of the neighborhood, and once satisfied, I followed him in.

Devon sprawled on a bench seat with a clear view of the two tech stations that ran along the opposite side. Roxie was in the chair closest to the driver's seat, where a curtain had been drawn across the front windshield as if she were camping overnight.

She pointed to the second seat, and I dropped into it, picking up the earbud lying on top of the ergonomic keyboard. I stuck it in my ear, then grabbed the mouse and activated the screen.

The display showed a street with houses, the movement jittery.

"Where you'd get the vest cams?" I was totally impressed.

"I had them provided." Devon put on a set of earbuds so he could listen to the communication.

"So, you're the sugar daddy." She gave him a rather seductive grin for a techie. "I should have known when I got a look at those baby blues." She hit buttons and swiped screens, then, in a voice any squadron commander would be proud of called out, "Test. Test. One, two, three. Come in, Hummingbird."

"Shit. How do I know if these are working?" Static hit our ears as Harlow did god knew what with the ear pieces.

"Stop hitting them," Roxie yelled.

"Yeah, yeah, luv. Hold your britches." A minute went by, and the screen changed on the display. They stood in front of a house, and based on the distance, they must be in the yard across the street. "Are you seeing anything?"

"Yes. Can you hear me clearly?"

"Yeah, and Trudy's giving a thumbs-up."

"Hold your position until I give you a go." She flicked a switch then turned to me.

I nodded and looked at the keyboard and screen in front of

me. Roxie pointed to a button on the display, and after selecting it, the phone rang once before a familiar voice answered.

"Testing. One, two, three. Come in, Twilight." When there was no response, I tried to smother a laugh and thought I heard a snort from Bella. I turned around and saw Devon's lips twitching. The silence continued, and I sighed. "Fine. Are you there, Sergi?"

"Yes." The one-word answer said everything.

"What's the word?"

"We have two eyes on Gheata in the club. It's crowded; I'm sending in two more. The club's front and back entrances are secure."

"Roger that." I nodded to Roxie.

"Hummingbird. The mark is in place. Give me five to cut the security. You can get in place."

While Roxie started breaking down the electronic security systems, the vest cameras started moving closer to the house. The team moved calmly, and when they reached the driveway, they split up. Harlow would enter from the front and Trudy from the back.

It had proved simple for Roxie to trace the security system, and though she'd been impressed by the sophistication, it wasn't anything she hadn't dealt with before. Devon and Sergi had both advised Harlow and Trudy to keep their eyes open. Gheata had been around a long time, and he probably had other surprises for an unsuspecting thief.

"Hummingbird. The net is down. Keep your eyes open for conventional systems."

"Roger."

I focused on Harlow's cam first and shook my head at how adept he was at picking a lock. I was fast; he was faster. I glanced over at Trudy's cam. She waited for her signal. Harlow wanted to go in first and get a sense for the place.

"I'm clear." Harlow's voice was a whisper.

Trudy worked the lock. She was equally good, though a few seconds slower than me. But she was in, the cam vests giving off a green glow of the room as she turned left then right. She was in the kitchen. Her movements were hesitant as she turned on her flashlight and swept the floor, the ceiling, and any other place where a wire or some other trigger might be.

"I'm clear." Then she moved around the kitchen, opening drawers, cabinets, the fridge, and freezer.

Harlow worked his way through the living area. Fortunately, Gheata was a bit of a neat freak, and it didn't take Harlow long to clear the room. The house wasn't large. The kitchen, a utility room for the washer and dryer, living space, and a small study. Harlow spent most of his time in there while Trudy waited by the stairs, checking them, the walls, and ceiling for trip wires.

"Nothing."

It was disappointing, but not unexpected for the first floor. They worked their way upstairs. I checked the clock. Ten minutes had elapsed.

"Sergi. Status."

There was silence, and I tapped my foot. I kept my eyes on Trudy's cam when she entered a second bedroom while Harlow took the master. The spare room was filled with storage boxes and a single desk. She went through the desk quickly, finding nothing.

"I'm here." I'd been so focused on Trudy, I jumped when Sergi's voice came through. "We lost the mark for a moment but have eyes again. He had some words with another vampire. Lucas thinks he's getting ready to leave."

The club was twenty minutes away by car, which was what Gheata used to get there. Their first distraction was an easy one. They slashed a tire. To make it look good, they slashed a couple others along the row. It was an inconvenience for the other customers, but it was believable for the area of town they were in.

I nodded to Roxie.

"Hummingbird. The target might be on the move."

"Roger." They picked up their pace.

When they came up empty, they worked their way downstairs,

where Harlow stopped in front of the hall closet. He flashed his light to the floor, then bent to pick something up.

"What is that?" I asked.

"Don't know," he responded. He ran the light along the seams of the door before opening it. It looked like a closet. A few coats hung neatly next to a shelf partially filled with light bulbs, stacks of batteries, and a couple umbrellas. Nothing of significance. He trained his light on the floor, the camera picking up the scratches on the hardwood. He handed the light to Trudy, who trained it on the wall as he ran his hands over it, pushing and pulling as he went. A click came over the mic.

"Bingo." Trudy's voice became excited, and I felt it myself. It was always thrilling to find a secret door.

"Be careful." Devon's voice was patient and calm.

Harlow took the flashlight and checked the door more thoroughly before opening it. It scraped the floor then revealed a staircase leading down. He checked it twice. This had to be it.

They were halfway down the staircase when the static from Sergi's radio made everyone in the van jump—except for Devon.

"He's at the car, apparently in a hurry to leave. Once he saw the tire, he checked the cars around him. He's changing it, maybe five minutes. Eight at the most."

I shook my head at Roxie, not wanting her to tell the crew yet. They had plenty of time to run. I didn't want them to rush. When they got to the basement, it wasn't as large as the upper floor. It appeared to be the size of the living room. Maybe someone's idea of a panic room.

Harlow ran his flashlight around the room. There were two metal shelves in the middle of the room filled with dusty jars and cans. Against the far wall, a compact refrigerator sat next to a desk topped with two stacks of folders, and above it, a corkboard overflowing with pictures, maps, and several pieces of paper with text impossible to read from where Harlow stood. The wall to the right housed tall storage cabinets.

Without wasting time, Trudy started on the storage cabinet while Harlow went to the fridge. When he opened it, my mouth dropped open. There were dozens of vials of blood. Harlow immediately started snapping pictures. He pulled out trays, one at a time, snapping pictures of the sides of the vials where coded labels had been printed. He was finishing up when Trudy called from the far side of the desk.

"Over here. You should see all of this." She flipped open files, taking pictures of the first couple of pages before moving to the next. "There's a file on Devon." She spread out the pages and took more pictures before shoving them back in the file and moving to the next one. She kept working while Harlow started on the second stack.

He was on his third file when he whistled. "Underwood, Christopher. Isn't that your father, Cressa?"

I was stunned, and it took me a minute to realize someone was yelling my name. "Cressa, he's on his way. Bella set up a traffic accident, but it won't hold him long. Get out."

I couldn't take my eyes off the image of Harlow shooting page after page from Christopher's file. Then he folded one of the pages and stuck it in his pocket.

"Tell them to get out," I yelled. "Gheata's on his way back." I couldn't seem to control my emotions, and I felt Devon's hand on my shoulder. He'd crept closer when Harlow started snapping pictures.

The crew put everything back in place, straightened the files, and turned back to the stairs.

Trudy stopped.

"Harlow?" Her voice was a whisper. "Did you hear that?"

"What is it?" I asked.

Roxie shook her head, and Harlow knelt by Trudy's feet.

"Oh god, I stepped on something. It's an explosive, isn't it?"

## *Chapter Thirty-Five*

"TELL THEM NOT TO TOUCH IT." Devon opened the back door. "Will the earbuds work if I run to the house?"

"Yes," Roxie said. "Do you want me to move closer?"

"No. You need to keep your distance. Cressa, tell Sergi to call the Eliminators and Sentinels and give them the account information to access the pictures. Can you patch me to Harlow?"

Roxie nodded.

"Do it. And I need to know where Gheata is every minute." The back door slammed shut, and he was gone.

I wanted to follow but focused on the video feed and tried to control my breathing.

"Harlow." Devon must have been racing down the street, yet his breathing was even. "You need to listen to me very carefully. I'm on my way. Keep Trudy still, but I need you to see if there's anything you can take a picture of that would prove the pictures came from Gheata's house."

"I didn't see anything with a name on it other than the files, and nothing with his name." His voice was remarkably calm, but Trudy's eyes were wide, when she wasn't squeezing them tight.

"I saw something I think." Trudy's voice quivered, and her

breathing sounded labored. "Far right side of the desk. Under a stapler. Or maybe one of those heavy tape dispensers." After a few seconds, she coaxed him. "It'll be okay, baby. Devon will get us out. You know those vamps know everything."

He snorted. "They just think they do, luv. They just like to impress." A bit of the fear left his voice, and he stood next to the desk, the camera moving back and forth. "I don't see anything."

"Wait," I said, and wiped beads of sweat from my forehead. "Back to your right. Under the mug, next to the stapler. It looks like a note." I switched the mic. "Sergi, what's the status? We need a blow-by-blow every minute. And I'm sending you the account information with Devon's instructions."

"He's just now moving past the accident." Sergi mumbled something, probably to the cadre, then he was back. "We have control of the stoplights, and we're stopping him every other block. You have fifteen minutes."

"Devon. Did you hear that? You have fifteen minutes."

"Got it." His breath was coming faster now.

Harlow jumped and turned. "Christ, man. Did you fly here?"

Devon chuckled. "It appears we have a bit of a time crunch." He knelt in front of Trudy, studying whatever she'd stepped on. After a few seconds, he said, "It's an incendiary device."

"Oh my god." Trudy's camera shook, and her breathing became raspy.

"Hold still," Devon commanded. "Any motion could set it off."

Her camera stilled, and she blew out a long, slow breath.

"This type won't destroy the room, just whoever's standing on it. I'm sorry to put it that way."

"That's all right," her voice was a shaky laugh. "Harlow always said I had an explosive personality."

"Now she jokes," Harlow growled.

"Ten minutes." Roxie was as cool as the proverbial cucumber.

"Harlow, you get everything you needed?" Devon moved

around the device, continuing to study it. His forehead wrinkled, or it appeared that way from the angle of Harlow's camera. I hoped the issues he'd been having with his foggy brain wouldn't be a problem now.

"Uh, yeah, right. There's a note with the name Boris on it. Then it might be the letter G, but the rest of it's hidden under the mug."

"That's good enough. Take a couple pictures, then I need you to wait at the top of the stairs."

"I'll wait right here with you, mate."

"Gheata is ten minutes out. We're going to cut this close. You need a head start to get the back door open and leave us a clear path. I'll be close behind with Trudy. Roxie, I need you to contact Jamal and tell him we're coming in five minutes and will need cover."

"Aye, aye, boss." Roxie switched her mic. "Jamal. Five minutes. Team of three requires cover. Over."

A couple of seconds went by before he replied, "Roger. Tell them to take a left out of the yard."

Then he was gone, and Roxie relayed the message.

"Harlow, go. I need to concentrate."

"Please, baby." Trudy's voice had softened to that tone she got when she wanted Harlow to take her home. From what she'd told me, those were their best sex nights. If it didn't do the trick now, nothing would.

"You'd better bring her up in one piece, vamp."

"Understood." Devon bent lower and blew dust away from the device.

Harlow stopped next to her and gave her the lightest of kisses before he was running up the stairs. He stopped at the top and turned, but the camera only picked up part of the stairwell.

The only video from the basement was on Trudy's vest, and it showed the cement floor, the tips of her steel-toed boots, and the occasional glimpse of either Devon's head or the explosive device.

"Five minutes." Roxie's voice continued to remain at an even keel. I would never have pulled that off.

Devon's fingers pressed a ring that circled the device and lights flashed blue. The light illuminated the ring then extinguished. A rainbow color of lights lit up, revealing multiple sections. Each section was equal in size and produced a different color. Devon paused and lifted his arm. Based on the motion, he appeared to be rubbing his head. Not a good sign.

Another minute ticked, and when he spoke, his words were steady and confident. "When the device turns a solid yellow, run. Do you understand?"

"Solid yellow, run. Wait. Does that mean the ring is a solid yellow? Could it be a flashing yellow?"

He chuckled. "Excellent question. No flashing. Just a solid yellow circle. Don't hesitate. I'll be right behind you."

"Got it."

He pressed a section and the entire ring changed to green for several seconds before returning to the multicolor. He repeated the action, the colors changing to white, then multicolor, another tap, and then a solid yellow. Trudy was on the move, her camera bouncing as she took the steps two at a time.

A loud pop.

"Devon?" I swallowed my hysteria.

No response.

Trudy turned to look down the stairs. A couple of nerve-racking moments later, the light went out, then Devon was racing up the stairs. Trudy turned, and Harlow could be seen at the back door, waving her on.

At the same time, I heard the distant sound of a car door slamming.

I might have been imagining it, but when I glanced at Roxie, she nodded. "I heard it, too."

"Run." Devon's voice echoed in my ears. Did they have enough time?

Harlow waved them through the door, then he locked it and quietly closed it behind him before running after Devon and Trudy. Devon had her by the arm and was dragging her past the back gate that had been opened for them. They turned left.

Harlow was several paces behind, but he stopped to shut the gate then took off. Jamal was a block down, waving his arms. He stood next to a dumpster.

When Devon got there, he lifted Trudy, giving her a second to realize where she was before he dropped her in. He waited for Harlow and boosted him over before jumping in behind them. A large tarp had been waiting for them, and they scrunched together underneath it. Then the lid came down, and the previous gray darkness turned completely black.

"Jamal. Can you tell us what's happening? Over." Roxie tapped her pen with a steady staccato rhythm, the only sign of her nervous state.

My leg bounced a hundred miles an hour, and I gnawed on a fingernail.

"I've moved back toward the mark's house. My box is all set up, and I'm tucking myself halfway in. No more contact until I give the clear. Over."

"Roger that." Roxie turned to me. "Now we wait and listen."

I figured I had a minute, and I switched the mic. I whispered for no apparent reason, "Sergi?"

"Here."

"Status on the photos?"

"The calls have been made. I expect the Eliminators will act first since they're already on the streets waiting for the command to pick up Devon."

Roxie turned back to the keyboard. She nodded. "Someone, make that two someones, have accessed the account."

"You're sure they can't trace it back to us?

"Positive. I've used it many times."

I'd have to trust she knew what she was doing. She hadn't let them down yet. The immediate concern was whether Gheata knew someone had been in the house. I didn't have long to wait.

"Hey, stay away from my box." Jamal sounded drunk and belligerent.

"You shouldn't even be allowed in the alley, you filthy waste of a human." The voice was definitely Eastern European.

"Law's on my side. Don't care what you call me." It sounded like Jamal was shifting stuff around.

"Did anyone come by here?"

There was a moment of silence then, "Now you want me to help you out? After all those names you called me?"

"Ten dollars for your time."

Jamal gave him a crazy laugh. "Well, now you're talking, brother. Money first."

Roxie rolled her eyes, and I grinned. A thief never turned down the offer of free money.

"Here. Now quick."

"Well, I can't say I saw any faces or nothin'. But I heard feet pounding the pavement. By the time I crawled out of my box, the guy was half a block away. Back that way. He was running like the hounds of hell was chasing him."

"You're sure there was only one person?"

"That's all I saw."

"How long ago?"

"Just now. That's why I'm out of my box. I was just getting ready to go to bed."

The sound of feet running. "Asshole didn't even say thank you."

Another minute, and Jamal was back online. "He didn't pursue. He went back in the house. Let's give it another five minutes."

"Cressa." Sergi's voice was urgent.

"I'm here. Gheata's here. The team made it out of the house."

"Are they back in the van?"

"No. They're hiding in a dumpster."

"Get them out. The Eliminators are two minutes out, and they'll block the whole street."

"Get them out. Eliminators two minutes out."

Roxie relayed the information, and as soon as the dumpster lid was raised and the tarp thrown back, the cameras came to life. There was nothing but blurry images as they ran. Jamal was in the lead, Devon and Trudy next, leaving Harlow to keep up.

A car blocked the end of the alley. Then a woman popped out of the driver's door and waved at them. Bella. Thank god. Jamal turned left and kept running, most likely heading for the Civic. Devon, Trudy, and Harlow jumped in, and seconds later the car took off.

I tapped Roxie on the shoulder. "Get us out of here."

She moved to the driver's seat while I shut off the feeds and computers then locked down the gear. The van started up, the curtains were slid aside, and headlights came on. She pulled away as if we had all the time in the world.

Harlow had rented a room at a motel near the Hollows. I knew the type before we pulled into the lot and drove toward the back near a tall conifer. Bella's car was already there, and she stood outside a room near the soda and ice machines. The lot was three-quarters full, but I didn't see any other car I recognized except for the gray Civic. But when Roxie and I entered, everyone was already there except for one. And I had to ask.

"Where's Simone?"

## Chapter Thirty-Six

I stood by the door and stared at the room of people—vamps and humans alike. It was strange to see Roxie sitting in the corner with her laptop, typing away. I'd never seen her out of her van. The vamps congregated on one side of the room and the humans the other. Devon sat between the two groups as the lone bridge between them.

"So, where is she?" I folded my arms across my chest, refusing to sit until someone explained. When Sergi gave a side glance to Harlow, I sighed. Secrets. Humans just risked their lives for them, and they still didn't trust them.

"Let's not worry about Simone." Devon waved me to take a seat, but I leaned against the wall near the window, too antsy to sit. "We need to review what we shared with the Eliminators and Sentinels, then split up so we're not seen in the area any more than necessary." Devon seemed his old self, though every so often, he glanced at Sergi as if confirming his comments. That wasn't good.

"I set up a secondary backup that's untraceable." Roxie continued to type, and then an LCD screen came alive on the dresser. Someone must have brought it in because the motel's cheaper version had been set on the floor. "I've sent the photos to the drop you gave me." She glanced at Sergi, who had his trusty tablet out. He nodded, which probably meant he'd received them. "I'm bringing up the photos in the order they were taken. This means they could be from either Harlow or Trudy, so they'll jump around as to what we're looking at."

She took us through each photo, and Sergi took notes as we discussed whether the photo had any value. We focused on the first set of files. The information was detailed and quite incriminating.

"This page appears to be in each folder," Roxie said as she zoomed in so the text was readable. "It names the target, common locations where they must spend most of their time, known aliases, and contacts."

This particular page had Devon's name on it. I couldn't corroborate all the information, but Devon did.

"This is more accurate than I would have thought. I'm only grateful the manor and a tea house are the only locations they've listed. The contacts aren't unusual and shouldn't be a surprise to anyone."

Roxie nodded. "The next two pages have more details about your whereabouts up until a week ago."

"When Boretsky was murdered." Lucas sat on one of the two double beds, and he leaned toward the display, his eyes moving across the screen. "They must have been planning something for Devon all along."

Sergi nodded. "My guess is that Boretsky played into their hands. But we have a larger concern with the number of files that were discovered."

"I agree." Devon relaxed against the skimpy headboard that seemed to bend beneath his weight. "I recognize most of the names on the files, but not all of them. It's not surprising Elijah from the Humboldt pack is on it." He slid me a glance. It had been Elijah and his pack we'd seen mutilated in a shared dream. With this evidence, The Wolf would have more than my mysterious text to ensure the pack remained on high alert. "Underwood was a surprise, and I recognize a couple other human names. They're all CEOs of fairly large corporations on the West Coast."

"Let's look at Underwood's file," Sergi suggested, and Roxie complied.

"They tracked his whereabouts during the same time period as Devon." Lucas pointed to the screen. "Scroll back up. That's it. Right there. Someone sent him the limo the night he was murdered."

After a quick review, Lucas was right. "What does the last line mean?" I had a feeling I knew, but I wanted someone to confirm it.

"It says Olfug Dilinae." Devon gave Sergi a glance before turning to me. "It's a remnant of an old vampiric language. It basically means 'finish it'."

I gulped. Christopher and I had our history. I wasn't sorry to see him dead, though the manner had been gruesome. But to see the order to kill him on the screen was another matter.

"Well, this should take the heat off Cressa for the murder, assuming we can find a way to get this to the police without a lot of questions." Lucas seemed pleased.

"Why would Cressa be a suspect in her stepfather's murder?" Harlow asked. "I read about it in the paper. Wasn't it the same night we ran into you and Ginger?"

I scratched my neck, thinking of something to say that would make him shut up. The last thing I needed was him mentioning the little job we did. The one I never told Devon about. Not that we'd had a lot of time to discuss it.

"Yes." Sergi was watching us both, and this wouldn't go well.

"I think we should focus on our primary issue, like getting Devon off the hook." I glanced at the others in the room, specifically Bella and Lucas. "We should look at what the vials of blood can tell us."

"Yeah." Bella finally joined the conversation. She knew I'd wandered off that night, and she had covered for me. It appeared she was still doing it. "The Council is going to want Devon to come in, and we need to know what the Sentinels know so we're not going in blind."

Roxie ignored the chatter and jumped to the photos of the vials from the fridge. Crisis averted for now as everyone refocused on the screen.

The labels on the vials appeared to be in code, which wouldn't be of much help.

"Nothing says Magic Poppy or even has the initials MP." Bella sounded as disappointed as the rest of them must have felt.

"But the first two characters are followed by numbers that could be dates." Devon moved from where he'd been leaning against the headboard to sit on the edge of the bed.

"That tray there. The first two letters are DT." Lucas's excitement spread to the others, and I felt it, too. We were on to something.

"I'll go through the photos and write down the first initials for all the trays. Let see if we can come up with possible names. Perhaps some will match the names in the files." Sergi frowned at the next series of photos. "Each label as two letters followed by what appears to be dates within the last month. They're all followed by the letters BP and another sequence of numbers that appear random."

Devon had paled, as did the other vamps.

"What is it?" I asked. "There's something there of significance."

"It's the BP," Devon replied. "It could be anything."

"Maybe." Sergi sounded doubtful.

"Tell us." It seemed obvious to me, but I needed someone else to say it.

"Blood Poppy." Bella's voice, as low as it had been, seemed to have an eerie effect on the vamps in the room.

"It's nothing more than a legend." Sergi kept his gaze on Devon, and something passed between them that had nothing to do with a mental fugue.

"It can't be a legend." When everyone looked at me, I shrugged. "There's a painting of it in the Renaud Library. I thought they only kept items important to the history and preservation of all things vampire." I also thought there was nothing better than forcing people—humans or vamps—into facing their own history. The good, the bad, and the ugly—humans had enough of it to spare. With the arrogance of vamps, there had to be some of that in their species.

"It could have been any flower. How do you know it was the Blood Poppy?" Sergi, who I'd always considered the stoic one of the cadre, might be playing devil's advocate. But considering his age, which was older than Devon's five hundred years, he might be a vamp whose whole philosophy on life was about to change.

"I've seen a rendition of one before. It was white with tips of red on the edges." Lucas seemed awestruck. I'd forgotten he was the historian of the group.

I nodded. "That was the same flower I saw. The painting itself was rather impressive, and for some reason, space maybe, had been tucked away in a corner. It was Erik who told me it was the Blood Poppy. I remember he thought it odd I didn't know what it was since I was a Blood Ward."

"Who's Erik?" Sergi asked.

"One of the Oslo twins. They were very helpful with our extraction from the library." I glanced at Devon, but he was staring at the unsavory carpet, and he was either someplace where no one could follow, or he was doing some of his quiet strategizing. I would have leaned to the latter if he hadn't been showing instability on the mental acuity front.

When silence descended—and I wasn't the only one watching Devon—he finally noted the lack of conversation. He shook his head and glanced around the room.

"I think this is all we can do for now. We need time to go through the photos in more detail." He stood and walked over to Harlow, extending his hand.

Harlow seemed surprised, but he clasped Devon's hand.

"I appreciate your help on this one." Devon's smile was sincere. "I should have known Cressa would only work with the best." He shook the hands of the rest of Harlow's crew, murmuring words to Trudy, Jamal, and Roxie that left them with odd smiles. I glanced away, hoping he hadn't mesmerized them.

Then Devon nodded to Sergi, and the two walked out the door. Not once did Devon look back at me, and I hated to admit it —it wrenched my gut. Or maybe it hadn't hurt until I saw the surprise in Lucas's and Bella's eyes when they shot a look my way.

I said my goodbyes to the crew, unsure if I should ask for a ride home. Wherever the hell that was. Instead, I watched Roxie drive away in her van and the rest jump into Jamal's car, Trudy hanging out of the window waving at me.

Lucas stepped up and bumped shoulders with me. "Ready to go home?"

Tears threatened out of nowhere, and I forced them back. I was sure I was reading too much into Devon's behavior. Maybe he needed time to discuss business with Sergi. But hadn't our relationship progressed to the point that he should have said something to me before walking out? He thanked Harlow's team but for some reason didn't feel the need to thank me.

"Cressa? Simone will be expecting us." Lucas took my elbow, steering me to the car.

He could take me back to the manor, but Simone probably gave him his marching orders. I glanced at Bella, and her gaze held mixed signals.

"I can't be of any benefit dealing with the Council, and I'd rather be with Ginger right now. I'll find my own way back to the manor."

I walked away, but Lucas grabbed my arm, which he immediately released when I turned on him with a sneer. I straightened my shoulders and lifted my chin. "I need what us humans call personal space. We just came off a risky job that was very close to being a catastrophe. I need space." The last three words were delivered with emphasis on each word.

He stepped back with hands raised. "The police are still looking for you."

I shrugged. "I know how to evade cops. And I don't need vamp babysitters." I hated to focus my anger on Lucas. It wasn't fair. I knew it. But I couldn't hold it in.

Devon blamed me for his impaired mental state. I knew it. I felt it every time he looked at me. But even so, I would have done what I did all over again. If he never spoke to me again, at least he wouldn't live the rest of his life in beast form.

I turned and walked off, almost expecting Lucas to come after me, but when I heard the doors slam shut from a block away, I'd never felt so alone.

# Chapter Thirty-Seven

I WALKED a few blocks before I called the one person I could always trust would be there for me.

"Cressa? What's going on?" Ginger's tone was anxious. "Lucas said you took off on your own."

"Well, he doesn't waste any time."

"That's not fair." She was hurt. "He's worried about you."

"I'm sorry. I know. I'm just so frustrated."

"He mentioned there was some strain between you and Devon."

"Let's see. I just left a meeting where he pretty much dismissed me in the meeting then left for Oasis without a backward glance. It's possible I'm imaging everything, but I think he blames me for his current mental state. And his behavior around me seems to be shared with Sergi and Simone. So, yeah, there's some strain."

"Where are you?"

I stopped and looked around. "I'm not sure." I wasn't familiar with this particular street but knew this part of town. "Somewhere near the Hollows."

"Why didn't you ask Lucas to bring you to the manor?"

"I don't know. I just needed air and time to think."

"Why don't I have him come get you? He won't mind."

I considered it, but anything that smelled of Devon would just irritate me. "Hey, is there a hide-a-key for the condo by any chance?"

"No. What kind of ID do you have on you?"

"None. I left it all behind since I was on a job."

"Okay. This might be a problem, but your name is on the rental agreement. Stop at security, I'll give them a call. Your name and password should be enough."

Thank god for this woman. "What's the password?"

She hesitated.

"Bono?"

She laughed. "You know me so well."

Her mother was a rock groupie, and U2 had been her favorite band when Ginger was born. Now it was one of Ginger's.

"Maybe I should meet you over there."

"Don't worry about me. You know I can handle myself."

"That's not why."

I had stopped to lean against a wall to speak with her. The better to keep my eyes on my surroundings. No sane person would walk around the Hollows lost in thought on the phone. Not unless they had body guards.

"I know. Like I said, I'm just feeling left out in the cold. Some time and space will help me work through it." I sighed. "Devon and I had gotten so close before he was drugged."

"He's had a traumatic experience. Just because he's a vamp and the leader of a House doesn't mean he can't get PTSD. He needs time, too."

"I know." Although I wasn't sure I did. "I'll call in the morning and see what's up." Then I hung up before she could say anything else. Confident I'd have a place to crash, I kept walking. As dangerous as the Hollows could be, I'd always felt safe here. These were my peeps—for better or worse. And I always preferred taking a walk on the wild side.

I'd walked a few more blocks until I was in the center of the Hollows. Even at this hour, the clubs were busy, at least those that catered to the supernatural. The area had been the affluent section of town before everyone moved mid-town decades ago. As the neighborhood shifted, the old homes had transitioned to clubs, shady businesses, and down trodden restaurants, some of which had decent food.

I turned down a side street to circle the block and make the long trek to the condo when I noticed another club farther up the street where several people were headed. A small sign in the window said The Den.

Decker's club.

Curiosity pushed me forward, and I blended in with the group as they entered the club. Two vamps were at the door, and other than give me a once over, let me pass without question. The Den was more than a normal club; it was a fight club, and the cages would most likely be in the basement.

The first thing I noticed was the high ceilings that even with the dark walls and low lighting gave the room an airier feeling. The place was crowded, but I found a spot at the end of the bar that gave me a view of most of the room.

The blonde woman at the end of the bar held up a finger in my direction. I nodded and turned to scan the room. Muffled yelling could be heard beyond the closed doors on the far side of the room. A sure sign fights were underway. When the bartender came over, I ordered a chilled vodka neat and scrounged through the bowl of nuts.

I was working on my second drink when the doors to the fight club opened, and the crowd pushed toward the cages. Once the doors closed, only a handful of customers remained that I guessed to be regulars—some sitting at the bar, others scattered among the tables, most with their heads down.

I was considering another drink when the bartender sauntered over to restock glasses. She gave me a side glance.

"I don't think I've seen you in here before."

I shook my head. "First time."

"Welcome to The Den. I'm Sabrina."

"Cressa."

We chatted about the club and the fights. After she poured my third drink, I worked up my nerve.

"By any chance, is Decker here tonight?"

She'd been refilling the olives in the garnish tray when she stopped and turned to me. "You didn't mention you knew Decker."

I shrugged. "He's more of an acquaintance through a mutual friend."

She eyed me with more interest than earlier. Then she paled a bit. "Your friend wouldn't happen to be a vampire."

"Why would you ask that?"

"Decker doesn't have many friends."

"And without this human, I might have had one less."

We both turned to see Decker, who'd stepped up from a hallway I'd assumed was for the staff.

"Decker. I'm sorry to bother you." I wasn't sure what to say. I'd been on the fence about whether to reach out to him and had been leaning against it until the vodka changed my mind.

"No, you're not. But I'm glad you came. Let's talk in my office."

Sabrina shot me a look that I couldn't read. I had a strange feeling she knew why I was here and also knew Devon quite well. Something told me Sabrina was another shifter and had been around for some time. I didn't want to know what kind of relationship she had with Devon. She seemed like someone I'd like to know better.

I followed Decker down the hall into an office large enough to hold a desk with the obligatory two guest chairs, a small mini-bar, and a less formal sitting area. He stopped at the fridge, pulled out a bottle of top-shelf vodka, grabbed a couple of glasses, and dropped into his desk chair. I sat in one of the two stiff-backed chairs, which were uncomfortable enough to discourage long visits.

He poured two generous shots and pushed one toward me.

I lifted a brow. "Are you a vodka man?"

"I am tonight. That's what you've been downing, isn't it?"

I nodded and sipped this one. I still had to stumble my way across town to the condo.

"I would have eventually come to you, but it's probably better this way." He downed his shot and poured another.

I was surprised by the statement but decided to let him continue in his own time.

He rested his forearms on the desk and pinned me with eyes that seemed to have an inner yellow glow. I'd bet a month's salary, if I had one, the color of that glow would match his wolf's eyes.

"I wanted to thank you for saving Devon."

I was speechless. That rarely happened to me. "No one else seems to think that. I get the feeling I made it worse."

He nodded while he topped off my shot and poured another one for himself. He was bright-eyed and didn't seem impaired, so these were either his first drinks of the night, or like vamps, shifters weren't hampered by alcohol.

He lifted his glass, I lifted mine, and we clinked them together, sloshing a bit of the clear liquid onto his desk. "I say fuck 'em."

I spit out a laugh. "I thought you were friends with the cadre."

He shook his head. "I'm friends with Devon. I put up with the others." He growled. "Sometimes they can be so narrow-minded. I get that they're vamps, and they think they know whats best for Devon. Like they know everything about their inner beast." He finished his shot, slid the glass aside, and began playing with a paper clip, bending and straightening it. "And I suppose they do to a point. But they haven't seen the true destructive power of the Poppy."

"You helped Devon through it before."

"And a few others." He leaned back in his well-worn but

comfortable-looking chair. "If the beast had only taken over for a day, I think Devon would have pulled through on his own. But it took more than a day before I was able to get him away from the Poppy. And I didn't see any noticeable difference in his physical appearance once it was out of his system."

He squinted as he studied me. "I don't know what you are." He lifted a hand against a protest I was forming. "I don't care. Devon trusts you, and that's good enough for me."

"He's got a strange way of showing it."

"That's pride getting in the way. I know he fed from you, and I don't know what's in your blood, but it was enough to satisfy the beast."

"And left him with brain damage."

He barked out a laugh that at first unnerved me, but then made me smile. "He's in a mental fugue. I got the same message as everyone else. The healer, who wasn't given the entire story on how the beast was put to rest, believes he just needs a few days of her potions and less stress."

"And what do you believe?"

He shrugged. "That everyone should listen to the healer rather than think they know better while blaming those that got him this far." He leaned over his desk as if he had a secret to share, and I couldn't help lean in myself. "I didn't know you knew The Wolf. He's quite fond of you."

My cheeks heated. "We're just friends."

"And Elijah isn't usually one to make friends in wolf form. He must sense something about you."

I knew Elijah was the alpha of the Humboldt pack, but I'd never met him. Then a feather knocked me over. "He was Mr. Black."

Decker gave me a strange look.

It was my turn to laugh. "The black wolf. There was a gray one, too."

"Don't tell me. Mr. Gray?"

"The Wolf didn't introduce us."

"It's actually Ms. Gray, just so you know."

"A female?"

He nodded. "Elijah's second. Remus asked the neighboring pack to keep an eye on Devon."

"He has good friends."

"Look. If you're here, I'm guessing it's because you're looking for redemption."

"Do I need redemption?"

"No. But that doesn't mean you're not feeling it, especially with the cadre being such dicks."

I played with a loose string from a seam in my pants. "Do you have any words of advice?"

"I heard from Sergi about an hour ago that the Sentinels have enough evidence to sway the Council on what really happened to Boretsky and who most likely killed him. The problem is that no one can predict how Lorenzo will take the news, but I'd give anything to be a fly on the wall at tomorrow's Council meeting."

"The meeting's tomorrow?" I sat up. Of course, it would be. No surprise I didn't get the memo. The hurt I'd felt earlier in the evening returned.

"Devon's time is up. Simone was contacted moments after the files were received with instructions for her, Lyra, and Devon to appear before them to hear the Sentinel's findings."

"Will this be the first time the Council hears the report?"

He nodded. "The Sentinels don't like to work that fast, but they understand the Council's desire to close the case."

"At any cost?"

"Yes. At least it was before new evidence came to light. And no one has seen Devon since before the murder, so Simone is going to be keeping an eye on Lorenzo when Devon is ordered to stand witness. I don't think even Lorenzo, the coldest vamp to walk the earth, will be able to shield his anger at Devon's recovery."

I gave him a wistful smile. "It would be something to see." I stood, feeling I'd overstayed my welcome, and the fatigue had finally hit. It would be a long walk to the condo.

"You going to the manor? It's a bit late to go all the way out to Oasis. You gotta a car?"

I shook my head. "I have a place in mid-town I can stay."

He stood and scooped a set of keys out of a bowl. "Let's go."

"You don't need..."

"Shut up and let me do something for you. To be honest, the cadre didn't think too highly of me when Devon decided to stay here for several years after he got clean. Us outsiders need to stick together—for Devon's sake."

Decker dropped me off a block over from the condo. It was his idea. He didn't think we'd picked up a tail, but he wasn't the trusting sort. He told me to take the alley to the left of where he'd parked, then work back to the condo. It was nice to see he could be as suspicious as me.

He gave me a gruff goodbye and took off, and I moved into the shadows to see if anyone followed him. Satisfied it appeared clear, I worked my way back to the condo. When I reached the security desk and gave them my name, they pushed a key card toward me without asking any questions.

Grateful I didn't have to go through the whole "prove it was me" scenario, I took the card, gave the guy a tired smile, and after a long elevator ride up, fumbled with the key card before I got the green light to enter. I was barely through the door when Ginger raced down the hall.

Tears erupted at her being there for me, and I collapsed where I stood. Ginger pulled me in for a hug, held me tight, and rocked me as I cried.

# Chapter Thirty-Eight

A KNOCK AT THE DOOR, followed by it swinging open with such force that it banged against the wall, spun Devon from the window where he'd been staring down at the garden. The warm memories shattered like so many others had in a very long week.

Lyra strode in, her eyes blazing with the same eerie blue of his beast. "Where's Cressa?"

He sighed and walked to the minibar, where he picked up his cup of cooling coffee. "I'd ask if you wanted a cup, but you seem more than awake this morning."

"Don't patronize me, brother."

"And now you're channeling Mother."

"And don't insult me." She came face-to-face with him, her breath rushing out in short gasps and her eyes still aglow. "She didn't come home with you last night."

"No. She didn't." He turned away, not only to get away from her condemning expression but his own guilt as well.

"In fact, not one of you brought her back. You just left her."

His anger, barely held in check since returning to himself, leaked out. "No one told her to go off by herself. But she's her own woman."

"She's under our protection."

"Which she flaunts in our face whenever it suits her." He forced his fists in his pockets before he slammed them into a wall and walked to the balcony. If he thought he could dodge Lyra so easily, he was a fool. Ever since she'd come back to herself, she'd grown stronger and more mentally aware every day. Or so Simone had told him.

If he wasn't so angry, he'd be proud of how she'd assumed leadership of the House. But he couldn't quell the rage, and it only burned hotter whenever he lost focus, which was too often and at all the wrong times. It was a wonder he'd gotten through the mission last night. His ability to disarm the incendiary device was more a miracle than skill.

Harlow's crew had remained calm and professional right from the start. Somehow, despite his salacious behavior, the man was a professional. He shouldn't have expected any less from Cressa. His irritation had flared knowing she had a life she could return to so easily. Then mention of the night she'd been out with his crew the same evening Underwood had been murdered made him question if they'd been doing more than having drinks. He remembered questioning Bella about the evening, and though he hadn't been able to poke a hole through her report, it had been obvious she'd left pieces out.

The whole damn House protected her. And for the life of him, he couldn't understand why it troubled rather than pleased him.

Lyra's hand touched his shoulder, and his body relaxed, the tension draining away.

"Is she safe?"

He closed his eyes, shutting out the garden and the lake beyond. "She's at the condo with Ginger."

"Not the manor?"

"I think she wants to put some distance between us."

"Was that her idea or yours?"

He turned and strode to the bed where the rest of his attire had been laid out. He picked up two ties, then tossed the crimson one away as he wove the royal-blue one around his neck. "I don't know what you mean."

"I might have lost my mind over the last several decades, but I'm much better now. And I can see a cadre that's splintering from the inside."

"Everyone will be fine once we get past the Council's ruling. Now that we've discovered who killed Boretsky, the Council should remove the orders against me, and we can get back to the mission."

"This isn't about the Council. This is about what happened with the Poppy. What happened when Cressa put the beast to sleep."

He turned on her so fast, he thought she might take a step back. She didn't. And once again, pride in her pulsed in his blood. "Did she cure me? Then why can't I focus? Why can't I keep track of the simplest things?"

"You're recovering. The beast was in control for days. You're lucky someone was able to put it to sleep at all. The healer said you'd require more rest if you refused to drink the healing blood." She stepped closer. "Why won't you take more? You know she wouldn't deny you. Not after everything she did to save you."

"She went to The Wolf."

Her musical laughter grated. "Because no one in the cadre would tell her where you were, and she couldn't get enough information from her dreamwalking."

He couldn't think. Too much information raced through his head. It didn't matter that his beast was put to sleep less than two days ago, he should be stronger than this. "We have more important matters to get through. Don't you think?"

A calmness came over her, and she straightened her shoulders. "You're right. We leave for the Council in fifteen minutes. Be on time."

She turned for the door, and he almost smiled at her dedication as House leader. "I told you once that Cressa would save you." She had stopped at the doorway but kept her back to him. "You should have listened."

~

Lyra's words continued to haunt Devon as he paced outside Council chambers. How had she known Cressa would save him or that he would require saving? It was a mystery. One he didn't have time to contemplate now.

He glanced up and down the hall. It was empty. He'd expected to see Eliminators or Sentinels waiting for him when he marched in with Lyra and the cadre. But the only ones waiting for them were the two Council pages, who stood next to the ornate double doors carved with a famous vampire battle scene.

If Cressa could see it, she'd have some smart-ass remark about the door representing a battle between the Houses. The thought made him look at it from a different perspective. Not a battle between Houses, but a dispute over philosophies that could end with the same amount of bloodshed.

Lyra and the cadre waited across the antechamber, giving him time to prepare for the Council. Jacques had stayed in the limo as usual, but this time for good reason. He was in charge of security while Sergi and Simone were in Council. This would be a prime time for an insurgence. Lorenzo knew exactly where the entire leadership of the House would be.

Lorenzo's mistake was that he'd always assumed Devon ran his House as the ancients did. As his Father had. And Devon allowed him to believe that. An ace up his sleeve. He was grateful Cressa and Ginger were at the condo, assuming they were being careful. He snorted. Which was why he had one of his own watching the place.

He chuckled. Then sobered when he recalled how angry he'd been when all she'd done was try to save him. He'd been shocked that her blood was able to cure him. Something that mere human blood couldn't have. He'd drunk from blood donors since he'd been back, but it had no more effect than its normal curative powers; it provided no relief from his mental fugue.

What risk was there to Cressa if she continued to feed him? Would the beast fall deeper to sleep or would her blood draw it back out? Until he could think clearly, he couldn't take the chance.

Footsteps approached, and he whirled around as a single Sentinel and two Eliminators strode toward him. They turned into the Council chambers before reaching him. The Council had been in session for forty-five minutes when they'd first arrived. The page had ensured them their case was the only one being heard. There should have already been Sentinels and Eliminators reporting their findings. The appearance of additional ones didn't bode well for him. His greatest fear was that they wouldn't accept the evidence from an anonymous resource. The chances of him walking out of this building seemed to shrink.

It was another thirty minutes before one of the doors opened and a diminutive man in the dress of a page called his name. Devon turned and followed the man into the room, Lyra and the cadre behind him.

He'd been in the Council room dozens of times—before and after his censure. In all those decades, nothing had changed, except this time his life was on the line. He followed the page, his gaze locked on the Council as a whole, refusing to look any of them in the eye. It wouldn't do any good; none of them would reveal their thoughts. He stepped onto the dais, Lyra standing next to him as the House leader, and the cadre behind them.

Four Sentinels sat to the right of the Council, and four Eliminators sat to the left. A computer was connected to a screen that was currently dark.

"Devon Trelane." Isabella Stanton sat in the middle of the Council members. She appeared pale, with the weight of the world on her shoulders. With the evidence the Sentinels should have been presented, all the Council should be feeling similar emotions. She peered down at him, the merest smile softening her stern expression. "It's good to see the Poppy has been removed from your system. The Council will restate its original decree and the resulting orders after new evidence has come to light."

Devon didn't twitch, but he did lift a brow. It would only be natural that his curiosity would be piqued at a possible reprieve. "I'm grateful the impact of the Poppy had no lasting side effects."

A sigh made him turn his head to Lorenzo, who appeared resigned. Was that a good sign?

"You were charged with the murder of Council member Boretsky while under the influence of Magic Poppy, an illegal substance." She used her bronze baton and tapped the gong once. "New evidence, provided anonymously, has brought conflicting data to light. Evidence that speaks to a larger problem than the death of a Council member."

She turned to one of two visitors boxes and bowed her head. "No disrespect meant."

He turned his head to see who was witnessing his fate and saw a man and a woman in the only occupied seats. It had been a couple of years since he'd seen them. Asher and Maya Boretsky sat proudly, and when they caught his gaze, they both nodded as if pulled by the same string.

He returned an imperceptible nod. "May I ask what evidence?"

"Various files and samples of Magic Poppy were seized. The files provided a direct link to various schemes, including premeditated murder and the distribution of the Poppy. Apparently, you were the victim on which the perpetrator hoped to hang their crime."

"Someone set me up? Why?"

"I'm afraid that is Council business."

He could argue that he had a right to know, but it didn't work that way with vampires. With Magic Poppy involved, the Council would want all evidence sealed for their eyes only. So, he simply bowed to her statement. What he preferred to know was the tally of votes cast, and that information he might never know.

"In light of the new evidence, the original orders against Devon Trelane and the House Trelane have been rescinded." Isabella swung the baton, and the gong rang once. She stood, and as one, the rest of the Council stood to follow her out of the chamber.

Devon remained where he was, as did all the remaining vampires, until the Council members left the chamber, which was standard ritual.

Lorenzo was the last one out, but before he exited, he turned and gave Devon a long stare before sneering and nodding his head. He was acknowledging that Devon had beat him, only solidifying the fact Lorenzo had been the actual instrument of Boretsky's death.

It was also clear the game was long from over. The death of a Council member and addicting him to the Poppy was his first strike at destroying House Trelane.

*Chapter Thirty-Nine*

THE POUNDING on the door made me want to curse and throw something at it, but it was Ginger and her third attempt at getting me out of bed. I rolled over, ignoring her while cursing Devon for having such luxurious sheets supplied in our furnished condo.

My chest hurt, and I rubbed it, as if that alone could remove the ache of loss. I was most likely blowing it all out of proportion, but even Ginger admitted to Lucas being tight-lipped and reserved around her. She blamed it on the Council meeting that was happening as I wallowed in bed.

I understood the stakes. Would the Council accept the new evidence or consider it suspect because it was provided anonymously. Was Devon going to come back, or was he receiving notice of his pending execution? I pulled the covers over my head.

My first thought last night after Ginger tried to talk me down was to dreamwalk. But his mind would be on the Council, and I didn't have a clue what type of construct was appropriate for the tension between us.

I threw the covers off and stared at the ceiling. Part of the problem was having nothing to do. There was a gym in the condo, as well as hot tub and pool. Nothing enticed me. Yeah. I was feeling sorry for myself.

The hammering returned.

"I'm not stopping this time. I'll beat on this door until you unlock it or the damn thing caves in."

I laughed, picturing Ginger in the hall with a box of tools she conned out of maintenance that she had no clue how to use but determined to try each one until she achieved her goal. Not wanting to cause Devon or the cadre any additional reasons to get rid of me, I crawled out of bed and stumbled over a robe I'd dropped on the floor the night before.

I unlocked the door then raced for the bathroom, making it there before Ginger realized she'd been granted access. If only I'd thought to lock the bathroom door—my mistake—because she barged in without remorse.

"Lucas called. Lyra's scheduled a meeting. A car will be here in an hour."

"Did he say anything else?"

She shook her head. "Nothing. He wouldn't even joke with me."

That didn't bode well.

When I was finished with my morning rituals, Ginger followed me back out to the bedroom and dropped onto the edge of the bed.

"About last night." She rubbed her head. "I'm sorry I was scared about the dreamwalking."

I threw on some sweats and moved to the kitchen, where half a pot of coffee was warming for me.

After I'd dropped into her arms last night, sad, miserable, and unsure of my future, Ginger had wrapped me in a fluffy robe, fed me hot chocolate and a scone, then made me tell her all about New Orleans. With all the urgency around Devon, I'd never had a chance to share what I'd learned about dreamwalkers.

I gave her a blow-by-blow description of the entire trip—the private jet, the Renaud library, the clubs, and three days with Colantha, describing each dreamwalking attempt as best as I could. For some crazy reason, I asked if she wanted to give it a try. She wanted to be supportive, but her enthusiasm for my new skill drained away at the suggestion, and she tucked her knees to her chest.

At first, I was disappointed that maybe she agreed with Devon and the cadre about my interference and the resulting damage it created. Then I remembered being on the ground in the mill with Devon. Neither of us able to call for help. What if I built a construct, called for Ginger, and then for some reason, couldn't back us out of it. How long would it take before someone found us?

"I shouldn't have suggested trying. Colantha only mentioned dreamwalking with vampires and others like me. I wouldn't think it would be any different with others, but I never asked. If I'd thought it through more, I've only tried creating a construct with Devon, and I wasn't sure it would work. And the only reason it did was because I'd subconsciously shared dreams with him before. It was foolish of me to ask."

She reached across the counter and grabbed my hand. "I was honored that you asked. Can you imagine if we tried, and then, I don't know, we got stuck there?" She waved her hand in a dismissive gesture as she popped her coffee in the microwave for a warm up. "Now that I think of it, we would have been fine. Lucas would have found us before we died from dehydration."

We both giggled at the thought, but we both knew it could have been a lot worse, and she thankfully changed the subject.

"What do you think it means that she's sending a car for you? The Council meeting must have gone well. I mean, would they be taking you back to Oasis if something bad had happened?"

I shrugged and stared into the mug. "Maybe they didn't want to share the bad news over the phone. Who knows what I might do? They all think I'm a bit crackers after facing the beast."

"I hadn't thought of it that way."

We ate bowls of cereal in silence, then I went back to my room to get ready. When the knock came, Ginger headed for the door but stopped when her phone rang.

"Oh, hey Lucas." She shrugged as she glanced at me then the door.

I peered through the peephole in the door, then nodded at her before opening the door to greet Jacques.

"How's Devon?"

"My orders are to bring you in for a meeting. I haven't been told anything else." He stepped aside, waiting for me to exit.

Ginger waved to me and turned to finish her discussion with Lucas. I checked my pockets, ensuring I had my phone and key card, then closed the door behind me.

JACQUES OPENED THE PASSENGER DOOR, forcing me to ride in the back of the sedan, probably to decrease the opportunity of me peppering him with questions. He drove us in silence, and I wondered if he was this chatty with Bella. Since I was tired and irritable and wasn't interested in playing games, I leaned back and watched the scenery. I'd been expecting a trip to Oasis and was surprised when the landscape became familiar, and he drove to the front of the manor.

No one waited to greet me. Not even Lucas. I got out, slamming the door behind me and dragging myself up the steps, bracing for what awaited me.

The manor was quiet, and I walked straight to Devon's office, took a deep breath and knocked once before entering.

The cadre formed a semicircle around the desk where Lyra presided with Simone by her side. Decker hovered on a barstool, pouring a shot of what was probably whiskey. It was in a decanter, so it could be any amber-colored alcohol. Devon sat next to him, accepting the shot. It was also impossible to determine if this was their first or fifth.

Devon glanced at me with a barely perceptible nod, and I masked my own feelings and leaned against the espresso bar.

"Welcome, Cressa." Lyra's voice was her usual grace and warmth. "We saved a seat for you." She pointed to one between Lucas and Sergi.

"I'm good here." I folded my arms across my chest. Not defensive at all.

She nodded as her smile slipped. "I understand. Let's catch you up."

After she covered the highlights, I breathed easier knowing our heist had worked, and Devon was off the hook.

"Did you notice the Sentinel and two Eliminators who arrived well after the hearing had started? Does anyone know what that was about?" Devon shoved his empty shot glass toward Decker, who refilled it.

Lucas was the only one to speak up. "Funny you should mention that. I'd been wondering the same thing. I spoke with a friend who works in the Sentinels office. The team that came in late were the vampires that had been on-site and were responsible for the collection of evidence. Several Council members wanted to hear directly from those with firsthand knowledge."

"Makes sense." Sergi had stopped fiddling with his tablet to listen. "If the Council has interest in pursuing the distribution of the Poppy, they might have had additional questions for those that handled the inventory."

"Or it could have been Lorenzo hamming it up to cover his own hand in it." Bella leaned back in her chair, a booted leg crossed over her knee.

"Either is equally possible, and not mutually exclusive." Simone had been abnormally quiet during the meeting. I'd considered calling her to see how she'd react. It might give me an idea of how big my transgressions were. But with the Council meeting looming, I'd chickened out.

"What do you think the Council did with the vials of Poppy?" Bella asked.

"They'll send them to Lorenzo's labs." Sergi had changed from the gallant bodyguard to the indifferent vamp in the space of a heartbeat. Maybe that would have happened once we were surrounded by the cadre. Or maybe it was my unsanctioned actions with the beast.

He wasn't the only one who seemed different. Simone was unusually quiet, and Lucas was more reserved, even with Ginger. The only exception seemed to be Bella, whose occasional glances suggested she still had my back.

"Back to the one who probably created it in the first place." Lucas ran hands through his hair. "It's like whack-a-mole."

I snorted, but I appeared to be the only one who got the reference.

"Remus has a sample." Devon had also been quiet except for the occasional question. Based on the stares from the cadre, no one had been prepared for his simple comment.

"How did he get a sample?" Simone asked.

Devon quirked a smile. "Harlow gave me one before we split up." His gaze met mine but moved away just as quickly, his grin fading.

"The Wolf's job will be more difficult without the data Lorenzo has at his disposal," Sergi replied, never taking his eyes off whatever he was reading.

"It's a start, and he has the blood from the shifter deaths as well as Underwood's." Devon sipped the whiskey, and shuttered his eyes as he swallowed, letting the burn have its moment. "We need to get back to the mission while Lorenzo is focused elsewhere. It won't be for long."

"Devon's right." Lyra closed a ledger she'd been reviewing. "It's time to transfer power back to you."

He shook his head. "Not yet." When the cadre grew restless, he waved them off. "Just temporarily. I think Lyra should stay for a bit longer. It will keep the focus off me for awhile." He didn't mention his fugue, and I wondered if that was the true reason. No one questioned him. "One thing I don't understand. What happened to Gheata?"

"He's in the wind." Lucas stood but stayed by his chair. "They have bulletins out, though I doubt they'll catch him anytime soon —or ever."

"He's probably left the country," Bella added.

"I wouldn't bet on it." Simone seemed to have rejoined the conversation. "Lorenzo will keep him close. He might even undergo reconstructive surgery to avoid recognition software."

I had a hard time imaging someone going to those lengths. How much was Lorenzo paying this guy? And if he was on retainer and living in suburbia with the middle class, what did he need money for? Elaborate vacations?

"We have one more matter to discuss." Sergi glanced at me, and I wished I'd sat in a chair when I came in. A deep one I could bury myself in.

As expected, all eyes turned to me.

"We didn't get enough information to clear Cressa in Underwood's murder. She's still wanted for questioning, and they've had enough time to determine she's not in Seattle."

"Harlow confirmed he was with her and Ginger the night Underwood was killed," Devon said.

"Does that cover the time of death?" Sergi asked.

I glanced to Bella, but she appeared to be busy texting someone.

"I don't know. You'll have to check it out." Devon tapped his fingers on the bar and pointed to the bottle of whiskey. Decker poured another shot. "We have the photos of his file."

"I've had time to review them, thinking along your same lines." Sergi fiddled with his tablet, most likely pulling up the file in case he needed to refer to it. "A handful of House names are listed. It appears Underwood had partnerships with more than Lorenzo, although they're all aligned with him. It wouldn't be good for the information to get into police hands."

"Did we get pictures from everything in Underwood's file?" The question came from Lyra. "Perhaps there were additional pages we don't have that could help. Since Underwood isn't connected to the Magic Poppy, perhaps the Council would allow us a copy of the file."

It was an excellent idea, though most likely a long shot. And her question reminded me of something I'd seen on the video when Harlow was taking pictures of the files. He'd taken a page from Christopher's and tucked it in his pocket. I'd have to pay him a visit and see what it was.

I stole a peek at Devon and found him frowning. He wasn't looking at his sister; his gaze had lowered. Maybe he was mentally checking a list of his questions. Or maybe he was reviewing what he had for breakfast. Without speaking with him, it was impossible to tell if he was improving.

"It's difficult to read the Council these days, but there are one or two I can reach out to." Sergi shut the case he kept his tablet in. "It will depend on which way the wind is blowing, but I'll get on it."

"That concludes House business for now. I suggest a special lunch to celebrate the good fortune that came to our House today. Cook has something special prepared, and a table has been set in the solarium.

When Lyra released us, I was the first one out the door. There was good cause to celebrate, but I already felt like a fifth-wheel, or the dead guy's mistress sitting across the aisle from his widow at the wake. I was a pentagram trying to fit in a circle. Instead of heading for the solarium, I found Jacques in the hall, and I snagged him.

"Take me back to the condo."

Chapter Forty

I PERCHED ON THE BENCH, the heavy scent of roses blending with the sea air. My knee bounced as I questioned whether this was the right approach. I ran a hand over my sundress, the periwinkle color something different for me.

This was the second time I knowingly attempted to bring someone to a construct when not expecting it. Devon and I never spoke of the first one, when he woke to find me in his bed. But so much had happened since then, we'd never had the chance to talk about much of anything.

My nerves were a mess. This was a big gamble considering the rift between us, but having this conversation in the waking world could be a riskier one. It was my own dream world. One I could shut down at any time. No awkward walking away. No slamming of a door in someone's face. Just stop the dream. Yeah. What could go wrong there?

I heard the footsteps on the gravel path, and I closed my eyes, sucking in a deep breath and sliding on my game face. When the footsteps faltered, I stood and turned around, the ocean to my back.

He was so breathtaking. His hair was rumpled from sleep, which was odd as it never looked that way before when we'd shared a dream. But the question of why slipped away as I skimmed over his clothing. He was in the same suit he'd been in at the meeting earlier. I'd waited until late to be sure he'd be asleep. I grimaced at the thought that I'd pulled him away from someplace while he was still awake. If I had, was it because some part of him wanted to come?

I took a step toward him, and then another. "Hello, Devon." God, that was stupid. I'd spent time planning the best construct but never considered how to start the conversation.

"Lyra was disappointed you didn't stay for the celebration. She considers you the reason for it."

*She* considered it. Did that mean he didn't think my part was worth a mention? "I didn't mean for our differences to upset her. She's been nothing but gracious to me."

His brow lifted. If I'd made it sound like she was the only one who respected my role in it, then I guess we were even. "I understand Cook had blueberry scones for the occasion, but when he heard you left, he had them returned to the kitchen."

Now he was making me feel guilty and terribly sad.

"Why the dream, Cressa? Why not come to me awake?" Devon stood his ground, but I could see his desire to take a step back for every step I took toward him. And for a moment, he appeared afraid of me.

If this conversation weren't serious, if we weren't in a construct I didn't know how long I could maintain, I might have laughed at the thought a vamp could be scared of an inexperienced dreamwalker. One who'd saved his life.

At first, the idea made my angry. But if I considered it from his point, of how confused and angry I'd been with the first dreams when I thought he'd been manipulating them, I could see his point.

"I never asked Colantha whether physical activity in a dream impacted the sleeping form." Instead of walking toward him, I moved toward a vine and plucked a rose, its heady scent touching on favored memories. "I was exhausted after each session with her, but it was a mental tiredness. I don't remember feeling tired after our shared dreams. Do you?"

He shook his head.

I nodded. "You've been through a lot in the last week, so I thought it best we meet in our dreams." I was such a liar. I gave him a shaky laugh. "That, and I wanted to see if I could initiate a dream world. It's been a few days since my last test with Colantha." I turned around with my arms raised to the sky. "This is a construct of my own making. What do you think?"

He broke his gaze from me and surveyed our surroundings. "Pieces of it seem familiar. Is this a real place?"

I'd hoped his curiosity would distract him. "It's a consolidation of real places. The pieces that blend the different landscapes together are of my making. How I imagine the puzzle pieces might fit. I don't have the experience, or power, to create from a blank canvas. At least, I think that's right."

"The roses?"

"From your garden at Oasis, and the sycamore—" I nodded to a point over his shoulder, "—from the manor. Most of it's from Newberry Park. That was one of the places I'd run to when I had to get away from my life. A place I always felt safe." I gave a self-deprecating laugh. "Poor little rich girl syndrome. It wasn't difficult to tell if Christopher was on a rampage from the minute he walked through the door. Some business fell through, he had a difficult overseas call, his mistress was too busy, so he had to come home. Pretty much anything that didn't go his way gave him a reason to strike out. And I was his favorite chew toy." I shook myself. This wasn't about me or my relationship with a dead man. "Even after I'd fled that life, whenever I questioned my direction, this place seemed to help."

"Why didn't you dreamwalk with me after we were taken to Oasis?"

His question surprised me. Had he been hurt that I hadn't before now?

"I'd considered it once before the heist, but you were still healing. And we had such little time, it seemed more important to focus on the job." I wanted to add that he hadn't made me feel welcome enough to share a dream. Although it wasn't any better now. The rift between us seemed to be widening, and this was a last-ditch effort to close the divide.

"Sergi tells me you were successful in New Orleans, so I suppose this shouldn't surprise me." He spread his arms out to encompass the construct.

"I'm not sure what he means by successful, but I have learned some control when wearing the necklace. Colantha pushed hard to take over my dreams. It's not foolproof. I'm strong enough to repel anyone trying to take over my mind, and I can retain control of my construct from those weaker than me. I'm not sure that's saying much, but it's a start."

I couldn't look at him. The longer he was here, all I wanted to do was run into his arms and beg his forgiveness. The problem was, I wasn't convinced there was anything to forgive. I turned to face the ocean. The wind had increased, and the waves grew turbulent. I pushed away my frustration that was bleeding into the construct. My mood could effect it, and I should have remembered that.

"It doesn't seem as if three days was enough to become an expert." He sounded closer.

"She wants me to return for additional training. I told her it would have to wait until my debt had been paid. There's a larger mission, assuming you still need my skills." I wanted to say if he still needed me, but I wasn't brave enough, terrified what his answer would be.

Warm hands caressed my shoulders and ran down my arms.

They wrapped around my waist and pulled me against his hard frame. I closed my eyes and let my head fall against his chest.

"If anything, I need you more now. Our timeline has compressed. Lorenzo will be upping the game, so we have to be more aggressive in our approach. You are still very much needed."

Then his lips touched my shoulder and traced a path up my neck until he nibbled my ear. They hadn't been the exact words I wanted to hear, but something told me it might be a long time before we shared another moment like this—if ever. I wasn't willing to miss it.

I turned and kissed him with every ounce of desire that yearned for him. If he didn't grasp the depth of my affection and understand why I would risk the beast, then maybe this would tell him.

I let his return kiss linger as I pulled him to me. Some things hadn't changed. He was just as eager, pushing the straps of my sundress down. I ran a hand through his disheveled hair as his tongue met mine. I worried for a nanosecond that my mindless lust might lose grip of the construct, but it hadn't before, and that was when I had no clue the dreams had been of my own making.

The grass was cool against my skin when Devon laid me down. For a moment, his movements were tender, almost reverent. His touches scorching as he slid the dress off me. Then he became more frenzied as he ripped off his own clothes, his gaze never leaving mine. His eyes glowed with their preternatural icy blue before warming into the color of a lake at twilight.

I arched when he entered me, and as I threw my head back, day turned to night. Stars filled the night sky. Millions of them that most never see. I could almost sense the other worlds before I returned to him and this moment.

We were in a whirlwind, making up for lost time, as if pushed by a fever until there was nothing but entwined arms and legs forging into one.

It wasn't the slow lovemaking we shared on other occasions, but it was no less passionate. When I laid my head against his shoulder and watched the heavens with him, I clutched my medallion.

He kissed my temple. "Did you discover what the symbols on the necklace mean?" His voice was rough from exertion.

"Yes." I held the medallion in my hand so he could see it. "I don't remember her exact words, but I think I can get close. The first symbol is the Blood Poppy." I felt his body tense at the mention, which didn't surprise me; I'd had a similar reaction. "Colantha called it the flower of life and knowledge. The bird is an ibis. Its meaning seems to be the most contested, but she believed it was a combination of rebirth, healing, and fertility."

He shifted, but didn't say anything.

"The last is the Dagger of Omar."

"I've heard stories. Most believe it to be a myth. The believers, who keep to themselves, thought it to be lost centuries ago." He repositioned himself to see the medallion better.

"There's a symbol on the hilt that symbolizes the connection between dreamwalker and vampire. There wasn't enough time to hear the stories, or so she claimed. Anyway, as you know, the symbols repeat on the back side but in reverse order. It represents a balance between dreamwalker and vampire. I wish I knew more about the dagger."

He was silent as he turned the medallion over, and his fingertips no longer held the warmth from earlier. They were stone cold.

"There's something else," I continued. "I asked if it was possible for a non-dreamwalker to create a construct if they wore the medallion."

I waited to see if he had a reaction, and I was intrigued that he picked up on its meaning so quickly.

"You mean like Lyra did when we saw the wolf massacre?"

I nodded. "She seems to think that once a non-dreamwalker is connected to a construct, they have the ability to do it themselves as long as they wear the medallion."

"But when did Lyra visit a construct? Did you have a dreamwalk with her?"

"No." I sat up. I didn't want to get to a point where I had to lie to him. I wasn't even sure Lyra knew she'd revealed that Hamilton, her lost love, had been a dreamwalker. He would have to get that direct from her. It wasn't my place to share.

I pulled on my dress. "That does seem to raise questions."

When I turned around, Devon was already dressed. He stepped toward me, and I didn't move. It was his turn to tell me something. Like why he was so mad at me, and as much as I wanted to ask, it was up to him to explain his unreasonable behavior. Let alone explain why the cadre had become so distant with me. Were they equally mad that I saved him, that because of it he'd been left in a fog, or were they so tied to his emotions that they were simply mirroring his behavior?

He fingered a tress, rubbing it lightly before running his knuckles down my cheek. "I know it isn't your fault my memory is hazy." And for a moment, I counted this dream as a checkmark in the positive column. "But you didn't talk to anyone about it first. You made a decision based on a dream and symbols on a medallion. And maybe it was the only path to take. You've dumped a lot of information on me, and well..." His smile was endearing. "I'm still a bit slow when too much information is dumped on me. I need time to digest everything I've learned since returning home."

It was impossible to not return his smile. Not when combined with his indigo gaze pinned on me. It was really unfair. "I get it. I'm still processing it myself. And I'm sure, even with your current state, my brain won't come to an understanding any faster than yours."

He chuckled. "Then come home to the manor, and we'll figure it out together."

It was tempting. And it would be exciting for the two of us to work through it, as long as we didn't have outside influences to color our judgment. But we wouldn't have that luxury.

I shook my head. "You need to gather your conclusions on your own. So do I. It's only then that we can compare notes and see where it leads us. The problem for you is that you aren't just Devon Trelane. You're Devon, leader of House Trelane. It will be impossible to prevent the cadre from slathering their opinions on you. Lyra is the only one who'd wait for you to ask."

He quirked a brow, and something told me the relationship between brother and sister had more fire to it than I first thought. I smiled back—good for her.

"Until you have everything settled, I'll stay at the condo. I don't know what Ginger will do, but to be honest, I think it would be good for everyone to take a break and consider everything that's happened and how far we still have to go. It's not like we won't see each other. There will be training, phone calls, maybe a private dinner or two."

He walked me to the vines, and he selected a rose with a strong stem. "I don't like this. Lorenzo was humiliated at Council, at least with his allies. He's not done with me. I don't feel comfortable with you outside the manor."

I hadn't thought of that. Before Devon was dosed with the Poppy, I'd only considered Lorenzo a slimy vamp. But he'd proven to be much worse. Devon's concern was valid.

"I'll tell you what. Place one or two vamps around the building for security. You can even place one on our floor. But we both need our space, whether you're willing to admit it or not. Maybe this will encourage you to give more thought to it."

He picked the thorns from the stem then slid the rose inside the sundress so it rested between my breasts. His languid kiss made my knees weak. I might have stumbled a bit when he released me.

"It won't be long." His promise sounded like the leader he was.

"I only ask one more thing. Whether the cadre gives you opinions or not, will you promise to seek Lyra out? Ask her about the wolf massacre. I think the two of you have a great deal more to discuss."

When he nodded agreement, I took a deep breath of the rose and waved my arm.

The construct disappeared, and I stared at the ceiling of my room at the condo. It still amazed me how real the constructs felt. I could still smell the rose.

When something scratched, I glanced down to find the rose. It had slipped across my bare breast, and the edge of where a thorn had once been must have nicked me. I picked it up and breathed deep.

The heady aroma held a spicy sweetness. The flower and the thorn. This was the first time something from the construct manifested in real life. The only other time I could remember it happening was the prick on my finger from another thorn in a dream.

Was this normal? I didn't know much, but I had a feeling Colantha wouldn't be able to answer this new puzzle.

I hugged the pillow, still sniffing the rose. The construct hadn't gone anything like I'd imagined. I was disappointed he wasn't at the same place that I was in our situation. But how could he be? I'd dumped a lot of stuff on him in mere minutes.

He was right on one point. The Lorenzo issue worried me. Ginger and I should be back at the manor. Or maybe they could move us to Oasis. That would be best. I don't know why I hadn't thought of that. I'd call him tomorrow.

Maybe living at Oasis would match the earlier prescient dreams we'd shared. A huge weight lifted. Somehow, being at the condo made our separation more real. At Oasis, his true home, we might live in different places, but our bond would be stronger. I smiled as I kissed the rose, being silly. Tomorrow didn't look so bad after all.

Thank You For Reading!
But don't go! Keep reading for more Cressa and Devon.

CRESSA WAKES from an accident with all her memories lost. She only has the word of an ancient and attractive vampire that she is his Blood Ward—soon to become vampire. The mystery of how or why that happened might forever be out of her reach.

Devon rages. His greatest enemy has taken something most precious to him. No other mission is as vital as bringing Cressa home. And he'll use every resource of the House Trelane to make that happen.

But first, he has to find her. And the only way he knows to do that is through her dreams.

AND NOW...

**Obsessed in Blood**
**Of Blood and Dreams - Book 4**

Keep reading...

*Obsessed in Blood*

## Chapter 1

IT WAS A NEW DAY, and my spirits couldn't be lifted any higher. The sun spread its early morning light through the condo, bathing everything with a touch of gold. Classic rock from the seventies and eighties blasted over the speakers. I danced through the kitchen, grinding coffee, adding water to the coffee pot, and laying out the ingredients for one of my special tossed omelets, which was nothing more than eggs, cheese, and anything else I could find to throw in.

While I wouldn't exactly call it a Cinderella moment, bluebirds might have twittered around my head as I set the table.

I jammed an air guitar solo, and when I twirled around to bring it home, I jumped in surprise when a disheveled Ginger appeared with one eye closed from eye crusties, mismatched knee-highs, and a sour expression.

"What in all that's holy are you doing so fricking early? Trying to wake the dead?" She stopped at the entertainment center and turned the volume down.

My lips twitched involuntarily. "One look at you says I accomplished my task. Didn't we both go to bed at a normal hour last night?"

"Lucas called around midnight, and we talked for hours." She shuffled to the table and collapsed into a chair. I filled a mug and then pushed it and the bowl of sugar toward her. Once the first sip was down, she wiped her eye until the lid popped open, and she gave me a typical Ginger smile. Her gaze twinkled. "He sounds so much like his old self again. We laughed, and he told me how stressed he'd been." She held the mug with both hands, savoring each sip as I chopped onions and avoided rubbing my own eyes.

"He'd been terrified the House might fall, and if he didn't have a choice of a new House, he was considering his options of going rogue."

I stopped chopping. "Oh, my god. I had no idea. That's a big decision."

She nodded, then her sunny smile returned. "But the House is safe, at least for now. He wanted to tell me everything he was going through as it was happening, but Simone and Sergi had everyone on strict orders of silence."

I rolled my eyes. Once the cadre discovered Devon was on the Poppy again, and his car was at the scene of a Council member's murder, the House had been in disarray. The Council had been eager to close the case as quickly as possible with threats of sanctioning the House. It was an all-hands-on-deck moment, and even Lyra, as the temporary House leader, had difficulty keeping the cadre from enforcing marshal law. I might be exaggerating, but it was a tense week.

If that hadn't been bad enough, they wanted me on ice until everything had been resolved. It would have gone much easier if they'd trusted me. After everything I'd done for them since first landing on their doorstep, I'd thought I'd earned it.

"Well, that's over for now." I poured eggs into the skillet and placed toasted English muffins on the table along with the butter and jam.

"What's with the happy homemaker? You haven't cooked in ages." She nibbled at the muffin and eyed me suspiciously as I flipped the omelet. Then her gaze widened. "You got lucky last night."

I grinned as I slid the omelet onto her plate. She cut it in half, pushing one of the halves onto my plate while I dumped the skillet in the sink and plopped into a seat across from her.

"I brought Devon to a construct."

She grimaced. "Was he mad?"

"He was a bit confused about why I chose for us to talk it out in a dream." I savored my first bite and washed it down with a swig of coffee. "We still have a lot to talk through, but we've formed a tentative peace."

"I think you did a bit more than talk."

I winked. "You know what they say about makeup sex."

She giggled. "I think I'll get a reminder this afternoon. Lucas is taking me to the city for a couple of nights."

We clinked our mugs together before focusing on the rest of breakfast. Everyone needed a few days to decompress, and I was thrilled Lucas was finding time for her. And while I felt good about where Devon and I left our own wacky relationship, I was a bit unsettled with how the cadre would deal with me.

"So, what will you be doing today?" Ginger picked up the dishes and rinsed them before stacking them in the dishwasher.

I followed behind her with the condiments, sliding s couple of them into the fridge. "Anna is restarting our study of the Houses, and Devon wants to reestablish a training schedule. He's serious about getting back to the mission."

"A routine will help with his mental fugue."

"I was thinking the same thing."

She bumped my hip and gave me a quick hug. "Hopefully, everyone has learned a valuable lesson that we're stronger working together than apart."

I snorted. "Something tells me the cadre might need more than a single lesson before it sticks. Sometimes they don't know as much as they think they do."

She sighed. "We can only work with what we've got. I'm going to take a nap and then a long bath. Lucas said he'd pick me up at three."

"Have a great time, and keep in touch. My transport to the manor will be here soon. I'll see you in a few days."

DEVON STRETCHED out on the sofa in his office, though it was currently Lyra's as long as she remained the leader of the House, which was why he didn't sit at the desk. He could have used the one in his bedroom, but he needed a change of scenery, and had scheduled a private meeting with Lucas.

The blinds were open, and the mid-morning sun washed the room with a bright light that only improved his mood. He should be more upset with Cressa's continued stubbornness, but after their dreamwalk the previous night, he couldn't argue her logic. His sleep had been the deepest and most restful since the beast had been put to rest. And though he hadn't tested it, his mental state seemed clearer this morning.

He stared at his tablet. The first thing that morning, he'd written down everything he could remember of what Cressa had shared about the symbols on the medallion. If this Colantha Dupré was to be believed, there was a strong tie between vampire and dreamwalker. He'd never heard of such a thing in his younger days. After Lyra had her psychotic break, he'd stumbled across an old myth of dreamwalkers in his search for something to help her. The medallion made it all the more real, as if the shared dreams weren't enough.

Sergi hadn't found any background on Colantha. Was that because this was all some sort of hoax? A group of psychics playing games? Or was it possible the Council had hidden a devastating secret so deep that after centuries, with part of their history unknown to them, its simple existence could tear the vampire world apart? If he'd never heard of dreamwalkers in his five hundred years, then whatever occurred to wipe them from written history happened with a Council centuries ago, possibly before his Father's time.

He refocused on the tablet and pulled up his task list for the mission, adding a note for further investigation into Colantha Dupré. This covert assignment would belong strictly to Sergi. If the meanings on the medallion were legitimate, this discovery would be highly sensitive information.

When the knock at the door came, he switched to his notes about the illusive book, *De første dage*. The title was Danish for "the first days" and had been cataloged at the Renaud Library. It was now missing, as was the museum's curator, Philipe Renaud.

"Morning." Lucas sounded chipper for the first time since Devon returned home. He assumed Ginger had something to do with that. "Can I get you another?"

He glanced at his empty cup of espresso. "Yes, thank you. Is the car on its way?"

Lucas glanced at his watch. "I sent Mateo with a second car as a backup for Jacques." He raised his voice over the sound of the espresso machine. "They should be on their way back."

Devon smiled, curious at what Cressa's mood would be like when she arrived. Either way, an hour or two of intense training should shake out any remaining irritation she had with him.

Lucas set the cups on the coffee table and dropped into the chair next to him. "It will be good to get back to a mission."

"Have you told Ginger?"

He shrugged. "I told her I had a job that might take me out of town for several days."

"It could be weeks or months."

Lucas sipped his espresso, refusing to meet Devon's gaze. "I've heard back from some old contacts of Philipe's. They're willing to meet, but until we know more, there's no reason to upset her."

Devon laughed. "Are you not giving her enough credit to be monogamous while you're gone, or have you become so smitten you've discovered you'll be the one struggling with a long-term separation?"

When a light blush touched his bodyguard's cheeks, Devon relented. "How confident are you with these contacts?"

Lucas opened his tablet and turned on the LCD above the hearth to allow Devon to see the list of names. There were twenty of them, and next to each name was a city.

"That's going to take some time."

The door opened, and Lyra stopped when she saw them. "I'm sorry. I didn't realize you had a meeting."

Devon held out his hand. "Come sit. I should have mentioned it. Old habits, I'm afraid. We're reviewing a task I'd like to send Lucas on, if it's all right with you."

She closed the door and sat next to Devon on the sofa, her gaze reviewing the names on the display. "I recognize some of them."

"Where from?"

"Father, I think. I don't remember meeting any of them, but I'm sure he mentioned them at least once or twice. It was a long time ago."

"My first step will be determining the last time any of them have seen Philipe." Lucas lifted his cup, and Lyra shook her head. "Maybe they can share some of the locations he used to haunt. Then I thought I'd ask them about the book and see if I get any flicker of a response. But I wanted your opinion and approval. Just asking about the book might be problematic. It could leak to the wrong vampires."

"What book is that?" Lyra asked.

Before Devon had a chance to answer, the door burst open. They turned to find Sergi standing in the doorway, his face pale.

He shot a glance at Lyra before turning his glazed eyes back to Devon.

"There's been an accident."

~

THE SCENE of the accident was barely ten minutes away. So close to home, and Devon wasn't able to prevent this.

A dozen of his vampires blocked the street. Whoever had done this selected a stretch of road with fir trees on both sides. One small side street ran west to the point, a location popular with birder watchers and the occasional surfers. Cars, as few as there were on this residential street, were either asked to turn back, or vampires ushered the vehicle past the debris if they lived on the road.

"I've spoken with the SBPD." Sergi drove the sedan past two other cars. "They've agreed to let us handle this as long as the road is cleared in thirty minutes."

Devon rolled down the window moments before the burnt husk of the car became visible. The acrid smoke clogged his senses, and he struggled to keep the beast down. He understood his beast's rage. Beneath his own anger, his heart clenched, and his breathing grew tight. She couldn't be in there.

The sedan hadn't stopped before Devon was out and marching across the blacktop, with Sergi rushing to keep up. Four vampires circled the remains, one at each corner of the vehicle.

"They were either sloppy or didn't have time." Sergi glanced around, then nodded at a vampire standing off to the side with two others. "The sedan was hit mid-section from the cross street. The fire started in the engine compartment, and we believe it was set rather than a result of the crash."

Devon glanced at the vampire approaching them. "What happened?" He kept his tone level, waiting to hear Mateo's report before making any judgment.

"We were about a block behind Jacques. There was no one

following us. A semi pulled out in front of us, and we narrowly missed it before stopping. Shots were fired from the cab, pinning us down. Rafael was able to go around and take out the shooter, but it took time to move the semi. I called Jacques once the gunfire started. He acknowledged the warning before I lost connection."

"Did he survive?" Devon asked.

Sergi grimaced and nodded. "Half his body is burned. They gave him blood. He should be at the safe house now. The healer is on her way."

Fire was not a vampire's friend and was one of the worst ways to die. But if one survived, the healing process, while painful, was quicker than for a human and didn't leave scarring. The restorative powers of fresh blood and healing herbs would repair the skin. He would be out of commission until he healed, which with the amount of flesh burned, would be about two weeks.

Bella would be a mess over his and was probably already at his side.

He took a deep breath and moved toward the vehicle, terrified of what else might be in the scorched remains. When he grew closer, he breathed a sigh that the back passenger seat wasn't as badly burned. He was six feet away when he spotted Cressa's backpack. When he noticed how singed it was, he was seized by an uncontrollable rage.

The beast roared. And his chest ached. The beast seemed to be shaking his ribs like bars to a jail cell, demanding release.

He dropped to his knees as if someone had rammed a sledgehammer into the side of his head. Sergi was by his side, but he held out an arm to stop him. The pain was excruciating, as if his brain was swelling inside his skull with nowhere to go, ready to burst through.

He grasped his head with both hands, the pressure continuing to build. Then, with one last push, there was a sound like the popping of a balloon.

All was quiet and fresh air filled his lungs. He blinked several times.

Sergi was on one knee; his brows squeezed, a hand resting on Devon's shoulder.

He stared at him in wonder, which made Sergi's forehead wrinkle more. He couldn't explain it, but his mind had cleared. It was as if all this time, he'd been struggling to breathe, then suddenly, out of nowhere, someone flipped a switch, and the bag over his head vanished. Instead of a slow stream of thoughts returning, it was a raging flood, erasing his previous foggy mental state and replacing it with complete clarity.

For now, he pushed the staggering experience aside and rose to his feet, stepping next to the open door of the back passenger seats. They were black with soot and wet from the foam of fire extinguishers. Bits of burnt leather had curled from the heat, and one of the windows had shattered, but the rear half of the vehicle hadn't burned.

"This is similar to another accident." Sergi stuck his head in as he surveyed what was left. "At least from the pictures I've seen."

"Lyra won't take this well." Devon glanced around, searching for anything that might have been missed. "I'd like the healer to meet us at the manor when she's done with Jacques. Bella can stay with him for now."

"What are you thinking?"

His thought was that the only thing that kept the beast at bay was that Cressa was still alive. She wouldn't have had time to wander away on her own with Mateo close enough to have put out the fire. The driver of the second car was also missing.

His laugh was harsh and full of menace. "There's only one answer. Cressa's been taken. And there's no question as to who took her."

"Lorenzo."

"And this time, he's gone too far."

Don't miss out on the next release of ***Obsessed in Blood*** - **Of Blood & Dreams, Book 4**

**As a special treat**, if you haven't already downloaded it, consider reading the free prequel to the Of Blood and Dreams series - *Lyra*. This novella is set one-hundred years before the start of the series.

Only available as ebook download.

Visit my website at www.kimallred.com

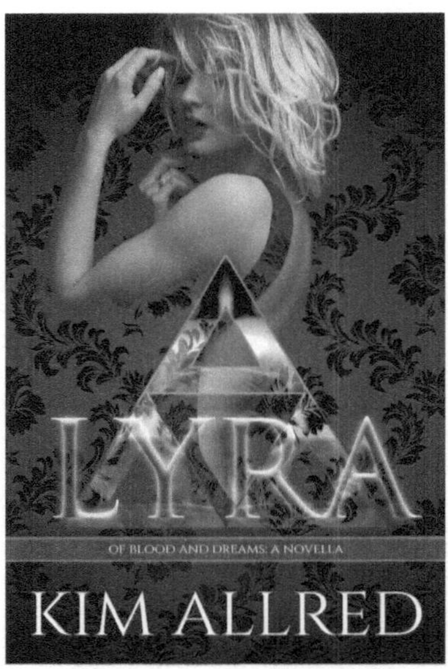

**The catalyst. The victim. The bridge.**

The Roaring Twenties. The time of flappers and Prohibition.

For Lyra, a young vampire and aspiring painter, the world is her canvas.

When she meets Hamilton, a sculptor and her family's gardener, time stops. He understands her like no one else.

But he's a human. And he's not the only one drawn to her. An ancient and powerful vampire has declared his desire to seduce her.

A perfect storm that sets the stage for all that is to come.

**Make sure you never miss a new release!**

Join my **FB Readers Group - Kim Allred's Heart Racing Romance**

Join my **newsletter**...I'm pretty much unobtrusive.

Follow me at **Amazon, Goodreads**, or **Bookbub**

If you can't wait and want to check out my other series, visit my **website**.

**Kim Allred** lives in an old timber town in the Pacific Northwest where she raises alpacas, llamas and an undetermined number of free-range chickens. Just like most of her characters, she loves sharing stories while sipping a glass of fine wine or slurping a strong cup of brew.

Her spirit of adventure has taken her on many journeys including a ten-day dogsledding trip in northern Alaska and sleeping under the stars on the savannas of eastern Africa.

Kim is currently working on the final books for the Mórdha

Stone Chronicles series and the next books in her paranormal romance series — Of Blood and Dreams. The first book in her new time travel romance series - Time Renegades - is on the horizon.

*For more books and updates:*
www.kimallred.com

facebook.com/kimallredwriter

instagram.com/Instagram

bookbub.com/authors/kim-allred

amazon.com/-/e/B07CQY2J8Y

pinterest.com/kimallredauthor

www.ingramcontent.com/pod-product-compliance
Lightning Source LLC
Chambersburg PA
CBHW031326210726
48287CB00005B/1715